PENGUIN CRIME FICTION

THE BOTTOM LINE IS MURDER

Robert Eversz has worked as a marketing consultant to numerous Fortune 500 companies and currently heads his own consulting business in Venice, California. He is at work on another Marston/Cantini novel.

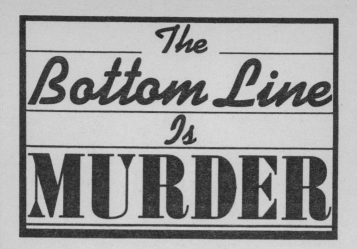

ROBERT
EVERSZ

PENGUIN BOOKS

PENGUIN BOOKS

Published by the Penguin Group
Viking Penguin, a division of Penguin Books USA Inc.,
40 West 23rd Street, New York, New York 10010, U.S.A.
Penguin Books Ltd, 27 Wrights Lane,
London W8 5TZ, England
Penguin Books Australia Ltd, Ringwood,
Victoria, Australia
Penguin Books Canada Ltd, 2801 John Street,
Markham, Ontario, Canada L3R 1B4
Penguin Books (N.Z.) Ltd, 182-190 Wairau Road,
Auckland 10, New Zealand

Penguin Books Ltd, Registered Offices:
Harmondsworth, Middlesex, England

First published in the United States of America by Viking Penguin,
a division of Penguin Books USA Inc., 1988
Published in Penguin Books 1989

1 3 5 7 9 10 8 6 4 2

LIBRARY OF CONGRESS CATALOGING-IN-PUBLICATION DATA

Eversz, Robert.
The bottom line is murder/Robert Eversz.
p. cm. — (Penguin crime fiction)
ISBN 0-14-010757-6
I. Title.
[PS3555.V39B68 1989] 813.54—dc19 88—37996

PRINTED IN THE UNITED STATES OF AMERICA
Set in Times Roman

For Mac and Marian

The business of America is business.
—CALVIN COOLIDGE

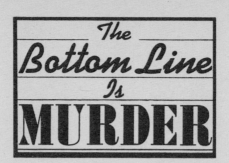

The
Bottom Line
Is
MURDER

Chapter
1

EVERYBODY STEALS. Most people steal small things. Like paper clips. Ashtrays. Things that have no value, except as stolen objects testifying like snapshots to the trespass of forbidden terrain.

Then there are those for whom the thing of no value is not enough. Executives augmenting six-figure incomes with a little graft have drilled my eyes with a salesman's sincerity and said that a million dollars isn't a lot of money these days. These are the people I love to nail.

I was in the law offices of Hansen, Holbrook and Hansen, and I had my hammer out.

"Mr. Hansen, I'm sorry to inform you that your partner has been embezzling from the company," I said.

"I knew it! The son of a bitch has been robbing me blind!"

Jason Hansen, a senior partner in the firm, slammed down the intercom button.

"Miss Weakly! Drop whatever you're doing and draw up Ray's retirement papers."

Her disembodied voice squawked back: "Yes, sir, Mr. Hansen."

Jason leaned back in a leather swivel chair and paged through the folder of evidence gathered during the investigation. His skin was deeply lined and coarse above the eyebrows but smooth around the eyes and mouth. His eyes were hard but friendly if you were on the same side as he, and hard and not so friendly if you weren't. The prominence of his brow and cheekbones suggested a large nose which had sometime during his life been changed into a small arrow-shaped nose. He was a vain man who didn't know how to relax, and in testament his face struck a precarious balance between hard work, excessive personal habits, and frequent trips to the plastic surgeon.

"How much did he get?" Jason demanded.

"About twenty thousand in fiscal year 1986, and twenty-five thousand this year, for a two-year total of forty-five grand," I answered.

Jason bolted to his feet, spinning the chair against the wall.

"That slime!" he shouted.

He crossed the room in three agitated strides and flung open the door to the hallway.

"Miss Weakly!"

"Yes, sir?" Her voice floated back from down the hall.

"I want Ray's pension provision canceled!"

Jason slammed the door shut, pulled the chair from the wall, and slumped over his desk.

"It could have been worse. How did Ray do it?" he asked.

"By underreporting his hours on a few key accounts. If he spent one hundred hours on a case, he'd bill for sixty through the law firm, and charge the remaining forty at a reduced rate payable directly to his personal account."

"You can't trust anybody," Jason said, unable to suppress a smile.

I wondered why the smile, and remembered that he stood to make a bundle from forcing his partner out of the firm. He leaned over the desk and shook my hand.

"Excellent job, Marston. You came highly recommended and lived up to it."

I thanked him.

"I'll get your check to you first thing in the morning."

A silver-haired gentleman in a crisply tailored blue suit stormed through the door and slammed it behind him with enough force to dislodge a painting from the wall. It was Ray.

"What's this bullshit about my retirement papers?" he demanded.

"Hello, Dad. Have a seat," Jason said.

"I will not have a seat. What the hell is going on here?"

"This is Paul Marston," Jason said with a nod in my direction. "He's a private investigator."

Ray looked at me sharply.

"He has no business here. Get him out."

"On the contrary, Mr. Marston's business is our business. Specifically, your little side business of embezzling from the firm's key accounts."

"Nonsense!" Ray bellowed, and stared defiantly at Jason, who opened the folder containing the evidence.

Ray's shoulders slumped when he saw the canceled checks and notarized statements detailing his guilt. He was very quiet for the minute it took him to examine the documents. Jason shrugged a halfhearted apology.

"Sorry, Dad. The evidence is incontestable. You'll have to step down."

"I won't do it, and you can't force me," Ray said, regaining his bluster.

"I could choose to pursue legal action."

"Not against your father you wouldn't. Don't forget I helped found this firm."

"And that will make your criminal prosecution all the more painful to me," Jason warned with a minimum of regret.

I decided to step into the fray.

"You should know that someone else is embezzling from the firm," I said.

Both Hansens were shocked.

"Holbrook?" they chimed.

"Not Holbrook. You," I said, straightening a forefinger toward Jason. "I estimate you siphoned almost sixty grand against Ray's forty-five."

Anger swelled Jason's face like a blowfish. His voice made a sharp strangling sound, and I thought he was either going to drop dead from a coronary or play ring around the collar with my neck. He found his voice, and when he found it, it was loud.

"But I didn't pay you to investigate me," he shouted.

"Don't worry. I didn't bill you for it," I said.

I hadn't made any friends. Both Hansens were shouting when I left the office. It was the beginning of a long day.

I drove Topanga Canyon east toward Santa Monica. It was the morning after a hard winter rain, and the sky was washed clear of smog and dust. Midway through the canyon, the needle on the old Mustang's gas gauge dropped to E, and I pulled into the Chevron station at the corner of Topanga and Henry Ranch Road. The attendant was a wiry young guy in blue overalls encrusted with enough grease for six standard lube jobs. I told him to fill it up and leaned against the hood of the car, enjoying the only outdoors I was likely to get until the weekend.

I heard the trouble before I saw it. A sound—the sudden change in pitch that props make when dropping from the sky—wrenched the air from my gut. I focused on the sound and spotted a small twin-engine aircraft diving over the far ridge up canyon. Out for a joyride, I thought, but as the plane began to spiral in a silent free fall, I knew I thought wrong. As if the pilot had awakened to find death rushing up, the engines caught hold and gunned violently as the nose tipped up and tried to claw back up the sky. The angle was too steep. The engines faltered. The plane hung in the air for several improbable seconds, as though gravity could be suspended, then the nose fell back, and it dropped.

The plane slammed to earth a couple of miles east of where I stood. I didn't see it hit. I heard the crush of metal echo down the canyon toward the sea, and a stillness swept through the oaks like a wind.

A siren began to wail far up canyon. I leaped behind the wheel, tossed a ten at the attendant and kicked the gas to the floor. Gravel spitting against the rear bumper, the Mustang slid onto the highway, and the tires bit into asphalt at a dead run.

A stream of black smoke spired through a clearing in a stand of oaks north of the creek bed. A fire truck swung off the road ahead and rumbled across a bridge built from an old railway car. I pulled to the side and parked. Several other cars had stopped in the middle of the road. A young woman with long brown hair and crooked teeth leaned against the fender of a pickup, holding a baby. At her side, drinking a can of beer, stood a man who hadn't shaved since birth. Up and down the road the idle and the curious stepped out of their vehicles, stretched, and craned their necks toward the smoke. The road was silent. A cicada trilled in the brush with a victorious beating of its wings.

I crossed the bridge and ran in the tracks the fire truck had laid through the wheat grass. It did not seem possible that anyone had survived the crash, but the improbability did not stop me from thinking that I might be of help. Or maybe I was drawn by the horror of violent death. I didn't stop to sort it out. Three firemen jumped from the truck and circled what had been an airplane. Two of them pulled brush away from the flaming wreckage, preventing the fire from spreading down canyon. The third struggled with a fire extinguisher, which had somehow clogged, and cursed as he neared the flames.

The fuselage burned white-hot. A wing curled up in the heat and fell back against the tail, sending sparks adrift like fireflies. The fireman got his extinguisher to work and shot a burst of foam into the center of the fire a few feet behind the cockpit. The inferno collapsed to a trickle of flame. Black smoke drifted by and snapped at my lungs. Pressing a handkerchief to my mouth, I peered through the smoke and into the wreckage. Something resembling a human form curled into a charred ball of flesh in the cockpit. I looked away.

A voice sounded to my left, and I focused on that. The voice was excited. It came from a blond fireman crouched in the grass a dozen yards from the wreckage. His partner trotted over with a red medi-kit and pushed away the grass. It was a body.

I crept closer. It was the body of a young woman. The medi-kit snapped open. The blond fireman's fist crashed onto her breastbone. He crossed his hands on her chest and lunged forward. He counted aloud and lunged again. A respirator wedged against her mouth. The mouth was slack. The third fireman, wearing a yellow slicker, knelt at the woman's side and cut away the sleeve of her suit. Needle up, he filled a syringe from a vial and found the vein with a quick jab. The voice, counting, became a chant.

"Who is it?" someone asked.

"A woman," someone else answered.

"Ever see her before?"

"Nope. She's gotta be a flatlander."

Locals filtered through the trees: young men in down jackets, beards, and bushy hair, and an older woman standing aside with her arms crossed. The deaths interested but did not concern them.

The counting stopped.

The blond fireman sat back on his heels. His partner felt for a flow of blood at the carotid artery, didn't find it, and shook his head. Yellow slicker began to pack the medi-kit.

"There's not a goddamn scratch on her," the blond said. He stood and, wiping his hands, walked away.

I looked at the dead woman. She was about thirty. Her long auburn hair spilled through the grass at her head. She wore a light-gray business suit, its cut softened by a ruffled mauve blouse. I looked at her hands. There were no rings. A faint pattern of freckles spread below her eyes, deftly concealed with a light rubbing of rouge. The eyes were closed. There were no marks of violence. Death had not made her ugly. Yet.

A fireman brushed past me and knelt at her side with a blanket. Bunching it first at the feet, he spread it over her and gently draped it over the face.

I turned toward the highway. The field was littered with evidence of the plane's impact. Sprung at the hinges, a leather briefcase spilled a sheaf of papers into the grass. Sheets fluttered in the breeze and blew away, one by one. I walked on. A man's shoe rested next to an apple. A pale blue shirt splayed around the base of an oak, as though its occupant had been clutching it before sudden vaporization. A yard beyond, something metal glinted in the morning sun. It was a thermos. I squatted next to it.

The thermos was a beautiful piece of workmanship, encased in hand-tooled leather burnished to a bronze gloss. There wasn't a mark on it. I picked it up. An engraving of Aphrodite rising from the sea was carved into the leather. I shook the thermos. Crushed glass rattled like ice. The damage was inside, the glass bell smashed under its perfect skin.

Chapter 2

THE WALL STREET JOURNAL was at my office door the following morning. I scooped it up, raised the blinds, started the coffee, and checked the messages on Shirley, the Japanese receptionist with a microchip for a heart.

"Tell me you love me, Shirley," I said, hoping to hear from a few past due accounts.

With her usual electronic efficiency, Shirley proceeded to the tape. The first message was from a credit card agency in New York complaining about an unpaid bill. The second was from an ex-client questioning a five-dollar expense account item on my final bill.

I pressed the rewind. Shirley didn't love me.

When the coffee was ready, I woke up Hal, fed him a spreadsheet program, and spent an hour trying to match accounts receivable to accounts payable. They were parallel lines that met at infinity. Most of my creditors wouldn't wait that long. Five years earlier I had abandoned the company pension plan and the keys to a BMW for a no-money-down Ford and the chance to die in debt as a free-lance corporate investigator. I still have the Ford, and no one is gambling I'll hit the Fortune 500 any time soon. The phone rang and I couldn't afford not to answer it.

"Did you see *The Wall Street Journal* this morning?" a voice asked.

It was Billy Bates, one of the principals in a local advertising agency. When he had a client who needed security services, he threw the business my way.

I told him I hadn't.

"Hang up the phone and look at page 30. Then call me back."

The line clicked off.

I spread the paper over my desk and turned to page 30. In a box in the lower right corner was a name I recognized. It was Jack Carlisle, president and chief operating officer of Western Shores Corporation. The first line in the box praised Carlisle as one of the bright lights of modern management. The second said he had been killed in a small plane crash in Topanga Canyon, with two employees. The third reported that his death was already fueling takeover rumors on Wall Street. How like *The Journal* to get to the bottom line in a hurry.

Carlisle had given me my first job out of the service. What credibility I had in the business started with him.

I looked up Bates's number in the Rolodex.

"What do you know about this that I don't?" Bates asked when he picked up.

"Just what I read in the paper."

"Don't stonewall me," Bates snapped. "Western Shores was my personal account, and all shit is going to break loose. You were in tight with the company once. I need information."

"Try dialing 411."

"Very funny. What do you know about the recent takeover move Carlisle was trying to force through?"

"It's no big deal. Western Shores has been acquiring companies for years.

"You know worse than nothing. Carlisle wasn't buying. He was selling."

The news shouldn't have surprised me. Companies are bought and sold like used cars these days.

"If you want to know why he was selling, call your broker."

"I know why he wanted to sell," Bates answered.

"Why?"

"I don't want to talk about it over the phone."

"How about your office?"

"Worse. I'll meet you for the Happy Hour at King Arthur's. You know the place?"

I told him I did and hung up. He called back ten seconds later.

"Marston, this is all under the table. Understood?"

"Understood," I answered, and hung up again.

I was puzzled by Carlisle's attempt to sell the company. It wasn't his to sell. Carlisle's power was limited by Henry Howard, the founding father, chief stockholder, and chairman of the board. Carlisle was supposed to have been Howard's man. He had been groomed for the position, married off to Howard's granddaughter, and handed the keys of power with much ceremony. It was hard to figure why he wanted to sell against family, and how he was going to do it.

For the balance of the day, in those moments when I would look up from my work, the face of Jack Carlisle dropped into my mind like a slide. I thought about how he had started with nothing but brains, charisma, and an M.B.A., and ended with everything that mattered in the corporate world before he was forty, and about how much I liked him despite that. And I also knew that now that he was dead, I had to know why.

King Arthur's Court was a theme bar, like a Disneyland ride for the sex-and-Seagram's set. The interior was designed to mimic the great hall of a medieval castle. It came as a surprise to me that such castles were equipped with bar stools, plastic tables, and six-foot diagonal Sony projection television sets. But then I've never been a great student of history. After six o'clock the bar was crowded with office workers, mostly single, and the occasional stray tourist. Most were there to get laid. Most were more afraid of rejection than of terminal diseases. I was reminded of the bubonic plague and how surviving villagers would copulate in the streets while their neighbors' houses burned.

I spotted Bates making time with a philodendron in the back booth, and joined him.

"Come here often?" I asked.

"Every now and then," he answered, and gestured for me to sit.

"How interesting. What's your sign?" I said, and sat.

"What're you trying to do, pick me up?"

"Just practicing."

"Go practice on someone with tits." He grinned.

Bates was a large man, wide at the shoulders and wider still at the waist. Advertising clients liked him. He told dirty jokes. He was sharp-witted, cheerful, and always prepared to laugh at a bad joke if told by the right person.

A waitress in a short skirt and breast-hugging black leotard dropped by the table. I ordered a beer. Bates handed her an empty and ordered another martini. His eyes drifted down her legs. She ignored him. Her smile was purely professional. He watched her walk, then absently scanned the crowd.

I had to prompt him. "You said you had some information on Western Shores."

"What do you say we forget about that and pick up a couple of girls instead," Bates said, and gave me a two-martini wink.

"I'm not that kind of guy."

"You like girls, don't you?" His smile stiffened into a leer.

"Sure I like girls. I like beer, baseball, and sometimes I even like you. But we didn't come to talk about that, did we? So cut the bullshit."

The waitress returned with our drinks. Bates cradled his like a poker hand and studied it.

"The picture has changed. I don't know if it's smart to talk."

"It doesn't matter if you talk or not. You've lost the Western Shores account already."

"What makes you think I've lost it?"

"The ad agency always gets the ax after a change in top management. You have six months at most before they announce the account is up for bid. They'll insist that you're in the running, of course, but you won't get it."

"Our contract expires in three months," Bates admitted. He drained his martini and, hoisting the empty like a chalice, proclaimed: "The King is dead. Long live the King."

"Who is the new King?"

"The old man."

"Henry Howard?"

Bates nodded. "He appointed himself interim president this afternoon. There will be a review board to screen candidates for the permanent position, but I don't think Howard will give up the reins this time around."

"Why does he want to come out of retirement? The guy is seventy-five, widowed, and a multimillionaire."

"If Howard was normal, he'd find some sweet young thing

to screw him to death in his declining years. But he's not normal. He spent three years in semiretirement when Carlisle took over, and he couldn't take it."

"Was Howard unhappy with the way Carlisle was running the company?"

Bates tried to roll another swallow out of his empty glass and carefully said, "There were fundamental differences in the direction each saw as best for the company."

"Such as?"

"Howard built the company on the manufacture of hard goods, like appliances, generators, that kind of thing. Carlisle saw the pursuit of leisure as a high-growth opportunity, riding the wave of discretionary spending as we Baby Boomers moved into higher income brackets. He moved to expand the company's recreational properties. Howard has probably never taken a vacation in his life. He had no feeling for leisure as a business. He couldn't understand it or control it, and that scared him."

"If he was in semiretirement and the company was profitable, what did he care?"

"He wanted to run things from the sidelines."

Bates leaned forward and turned his glass upside down on the table. "Howard organized the sale of the company's resort properties in Las Vegas and Hawaii behind Jack's back, and tried to push it through during the last board meeting. Jack blocked the sale, but the board was badly divided, and it was questioned whether he could effectively operate the company under the circumstances."

Righting his glass, Bates frowned and looked for the waitress. I caught her eye and signaled for another round. Bates relaxed and continued.

"Carlisle knew this was going to be the big showdown. He would have to resign or be fired. So he found a third alternative: organizing a take-over attempt. That was what he was doing in San Francisco before the crash."

"I thought Howard was majority stockholder."

"He is. But he only holds sixteen percent. His daughter and granddaughter hold another fifteen percent, with the balance owned by institutional investors."

"With Carlisle married to the granddaughter, that makes for some interesting family politics."

Bates nodded vigorously. "Howard couldn't count on his own family. The vote would have been thrown open to the stockholders."

"Whose shares are controlled by the banks."

"Exactly. With the promise of a tidy profit, and Carlisle's reputation as a profit-maker, the banks would have backed the take-over."

"Instead, both Carlisle and the take-over attempt are killed in a plane crash," I said.

Bates shrugged.

"Could be coincidental," I suggested.

"I'm not suggesting it was anything but coincidence," Bates replied. His mouth said one thing, but the gleam in his eyes said something else.

"This is a little out of my line, but I could ask around and maybe come up with an answer in a couple of days."

The humor ironed out of his face. He shook his head. "I'm not asking you to do anything. Neither the agency nor I have a position on this. As far as we're concerned, you and I are just having a couple of drinks, shooting the shit."

"It's not easy to work without a client," I said.

Not profitable, either.

"Carlisle gave you a couple of good breaks. I decided to talk to you because I thought you'd like to return the favor." Bates caught my eyes with a shrewd look. "And if I'm lucky, you'll find out something that will help us keep the Western Shores account."

The waitress returned with our drinks. Bates smiled happily at her legs.

He asked, "Are you busy tonight, sweetheart?"

"I'm married," she briskly replied.

"Okay by me. I'm open-minded about adultery."

The waitress set his martini carefully down on the table. "Why don't you go jerk-off with a belt-sander," she suggested.

Bates reddened, then laughed.

"I could fall in love with a girl like that," he crooned, and sunk his martini in one swallow.

Chapter
3

IT WAS RAINING in San Francisco when I landed. Before nine o'clock I was paddling a rented Detroit econo-box through morning rush-hour traffic on highway 101. It was one of those cars that lists the engine as optional equipment. I took the Van Ness off-ramp and, with a blurred view of taillights stretching like a slow river ahead, drifted with the traffic into the city.

I parked in an underground lot beneath the Bayshore Hotel and rode the elevator up to lobby level. The Bayshore was one of Western Shores' flagship properties, located in the financial district. As a company man, Carlisle would have stayed there during his trip to San Francisco. The chief of security, an ex-desk sergeant named Mankewitz, owed me a favor, which would get me in the door and not much else.

The registration desk was at the far end of a lobby that aspired to turn-of-the-century grandeur. It had the trimmings—crystal chandeliers, plush gold carpeting, and burnished oak paneling, against which leaned the requisite dozen bored bellboys. But the clientele was wrong. The men wore blue suits and carried black briefcases. The women wore gray suits and carried black satchels. The bellboys had a right to be bored. The business crowd pays the rent but doesn't add much to atmosphere. The lobby needed a Joan Crawford type slinking in a long gown, and a couple of seedy aristocrats gadding about with a racing form to be really first-rate.

A pink-skinned blonde stood behind the registration desk. Her red nails scurried like garish mice over the keyboard of a remote terminal. When she looked up, I asked for Joe Mankewitz and handed her my card with what I thought was a charming smile. She examined the card, then looked at me doubtfully. I thought she might ask me for a better piece of identification, something with a picture on it.

"Is Mr. Mankewitz expecting you?" she asked.

"He's a friend," I replied.

She nodded and, without looking my way again, passed through a door behind her. Sometime later she returned without my card and told me to wait. I did. The door opened again, and Mankewitz strode out.

"Long time no see, Paul," he said in a friendly voice.

I said, "I found it, Mank."

He stepped back with a quizzical smile. "What did you find?"

"The case I can't solve. Only the great Mankewitz can help me now."

A loud laugh burst out of him. He swung open the half door next to the registration desk, and invited me in.

"The only thing I ever solved was a case of the clap," he joked and, under the blonde's scathing glance, led me to his office.

Mankewitz settled in his chair and promptly kicked his feet up on the desk. He had not lost any weight since I had seen him last. In his youth Mankewitz had been barrel-chested, but now, past his fiftieth year, most of it had comfortably settled front and back of his belt. What remained of his hair was gray and retreated to an open-faced crown. His face was round and flat, and the flesh sagged around his chin like rubber that has lost its snap.

"I read in the papers that Jack Carlisle was killed," I said after asking him about his wife, kids, dogs, and Winnebago.

Mankewitz shrugged as though he didn't care much and said, "It happens."

"Did you ever get a chance to meet him?"

"Mr. Carlisle stayed here when he came to town. I recall he and you were pretty friendly once."

"He was friendly to everyone who worked for him."

"Particularly the women," Mank grunted.

I watched him shake a smoke out of a pack of Pall Mall nonfilters and light it.

"I read that a couple of people went down with him. One was a woman. His personal secretary?"

Mank picked a speck of tobacco off his lower lip and came close to leering. "Miss Rogers. Special Assistant to the President. She was a real looker."

"I'd guess she had brains to match, unless the title was pure ceremony."

"Depends on whose keyhole you've got your ear next to," he suggested, and slowly rolled his cigarette to conserve the inch of ash gathering at the tip.

"Did they share a room?"

"Not by the books. They always paid for two across the hall from each other."

"But you can't help noticing things, I'm sure," I suggested.

"Particularly when they don't try very hard to hide it."

"Maybe they were just amateurs at that kind of thing."

"They weren't wearing neon, but I wouldn't have opened my mouth if it was a big secret."

The ash on his cigarette grew to a couple inches. Mankewitz carefully let it fall, whole, into the ashtray, then asked, "What's your interest in this? Got a client or something?"

"Or something," I answered.

"Like what?"

I shrugged.

"I'm not gonna play poker if you don't show your hand when I call," he said.

"Business is slow. A guy I knew gets killed, so why not look into it? I need the practice."

"What if something turns up?"

"Depends on what it is."

Mankewitz took turns examining the new ash growing on his cigarette and watching me. I waited for him to say what was on his mind.

"I don't want what I say to get back to me. What with Carlisle gone and Mr. Howard in charge again, things are pretty shaky. Nobody's job is safe."

I nodded. Mankewitz stabbed out the cigarette and spun his chair around to a file behind him. He pulled a couple of folders out, slapped them on the desk, and read a few names and addresses of people he thought I'd like to contact. Pausing at Valerie Rogers' file, he lit another cigarette.

"Rumor has it she's got a boyfriend living with her."

"It's a modern world. I hope you're not shocked."

"I hear he's an actor," he added.

"Employed?"

"Do you know very many who are?"

Someone knocked lightly. Mankewitz slipped the papers out of sight and acknowledged. The man who stepped through the door wore above the breast pocket of the hotel's trademark light brown jacket a yellow badge which read "manager." His face was thin and had angles like a bad cubist painting. One of the angles was his nose, and supported a pair of gold-rimmed glasses. He looked about thirty, and his mouth was an angry streak below his pencil moustache. Spotting me, he wiped a smile onto his face.

"Sorry to interrupt, Joe. I didn't know you had a visitor."

Mank stood and made the introductions, and we shook hands. His name was Jim Johnson. He managed the hotel.

"Marston used to work with us a couple of years back. He stopped in to say hello," Mank continued.

"Were you one of the security men here?" Johnson asked, his eyes drifting down the cut of my suit.

I was wearing my brown travel suit, the one woven from a miracle fabric impervious to stains. It was the type of suit your tailor warned you about.

"More or less," I answered.

"He was the director of security at headquarters," Mank explained, clearing his throat.

Johnson smiled appropriately, but his eyes fogged. He missed just enough of a beat for me to notice it, then played the polite diplomat.

"I hope you're staying with us this evening. We're always happy when old friends come to visit."

"Just in town for the day, I'm afraid."

"Maybe next time." he said. He turned toward the door and looked back over his shoulder as though just remembering an unpleasant detail.

"If you have a moment, Joe, I'd like to see you before lunch."

"No problem." Mank beamed.

When the door snapped shut, Mank's smile dropped from sight.

He grunted and said, "The guy's got a terminal case of the ambitions. With any luck, he'll get himself promoted out of here soon."

I asked Mank a few questions about Carlisle's movements and didn't learn much. He started to relax. Then I told him about the Carlisle take-over attempt.

"Was that what he was up to?" he said, stunned.

His last still smoldering in the ashtray, Mank reached for another cigarette. He scratched the flint three times before striking flame, lit the cigarette, then noticed he had two going and stubbed out the first. "Shit," he finally sighed in a breath of smoke.

"Something bothering you?" I asked softly.

"Nothing's bothering me," he said, annoyed. "Just that it puts a different perspective on things."

"Such as?"

"Such as I'll be out of a goddamn job if anything gets tied back to the hotel," he snapped.

"How could the hotel be implicated?"

"You could shoot your mouth off in the wrong place, for one thing, about how helpful old Mank was. I've been playing it stupid. I should have kept my mouth shut."

Mankewitz scooted his chair back and stood. I didn't know why the take-over news had bothered him, and he wasn't in the mood to tell me. He escorted me into the lobby, and when we shook hands, there was trouble in his eyes.

"I want you to do me a favor," he finally said.

I listened.

"If you find out something that concerns me or the hotel, let me know about it. I don't want to be hit by something I don't see coming."

"What are you afraid I'll learn?" I asked.

"Nothing. Just let me know, okay?"

I tapped him on the arm and, with a short wave, plunged through the double glass doors onto Market Street.

———

I spent the early afternoon driving north to San Rafael to interview the widow of the third crash victim. She was a plump woman of about forty-five who lived in a suburban house with carefully raked carpeting and plastic-covered furniture. When I asked her about her husband's job, she said that she never allowed him to bring his work home with him, didn't know anything about it, and then went into hysterics.

By midafternoon I was back at the airport, where an hour's wait and a twenty-dollar bill bought me a few words with Carlisle's mechanic. He told me that the plane had been in mint condition and that Carlisle could fly it. When I asked him why the plane went down, he speculated that it was karma. I regretted the twenty dollars.

Flying back to Los Angeles, the only gut feeling I had was the kind you get from eating airplane food.

Chapter

4

THE STORM THAT DRENCHED San Francisco never made it to Southern California. A house down the block from my apartment was running the lawn sprinklers. In February. The weatherman forecast a high of seventy-five Fahrenheit with a four-foot surf. It was the kind of weather that made you want to slip western civilization a Valium, forget to shave, and hang around the beach all day. Or longer.

I didn't have any Valium. I pulled on a pair of jeans, an old sweater, and headed for the car.

Mankewitz had given a West Hollywood address for Valerie Rogers and her actor boyfriend. I drove east on Fountain and turned south onto a quiet residential street lined by vintage 1930s fourplexes. Valerie Rogers' address was painted on a fake Mediterranean two-story, flanked on the street corner by two imitation French Provincials.

The mailbox to apartment number 3 carried two names: Rogers and Manly. I climbed the short set of stairs, and a pair of angry voices led me to a door with a number 3 on it. The argument didn't fool me for long. The voices lacked menace and stumbled over the wording of a scene from *Death of a Salesman*. I knocked lightly, then a little louder. The door swung open to a blond adonis in tennis shorts. He was two inches taller than my six feet, had the muscle definition of a health club regular, and a tan that looked like it came out of a bottle labeled "Liquid Sun." He didn't look much like Willy Loman.

I lied.

"I'm from the *L.A. Weekly*. Maybe I should come back later, when you guys have finished your argument."

Adonis flashed a proud smile. His teeth were so perfect and white that I thought they were painted on.

"It's okay," he said. "We were just rehearsing a scene."

It sounded real enough to me. I thought I was going to see bodies crash through the door on my way up."

A guy who could have passed for Superman's twin stood next to the couch, penciling a script. The pencil looked like a pin in his fist.

Adonis called, "Hey, Larry! The guy says he thought we were having a real fight."

Superman gave him thumbs up and returned to penciling the script.

"You said you were from the *Weekly*?" Adonis asked.

"You're Mr. Manly, right?

"Right. Chris Manly."

"Real name or stage name?"

"Both. The only thing harder than trying to pronounce my family name is trying to spell it, so I go by Manly," he explained with a well-practiced smile.

I pulled out my notebook and started scribbling.

"I'm doing an article on the death of Jack Carlisle and the corruption of ethics by corporate politics."

The *Weekly* had a reputation for left-wing muckraking. It must have sounded right to Manly. He nodded.

"I see you as a key source in the article. From what I've heard, you must be an actor."

Free publicity. Manly turned his smile up to full intensity.
I fumbled for my sunglasses.

Manly motioned me in and announced to his audience of
one, "If it's okay with you, I have to do an interview."

Superman rolled his script and crushed it into his back
pocket. His shoulders barely cleared the doorway on his way
out. Manly shut the door behind him and offered me a seat
on the couch.

I guessed that most of the furniture in the apartment belonged to Valerie Rogers. Under the window, light spilled
over a waist-high vase holding half a dozen dried pussy wil-
lows. The couch and matching chair were upholstered in a
tropical print of birds of paradise. Four reproductions of
Nagel, portraying men and women with great cheekbones
and flawless skin, clustered like a clique of the Beautiful
People on the inside wall opposite the window. The glass-
topped coffee table, framed in mahogany, carried a four-
figure price tag on Melrose Avenue. It was not the apartment
of an unemployed actor.

I began, "How long have you known Miss Rogers?"

"About four years," he replied, draping a bare arm over
the back of the chair.

"Describe your relationship. You were more than just
roommates, right?"

"We didn't just share space, if that's what you mean."

Manly thrust his chin forward and said, with a theatricality
that passed for feeling, "We were lovers."

"Uh-huh," I said.

"We weren't like other couples, you know, hung up on
jealousy and negative head trips. We were real positive with
each other. I could talk to her and work things out. She'd
help with the career, and I'd help her with her business life,

you know, give her a massage and stuff when she'd come home all tense."

"Sounds meaningful," I said. "A little like Tracy–Hepburn, or maybe Gable–Lombard."

I'm a bad liar. If I get away with one, I try to top it with another. Manly just nodded, however, and I resisted the temptation to liken the relationship to Bambi–Godzilla.

"When we first met," he continued, "it was at this party, and I guess she turned on to the fact that I was an actor. Whatever it was, we started going out together until it got to be a real drag, you know, always going home in the morning—my apartment was a real dump then, so we always came over here—and I decided to pack myself up and move in."

He smiled with a bright, empty charm. "And that's it. End of story."

I sucked on the tip of my pencil like I had seen other reporters do and delivered my next line.

"Did you ever meet Jack Carlisle?"

Manly brightened. "I never actually met him, but I really felt as though I knew him. I mean, Val had a close working relationship with him, so she'd always come home with her stories, or tell me what kinds of things they were doing at the company."

"I heard she was a secretary."

"She was more than just his secretary." He threw his right hand out in a gesture suited to a proscenium arch and audience of two thousand. "She was his right arm. He didn't make a single decision without talking it over with her first. There was something really solid about her that you could depend on. She gave good feedback, you know?"

"I've heard that they worked very closely together."

As I spoke, he nodded in agreement.

"So close, in fact, that they took their work to bed with them."

The actor in Manly lost his lines. His smile went into a holding pattern, and as his eyes blanked, he hid behind the expression, as though time would stand still if the smile remained.

"I don't think I understand," he finally stammered.

"You know how it is when people work close together. They become emotionally and physically involved."

The smile dropped from Manly's lips. His look was wary.

"Are you going to print that they were sleeping together?" he asked evenly.

"Were they?"

"Of course."

Manly stood up, crossed the room, and pulled a T-shirt over his golden tan. When he faced me, there was a narrow cunning in his eyes that I hadn't seen before. Maybe it had been there all along. Maybe he was a better actor than I thought.

"I just don't want it spread all over town that I was cuckolded. It's not good for the reputation."

"If you knew, why did you go along with it?"

I dropped my pencil and placed more of my weight on the balls of my feet to move quickly if he decided to try to throw me out. He watched, calculating what his attitude should be, before he finally shrugged, took the path of least resistance, and slouched back in the chair, as relaxed and informal as before.

"Why should it bother me? I told you we weren't into any jealousy trips."

I didn't believe him this time, and he knew it. He resumed a casual, gossipy tone.

"I mean, it was an important career move for her. The

guy was a real bigwig. He was married, so it was kind of safe. Everybody says they won't compromise themselves by sleeping with someone to get ahead, but they do it anyway, you know? You sleep around, you get around."

I pulled the judgment out of my voice and asked, "Was Ms. Rogers seeing anyone else, in addition to you and Carlisle?"

Manly shook his head with a sly grin.

"How do you know?" I pressed.

His voice turned smarmy. "She told me everything about Jack, from favorite positions to pet names. She had nothing to hide. We were very open and trusting."

I fought the urge to retch.

"Did she give you any reason to think something was wrong when she flew up to San Francisco?"

"She was really positive about it," he said, then fearing I would misinterpret the remark, hurriedly explained, "But not because she was going to be with Carlisle. That wasn't it at all. Something else was happening. She told me all about it, but I wasn't listening very carefully. She said it was a little frightening, but a real opportunity. There was something about a promotion and a big raise in salary."

I flipped my notebook closed and pocketed the pencil.

"Is that it?" Manly asked.

I nodded and stood.

"Where were you when Ms. Rogers was in San Francisco?" I asked.

"Around here," he said and, escorting me to the door, saw his last chance for a plug. "I have this Stanislavsky workshop on Saturday, and I had an audition on Tuesday, so I keep pretty busy."

"Did you get the part?" I asked, guessing that a small thing like the death of a lover wouldn't get in his way.

"I'll hear sometime this afternoon."

He smiled with perfect confidence. He must get tired of watching himself smile in the mirror, I thought. Probably not.

"Your concentration must have been ruined by the accident," I said.

"Not at all. I was devastated, but I was able to use that in the scene," he answered, and assumed a grieving look.

I was out the door and halfway down the stairs before he had the chance to work up the full complement of tears.

"You won't forget to mention that I'm a working actor, will you?" he called out.

I didn't answer. With all his Stanislavsky, I doubted he'd get a part weightier than crowd atmosphere in a muscle beach movie.

Chapter 5

I CALLED THE CORONER from my office. When I identified myself as a reporter from the *Weekly*, the receptionist routed me to an assistant. I expected Bela Lugosi. The woman who answered had a warm and friendly voice. She read the coroner's report on Jack Carlisle like it was a page out of *Alice in Wonderland*.

It had been difficult for the coroner to pinpoint the exact cause of death. There hadn't been much of him left after the fire gutted the cockpit. Formal identification had been achieved through dental records. Most of the blood had boiled out, eliminating all but the most basic toxicology tests. The official cause of death was ruled to be multiple trauma to the major body organs, complicated by third-degree burns over 100 percent of the body.

Death had done a pretty thorough job on Jack.

As an afterthought, I asked her to give me the official cause of death on Valerie Rogers.

She pleasantly said, "Myocardial infarction."

"I beg your pardon?"

"Cardiac arrest. Heart attack. Her ticker quit."

"No other injuries?"

"A few minor abrasions."

"What do you make of that?"

"It's not as unusual as you might think. The shock was too much for her heart. When the plane hit the ground, she was as loose as a rag doll. It's kind of like rolling with a punch."

Some punch.

When I disconnected, the clock said it was lunchtime, but my stomach told me to forget it. I bought a carton of milk in the building commissary, and it kept me company through a quick reading of *The Wall Street Journal*.

On page 13 there was a one-column article reporting that Henry Howard would assume temporary command of Western Shores.

"Although I understand the market's initial reaction to the death of our esteemed colleague," Howard was quoted as saying, "I want to stress that the company is assured of a strong continuity of leadership and is eager to put this sad chapter in our history to a close."

I fed Hal a communications disk, switched on the modem, and dialed into a computer service that ran updated stock market quotations. As of noon Eastern Standard Time, Western Shores stock was dropping like a dead bird. I looked up the number in the Rolodex and phoned my ex-broker, Ian Waddington. Ian was a young turk in a big brokerage firm. Back in the days when I had money instead of my own business, I invested in a few stocks on his advice. The return was better than 20 percent in a bear market, but when it came down to keeping the stock or paying the rent, I paid the rent. He took it as a personal insult when I pulled out.

It took a few minutes to work through his secretary. I was ready for the run-around when Ian finally came on the line.

"Paul! I hadn't heard from you for so long I thought you had died, or worse, gone to debtors' prison."

"I was thinking you might like to do me a favor."

"I do favors for clients. You're not a client anymore."

"It concerns Western Shores."

It piqued his interest. He paused.

"We're taking a real bath on that one. What have you got?"

"I'm investigating the accident."

"Who for?"

"Myself for now. I used to work there."

"You mean you don't even have a client?"

I pulled my ear from the phone while he screamed: "Didn't anybody ever tell you that you don't do anything for free unless it's tax deductible?"

"My accountant is a sharp guy. He's been writing off my sense of moral responsibility for years."

"Deductions are irrelevant if you don't have an income."

It was a no-win argument. I changed the subject.

"I heard that Jack Carlisle was organizing a take-over attempt before the accident."

"That's an interesting piece of information," he admitted. "Who's your source?"

"Somebody close enough to the company to ask for confidentiality."

I hung on while Ian breathed heavily into the line, working through the possibilities. A lot of money could be made on a good tip.

"You want me to confirm or run up the details?" he asked.

"Both. It would take me half the week. I figure you could do it with a couple of phone calls."

"Sounds fair. You'll hear from me tomorrow or the day after."

"Tomorrow is Saturday. You'll be out playing golf."

"Tennis actually. It's better for my heart."

"Glad to hear you have one."

"Very funny."

"This afternoon, then?"

"I'll see what I can do."

I thanked him. He grunted, then disconnected.

The National Transportation Safety Board occupies a suite of offices in the Federal Building on Aviation Boulevard south of Los Angeles International Airport. I rode the elevator to the fourth floor, took a wrong turn down the hall, retraced my steps, and found the correct office by the writing on the door. I gave my card to the receptionist, who sat surrounded by pictures of her twenty grandchildren.

"I need to speak with the investigator in charge of the Topanga Canyon crash," I announced.

She looked at me doubtfully. "Do you have a case number?"

"I didn't know it had one."

She shook her head and frowned. "I need a case number."

"It can't be very difficult. How many Topanga Canyon airplane crashes do you get every week?"

She didn't return my smile.

"That's not the point. I don't know who to send you to unless you have the case number."

I shrugged and looked lost, imitating an average American taxpayer swamped by government red tape.

"If you'll have a seat, I'll see what I can do." She sighed and buzzed through on the office intercom.

I backed away from her desk and, briefly examining the reception room chairs, was assured that little of my tax money was spent on office furniture.

The receptionist returned the phone to its cradle.

"Mr. Thompson will be out to see you in a moment," she announced, and swiveled back to her typewriter.

The man who came out to meet me was about forty. His hair was short and curly. An attempt had been made to sweep it back with a part on the side, but it resisted control and sprang in unlikely cowlicks at the front, back, and sides of his head. He wore a pair of government-issue steel-framed glasses. The glasses had bottle-thick lenses, and his eyes jumped out at me like bug eyes.

"What can I do for you?" he asked with a high crack in his voice.

"I'd like to ask you a few question about the Topanga Canyon crash."

He nodded and waved me back to his office. With the door closed, his office had the dimensions of a closet, and not the walk-in kind. Thompson settled his elbows on the desk and clasped his hands. With his huge eyes, wild hair, and thin, bony arms, he looked like a praying mantis settled on a branch.

"I'd like to know if you've determined the cause of the crash yet," I began.

Thompson laughed. It was a high, cackling sound.

"No, not yet."

"When will you know?"

"In about six months." He laughed again, and his huge eyes danced gleefully. "That's if we're lucky."

"Still tied up with the Hindenburg crash, I suppose, and now that they make these things with wings, the job is even tougher."

"We move as fast as we can," Thompson said, slowly enunciating each word. "There are tests involved. Autopsies take time. We have to tear down the engine and poke into the structure of the plane—or what's left of it—and contact what eyewitnesses we can."

Thompson unclasped his hands and opened a file on his desk. "If you're the same Paul Marston, you're one of the witnesses."

I nodded. Licking his thumb, Thompson flipped through the file until he found the form he was searching for.

"A real coincidence that you're checking into this case. What's your interest?" he asked.

"I knew Jack Carlisle."

"Interesting," he said, stretching out the syllables.

"Have you seen the autopsy report on the Rogers woman?" I asked.

He nodded and tapped the file.

"What's your opinion?"

"Inconclusive. The heart attack is interesting, but it doesn't mean anything yet. Hard to say what happened. We're doing a toxicology test right now in Oklahoma City. That might help, or it might tell us nothing."

"I thought the coroner already did a toxicology test."

Thompson folded his hands again and smiled patiently. "We like to do our own."

And that took time. In business, time is money. In government, time is relative.

"I'd like to take a look at the list of articles found at the crash site. Nothing mechanical. Just personal effects."

Thompson's hands didn't move toward the file.

"We don't handle that," he said.

"Who does?"

"The local police." He cleared his throat and absently brushed invisible dust off the desk. "We sometimes don't visit the site until a couple of days later. Usually the local police make a list."

There was no confidence in his voice.

"What do you mean, usually?"

"It depends on the police. Sometimes they're sloppy. I've seen all kinds of stuff lying around a couple of days after the crash. If I see it, and it seems important, I'll pick it up."

"If it seems important, like a smoking gun."

Thompson smiled uncomfortably.

"Has anyone from your department been at the crash site yet?" I asked.

"I'm scheduled to go out there tomorrow."

"Did the local police make a list?"

"Not that I'm aware of."

"Do you want me to draw you a picture of a smoking gun, so you know what one looks like?"

Thompson heaved a bureaucratic sigh, heavy with the weight of triplicate forms and an unappreciative public, and pointed to the door. I used it.

The ten-mile stretch of the San Diego Freeway nearest the airport is never an easy drive. At four o'clock in the afternoon you need a tank to get through. The Mustang wasn't big enough to qualify, so I squeezed through the Centinela off-ramp, turned right at the light, and parked in the Pacifica Hotel lot. I knew most of the pay phones on the West Side, and the Pacifica Hotel phones were among the best. They were quiet, uncrowded, and comfortable. Everybody is an expert at something. I know pay phones.

I dialed my office and, fumbling with the beeper, played back the messages on Shirley. The first call was from an office supplies salesman. The second was from Ian Waddington. Dropping the last of my change into the slot, I dialed his number. The secretary must have gotten the word that I was okay. I was put straight through.

"Where the hell have you been all afternoon?" Waddington barked the instant he picked up.

"Sounds like you found something interesting."

"I haven't seen this much intrigue since the Columbia Pictures debacle a couple of years ago. When this story goes public, you can use your Western Shores stock for wallpaper. How much do you know already?"

"I heard that the fight between Carlisle and Howard centered on the sale of resort properties, and that Carlisle was looking for outside backing to stage a proxy fight."

"What you don't know is who the buyers were."

"And you do."

"Correct. I heard that Carlisle was within an eyelash of securing a deal with TransNational. They had worked out a rough agreement by Sunday night. TransNational pulled all their lawyers in over the weekend, working out the legal implications of the take-over—the tender offer price, potential problems with the FTC—you know the routine. Carlisle was to have landed in L.A. Monday morning and shopped the proposal to the more sympathetic board members to see if they'd go along with it."

"He picked a blue-chip company to deal with," I said.

"Number 122 on the Fortune 500. But there is something even bigger."

Waddington let a few seconds drag by to impress upon me the import of his news.

"Okay. How big?"

"There were two companies significantly interested in making a deal with Howard for the company's resort properties—a Florida company named International Properties, and American Sun Corporation out of Las Vegas. Looking at the 10-K's, I don't think International Properties could raise that kind of cash. The most serious offer would have come from American Sun. Nobody can prove it, but the word is that American Sun has some unsavory connections with the underworld."

The government had tried to prove it ten years ago, indicting American Sun's president on bribery charges. The president had resigned, but was acquitted. His brother had succeeded him to the presidency.

"They've been looking for an opportunity to expand out of Las Vegas for several years now," Ian continued. "I wouldn't want to get in their way. While we're on the subject, what shape is your life insurance portfolio in?"

"I have enough to cover burial costs."

"Be careful you don't cash it in," Ian advised.

I didn't need the warning.

Chapter 6

I DIDN'T SLEEP WELL the night after Jack's funeral, and when Saturday morning finally rose above the San Gabriel Mountains in the east, I stepped into a pair of swimming trunks and walked six blocks to the beach. The breeze blew crisp and clean off the sea. To the north, the coast mountains curved like a cupped hand around the bay. Past the breakers, the sea was smooth and sparkled in a sheen of red and gold from the rising sun. I swam slowly, forcing my body to relax in the cold waters. My joints ached for the first mile. By the second mile my blood began to warm, and I could feel my toes again. I doubled back and caught a curling four-footer to the shore.

A warm shower massaged the circulation back into my skin. I turned on the television and caught the last half hour of a John Wayne film. John Wayne versus the Indians. The Indians lost. The rest of the morning I stared at the phone, wondering what I would say when I finally got the guts to call. In every line of work there are ambulance chasers: guys who follow in the shadow of private tragedy with a business card, a long face, and a hustle. That morning I felt like one of those guys.

By noon the feeling hadn't gone away. I picked up the phone and dialed Leslie Carlisle's number, expecting to hear her tell me to go to hell. She picked up on the third ring. Our conversation didn't last long. I told her who I was and she told me to be at her house in an hour.

Leslie Carlisle lived in a two-story colonial in Cheviot Hills, between Culver City and Beverly Hills. Cheviot Hills is a community for those who haven't quite made it to Beverly Hills, but probably will with the next million.

Stepping out of my Ford, I straightened my tie and pressed a vagrant crease out of my suit coat. With a covetous glance at the red Targa-style Porsche parked in the driveway, I stuck my thumb in the door chime. The woman who answered the door was dressed in white tennis shorts and a blue sports shirt with a famous reptile over the left breast. A racket leaned handle up against the stairwell to my right. Nothing like a good game of tennis after you bury your husband.

When I handed her my business card, she said, "You knew my husband?"

Her strawberry-blond hair was worn loose, ending in a curl at her shoulders. The face was pretty in an ordinary way— it could have been worn by a model, though to no great fame—but the eyes were startling. The eyes were cobalt blue and, with flecks of white ringing the iris, seemed like gems shot through with light.

"We worked together. He hired me when all I had going for me was a good service record."

"What did you do in the service?"

"Military investigations, mostly in the Saigon black market."

She nodded and, with an abrupt turn, swept into the living room. I gathered I was to follow.

The living room looked like a page out of *Architectural Digest*. A gray leather sofa stretched under the white-draped

front window. Opposite the sofa, two armchairs sleekly reclined in matching wave shapes, a motif repeated by twin
black floor lamps with attenuated swan necks. The center-
piece of the sitting group was a crystal coffee table. The glass
was clear as rainwater, three inches deep and beveled at the
edges. An end-of-day vase held three yellow roses at the
table's center. On the far wall hung a Chagall oil, its blue
paint a shade darker than the blue of its owner's eyes. There
were no books, magazines, or personal objects to obstruct
the austere clarity of the room.

Leslie Carlisle draped her body over the sofa, resting one
leg on the leather and the other on the carpet. They were
nice legs, lightly muscled and polished like redwood. I wedged
myself into one of the armchairs, which proved to look better
than it sat.

"I don't trust many of Jack's so-called friends," she said,
"so I'll begin by not trusting you."

"Okay," I said.

I was surprised by the emptiness of the house, and the
careful avoidance of any visual reference to Jack's death.
Leslie watched me or, more exactly, was aware of me without
moving her eyes.

"In case you're wondering, I threw everyone out this morning. I can't stand funerals. Sympathy I like even less."

"I haven't come to offer you my sympathy."

"I know I should be curious about your visit, but I'm not.
I'd rather just talk for a few minutes."

Her forefinger traced the bridge between her thigh and
white shorts, a simple caress that seemed to require her concentration. It occurred to me that she might not have talked
to anyone about the things that mattered, since Jack's death.

"Okay, we'll talk," I said, and struggled to discover how

the chair wanted me to sit in it. "Let's start with why you don't trust Jack's friends."

"Jack wasn't a shrewd judge of character. He liked everybody."

"Maybe that was because everybody liked Jack," I offered.

"That was one of his many faults."

Though there should have been irony in her voice, I didn't hear it.

"It's not a bad thing to be well-liked."

"You weren't married to him." Her voice had a bitter taste in it. "People didn't just like Jack. They adored him. He was smart and knew what he wanted, but it was his charisma that made it all work. And it worked beautifully. I'm a great example of the power of Jack's charm."

"You mean because you fell in love with him."

Leslie lifted her hand from her thigh and guided it across the table to the vase of yellow roses. A silken petal stretched taut at her insistence and fell to the glass surface. She looked up at me, once, and found the roses more to her liking.

"Jack knew what he wanted. He always knew what he wanted. He's like Grandfather. That's why they were such great pals when they both wanted the same thing, and enemies when they didn't."

"What did Jack want?"

It was such an obvious answer to her that she paused, pulling free another wing of the rose.

"He wanted the company. To get the company, he had to win me first. That was Grandfather's rule: only family runs the company. So Jack turned on the charm, and it was easy. I wanted to be the president's wife, and I knew Jack would be a great president. What I didn't know was what a lousy husband he'd be."

"So the day after his funeral, you put three yellow roses on the coffee table, a touching gesture of remembrance, and go out for a good game of tennis to sweat him out of your system."

Her hand jerked from the roses, and the leather sofa cracked when she sat back hard. Sorrow, or maybe just shock, veiled the bitterness in her eyes. There was a good cry in her somewhere, but the bitterness won out.

She bluntly said, "You haven't told me what you want."

"I want you to hire me to investigate the crash that killed your husband."

She swept the hair from her forehead. Her eyes turned as cruel as my remark.

"It's amazing what crawls out of the woodwork at times like this. Are you that desperate for work?"

It was a fair question under the circumstances, but I resented it.

"I do okay, but I'm not getting rich. I had a BMW once, but it was repossessed because my clients don't pay on time and some of them don't pay at all. My bank account shows a balance of five thousand dollars, and I owe at least twice that to other banks. I have a list of references, and any one of them will tell you that I'm hard to work with but I'm good at what I do."

She looked at the wall, the floor, the ceiling, anywhere but my face.

I added, "The name at the top of that list is your husband's."

She looked at my face and then was gone into her private world. Though her eyes fixed at a distant point somewhere over my head, they were vacant as stones. I guessed that she was thinking, but there was something so distant about her that she seemed beyond thought. She didn't much care whether I was there or not.

After fifteen seconds of it, her head snapped back.

"I'm a lousy hostess. Would you like something to drink?" she asked, and rose in a single graceful movement to her feet.

I told her I'd have a beer, and watched her stride out of the room. There was more athlete than woman in her walk. Her body was slim and hard, and almost masculine except for the curve of her hips. She returned with two bottled Becks, handed me mine, and dropped back down on the sofa.

"You didn't want a glass, did you?" she said, wiping the lip of her bottle with her shirttail.

The rich can afford to be casual. I shook my head. She took a long slug at the bottle, then said, "Why shouldn't I let the authorities handle this?"

"That depends on how long you want to wait, and whether you think they'll do a good job of representing your interests."

Her eyes were cynical. "Is that what you'll do? Represent my interests?"

"Within limits."

"What limits?"

"I won't break any laws I don't want to break. I won't hide something I don't want to stay hidden. I won't take any falls I don't have to take, and I won't die for you."

She laughed. "I wouldn't ask you to."

She lost the laugh somewhere in the back of her throat.

"You're either a cheat or a spy, Mr. Marston, and I can't figure which it is. You have a good act. Maybe it's both."

And here we were, getting along so well. A great amusement moved behind her eyes, as though she could read me as easily as a spider crawling along the floor. I stepped over the coffee table and, sitting on all five thousand dollars of it, pinned her against the sofa.

"What are you doing?" she asked.

Surprise flattened the archness in her voice.

"Shut up and listen to me. You probably have a very good reason for trying to provoke me, but the hell if I can figure out what it is, so I'm going to tell you what I have to offer, and if it doesn't interest you, be civil enough to tell me to get the hell out."

The mocking look was gone. Her breath came rapidly, and a glint of excitement mixed with the cobalt blue of her eyes. She nodded once.

"When I learned of Jack's death, I had no intention of getting involved. There are a lot of things that happen in life that you don't like, but there's nothing you can do about it. Then I got a call from a mutual friend who told me that Jack was fighting for control of the company with your grandfather. I decided to do a little research. I learned some things that you probably already know and some things that you don't."

She didn't faint or gasp with surprise. She didn't even blink. Pinned against the sofa, she twisted her mouth into a wry smile that seemed erotic. It was something I didn't want to think about.

"When Jack was up in San Francisco, he was twenty-four hours away from organizing a take-over deal with a Fortune 500 company," I continued. "That made the crash a very convenient accident. I needed to find out who could benefit from his death, so I called a stockbroker friend who did a little looking on his own. He reported that Jack was opposing the sale of some resort properties and that one of the frustrated buyers was a company with underworld connections. That company and your grandfather would both have strong motives for wanting him out of the way. I also heard that Jack was sleeping with his secretary, so I visited her boy-friend. He's enough of a flake to do something stupid if he thought it would do him good."

She didn't flinch at the mention of her husband's affair. She either knew about it and didn't care, or had long since learned how to conceal the pain.

"Do you think he was murdered?" she asked, and her eyes searched mine for something more than an answer to her question.

"All I know is that too many people could have benefited by his death, and that an airplane crash would have been a hell of a smart way to kill him."

"You really don't know anything."

"Not yet."

She bumped my leg with her knee.

"Then would you mind getting off the coffee table? It's one-of-a-kind, and if you scratch it I'll kill you."

"Sure I don't mind. But it's a hell of a lot more comfortable than that Italian torture rack I was using as a chair."

"Those are one-of-a-kind as well, imported from Genoa."

I wandered to the Chagall. I was betting it wasn't a copy.

"You're too much of a bastard to be anything other than what you say you are," she said, and laughed with a sharpness that startled me. "If I wanted to hire you, what would it cost me?"

"I charge five hundred dollars a day to corporations. This is a little different, so I'll drop my rate to three hundred, plus expenses. I start today."

"Agreed," she said, and, reaching behind the sofa, pulled a wine-red purse into her lap.

I had never been a great closer and couldn't believe it was that easy. Then, again, I rarely physically threatened my clients while making my pitch. Aggression sells. I went into my standard warning.

"I may learn some things that you won't want to hear."

"I want to know everything. Jack didn't spare my feelings in life, so I don't see how it should be any different now."

"Did you know about his affair with Valerie Rogers?"

"He didn't try very hard to hide it. There was always someone else. His tastes in women were very democratic. He loved them all."

"Was he recently involved with anyone else?"

"Just the occasional chambermaid, I'm sure."

She found her checkbook and poised the pen over it.

"How much do you want in advance?"

"One week," I answered. "What do you know about his trip to San Francisco?"

She wrote my name on the check and signed it.

"Not much more than you do. You might want to talk to my father. He sat in on the meeting."

"Did your father mention where he stayed?"

"Jack's hotel. The Bayshore."

She handed me the check. I pocketed it without looking and wondered for a moment about Joe Mankewitz.

"Tell me why your father was invited."

"My mother is a major stockholder in the company. For that matter, so am I. Jack made sure he could count on other members of the family. Grandfather froze Father out of the company a long time ago, so Father was going to get Mother to vote her shares with Jack."

"Would she have?"

"Mother would have gone where the money was. If it looked like it was going to go with Jack, she would have backed him. She would have cut his throat, though, if it was in her best interest."

"It sounds like you have a lovely family."

" 'We have dozens of relatives, but only one company' as Grandfather used to say. Still does." There was irony in her voice, but none in her eyes. Her eyes were just sad.

Chapter 7

FROM THE AIR AT NIGHT, Los Angeles is a vast glittering of lights, with the Santa Monica Mountains stretching like an archipelago through a luminous sea. As the plane banked north toward San Francisco, I caught the faint lamps of an oil tanker cutting through the black Pacific toward harbor in San Pedro. After it passed, there was nothing but night and stars. I closed my eyes and awoke in San Francisco.

Just before midnight I parked the rental car beneath the Bayshore Hotel and, with an overnight case slung across my shoulder, rode the elevator up. The lobby had an empty late-night brightness that hurt my eyes. I collected my room key from the night clerk, left a six o'clock wake-up call, and followed the numbers to my room. I stripped, and after a few hours of dark forgetting, woke to the ringing of the hotel operator.

I did all the things you have to do in the morning to feel human again, and at a few minutes before seven I bought a newspaper and joined the business crowd for an early break-fast at the hotel coffee shop. I sat at the counter, and as most people who wear suits believe their business is important enough to rate a table, there wasn't much company. The woman who took my order was in her late forties. She was the type of waitress you never see in a restaurant but find in coffee shops—efficient, opinionated, and motherly without being soft about it. I was her only customer at the moment. She kept my coffee cup full and my ears busy. We talked the favorite topics of strangers: the weather, marriage, kids, and the problems of making ends meet. By my fourth cup of coffee, when my kidneys were raising the white flag of surrender, she asked me what I did for a living. I told her and asked about Jack Carlisle.

"Breakfast is a lost art to most of these executive types. They say they don't got the time, but I say, if you don't got the time for a little bacon and eggs, what's the use of all that money you're makin'?"

"Ever wait on him?"

"Once. Sometimes I'd see him if he came down to get his thermos filled with coffee. He always had a nice word or two, and made a point of asking if people were happy with their work."

"Did you see him last Monday?" I asked.

She lifted a pot of coffee off the burner and refilled my cup.

"I didn't see him at all. I didn't work Sunday, so I didn't hear that he'd come into town until he was on his way out. I wouldn't have known he was here if it wasn't for the thermos he sent down."

"What did the thermos look like?"

"It was a real fancy job. The outside was done up in leather, and there was a picture of a woman"—her eyebrows arched in mock disapproval—"standing there as nature made her, without a stitch of clothing on."

"I didn't figure you to be the prudish type," I said, raising my eyebrows back at her.

She threw her head back and laughed. "I'm not. Honey, you don't get three kids and two husbands by blushing every time the lights go off."

I laughed with her.

"What went into the thermos?"

"Coffee, of course. But not the same stuff I've been filling your cup with. We have a machine back in the kitchen, a whatchacallit—expresso machine. We don't serve it to the customers. It was there just for Mr. Carlisle, because he liked his coffee thick as mud."

"Did you fill it for him on Monday?"

"Wouldn't know how. Carlos always takes care of it. He's the head cook and the only one who can work the machine."

"If you didn't see Mr. Carlisle on Monday, he must have sent someone down with the thermos, then had it brought back up to him."

She stuffed her order book into her apron and leaned against the counter with her arms crossed.

"I don't really remember. I can ask Carlos, though. He'd know how it went back and forth."

"That would be helpful," I suggested.

She patted my hand. I'd made a friend.

"My pleasure, darlin'," she said, and with a wink, backed through the swinging double doors into the kitchen.

I flipped open the newspaper while I waited for her to return, and scanned the business section. Nothing caught my eye. I turned to the sports section to see how the Lakers were doing, but before I got there, a hand grabbed my shoulder. Twisting away, my hand balled into a fist before I noticed it was Joe Mankewitz.

"What the hell are you doing here?" he asked with a worried smile.

"I couldn't get enough of the rain and fog you have here. All we get in Los Angeles is miserable sunshine," I said, and relaxed my hands.

"And smog," Mankewitz added, and hitched up his belt. He plopped down in the chair next to mine and folded his hands carefully on the counter.

"I didn't expect to see you back so soon. You here on business?"

I nodded.

"Stupid question," he said, and cleared his throat. "You got an expense account this time?"

I nodded again, and folded my newspaper.

"Mind if I ask who is footing the bill?"

"You can ask, but if I gave you an answer, it wouldn't be the truth."

Mank grunted. "At least you don't bullshit me."

He pulled a pack of Pall Malls out of the breast pocket of his brown blazer and lit one.

"I heard George Wentworth was here with Jack Carlisle," I said, and watched him breathe smoke.

"Yeah? Who's he?" he asked casually, and picked an invisible speck of tobacco from his lower lip.

"Jack Carlisle's father-in-law."

Mank nodded in a cloud of smoke. "Yeah, I saw him."

"You didn't mention it when I talked to you."

"I didn't think it was important enough to remember."

The waitress pushed through the kitchen doors and hesitated when she saw Mankewitz. I guessed she didn't want to give me any details about the thermos with the hotel security man sitting at my elbow. She turned toward the coffee, neatly lifted it from the hot plate, and filled Mank's cup.

"What can I get for you this morning, Joe?" she asked, and when he glanced at the menu, she rolled her eyes at me.

Mank ordered ham and eggs. With her right hand she filled my coffee cup, and with her left, she slipped my bill off the counter and into her front apron pocket.

"Did you ever meet Wentworth?" I asked as the waitress backed into the kitchen.

"Not more than to nod. He's been here a couple of times before, so I could recognize his face."

"Why didn't you mention him before?"

"How the hell was I to know what he was here for? I don't have all the goddamn answers. Hell, he wasn't even on the same floor as Carlisle. So what if I didn't tell you? I don't exactly owe you my left nut, you know."

"What are you so testy for?"

He flicked his ash and puffed on his cigarette, looking at me out of the corner of his eye.

"You make me nervous. The way I see it, you're bound to make trouble here sooner or later."

Something had happened since the last time I had seen him. He was wary. Maybe he was just taking me seriously this time.

"I won't make any trouble. But if it's here, I'll find it."

"You'd be lucky to find your ass with a sheet of toilet paper. I think you're wasting your time here. I've told you what I know, now return the favor and keep me out of it from here on."

"I'm just doing my job."

"And I'm doing mine."

The waitress set a plate of ham and eggs in front of Mank. "More coffee?" she asked.

I shook my head. She slapped the bill face down on the counter, and scurried back into the kitchen. I turned the bill over. Something was written on the receipt. It was the name of the person who had picked up the thermos. I slipped the receipt into my wallet.

"What was the name of the guy you introduced me to, the hotel manager?" I asked, signing the room tab.

Mankewitz paused, a forkful of ham arrested in mid-flight between plate and mouth.

"Jim Johnson."

"Is he around today?"

Mank smiled like a wise guy and stuffed his mouth with ham. "He's got the day off," he said.

"How would you answer a request for his phone number and address?"

"I'd refuse it."

"Then I guess I won't ask."

Sliding a twenty under the coffee cup, I rose to leave.

Mank wiped his mouth with a napkin and looked up at me. "If you happen to run into him, I'd be happier if you didn't mention my cooperation."

I nodded and left him to finish his eggs.

Returning to my room, I found the bed had been made and fresh towels laid out in the bathroom. I drew open the shades, and a diffused, overcast light seeped into the room. I spread a map of the Bay Area on the table, pulled out the telephone directory, and flipped to the three pages of Johnsons. There were forty-four "Johnson, J." listings, but only eight variants of Jim Johnson. I dialed them. Four were no-answers, one a disconnected, and three were not the Jim Johnson I was looking for.

With a pen, I outlined the areas in the map covered by the phone book. Most of the cities surrounding San Francisco fell out of the circle. I called information a dozen times and compiled a list of ten more numbers. If none of them panned out, it would take me the rest of the day to wade through the "Johnson, J." listings. Even then, there was no guarantee that his number was not unlisted or that he would be at home. Exciting work.

I was lucky. The eighth number I dialed, listing a San Anselmo address on Tamalpais Avenue, connected to an answering machine that played back Johnson's recorded voice. I circled the name, found the address on the map, and closed up shop.

Chapter
8

I DROVE THE 101 FREEWAY north across the Golden Gate Bridge to San Anselmo, pulled off at Sir Francis Drake Boulevard, and followed it west. A few wrong turns circled me around and then a right dropped me off at Tamalpais Avenue. I parked the rental at the numbered curb of a modern ranch-style house. It looked like the kind of neighborhood that would attract doctors and lawyers. None of the cars on the street grew up in Detroit. The car in Johnson's driveway was an Rx-7. I wondered what kind of money hotel managers made and where I could sign my name to the bottom line.

There was no answer to my knock on the front door. I crossed the driveway and followed the walkway through the gate and along the side of the house to the backyard. The curtains behind a sliding glass door off the patio were drawn half open. I peered into the darkness. It looked all wrong inside. Books from a bookcase on the far wall were scattered on the floor. A television had pitched over its stand, the top corner digging into the carpet. Johnson either had an avant garde taste in furniture arrangement or there had been a wild party the previous evening. I didn't want to think about what kind of party it was.

The sliding glass door was locked. I searched the corners of the glass for alarm wiring. It looked clean. Nudging my

hip against the glass near the lock, I pressed in and lifted
up. The door slid open smoothly on its track. I stepped inside
and held my breath for thirty seconds, listening. A car passed
by out front. A couple of houses down, a lawn mower chugged,
misfired, and caught with a droning roar. I shut the glass
door. Inside the house it was quiet. The telephone handset
dangled off the edge of an end table. Stepping over the books
littering the floor, I glanced left into the kitchen. Silverware
jumbled in a heap on the tile. My apartment had been broken
into before. I knew what it looked like. This was it.

My voice died in the house when I called out. The living
room had been gutted. A framed poster of a nude woman
spread-eagled over a Porsche hung by its corner on the wall.
Stuffing from the couch, slit tail to head like a fish, spewed
onto the carpet. Torn wiring was all that remained of the
stereo.

I wandered into the hallway. The door to the bathroom
was open. The medicine cabinet swung off its hinge. Bottles
and pills were scattered on the linoleum. The next door off
the hallway was closed. I twisted the knob and eased it open.
The feet—bare and ivory-white—were the first I saw of Jim
Johnson. A blue robe, still modestly tied at the waist, began
at his knees and stretched over the still body. There was a
patch of red matting the back of his sandy-brown hair. I knelt
at his shoulders and felt his neck for a pulse. The skin was
cold and empty. His gold-rimmed glasses were twisted away
from his face, the round lenses mirroring the pillage of his
study. I gingerly felt the back of his head. It had been crushed.
The blood was still tacky and stuck to my fingers like glue.
I stood and walked to the bathroom. Aspirin tablets cracked
under my feet. I dug a handkerchief out of my pocket and
used it to cover the hot-water faucet.

I looked at my face in the mirror. It was still there. Just

a little paler than before. I ran my hand under the hot water to wash off the blood, then dried it with my handkerchief. I wrapped it around my right hand like a mitten, to avoid leaving prints, and returned to the study.

The desk drawers hung half open, the contents littering the floor. I poked through the scattered papers, without knowing what to look for. Nothing clicked. I found a photograph of Johnson under the desk and slipped it into my pocket.

I picked up the phone and called the police. The dispatcher took down my name, the address, and the complaint. Hanging up, I stared absently at the flashing red light on the answering machine. My hand reached for the play button but stopped short. Tampering with evidence is not one of the heavyweight crimes, but it wouldn't endear me to the local cops.

Noting the number, I returned to the phone in the room adjacent to the sliding glass door. It had been kicked over. If there had been only one line in the house, I would have gotten a busy signal when I called earlier in the morning. A different number was typed on the cradle. In the study I found Johnson's briefcase flung open on its side. The remote message beeper was in the side pocket.

Holding the beeper to the receiver, I dialed the study phone and waited for the machine to pick up. Johnson's recorded voice began its announcement. I pressed the beeper. His voice abruptly halted in mid-sentence. The machine changed gears. A playful voice, identifying herself as Sharon, left a message to call her at the salon and recited the number. I jotted it down in my notebook. The next voice was Mankewitz's. He had placed the time at 9:00 A.M. and requested a return call. The last caller hung up without leaving a message—my call from the hotel.

I disconnected, left the phone dangling on its cord, and dashed into the study. The machine was rewinding. It stopped with a piercing beep tone. The red light flashed on and off. I wiped my prints from the beeper and placed it back in the briefcase.

I was waiting in the front driveway when the first squad car parked at the curb. Calmly, as though they answered a dozen homicide calls a day, the two cops, the first a tall, curly-haired man and the other a short and squat woman with a flat nose, strolled up the walk. The curly-haired cop glanced at his notebook.

"Did you place the call?" he asked, halting out of arm's reach.

I nodded and gave my name.

"Did you touch anything inside the house?"

"A few things. I can show you what."

"How did you gain entry into the house?"

His voice was flat, as though everything human had been filtered out of it.

"The back door was open," I lied.

"Could you show us, please?"

I led them around the side of the house to the sliding glass door.

I said, "I came in through here."

"Was it open or just unlocked?"

"Unlocked."

Nodding, he slid the door open with the back of his knuckle and stepped inside. I followed the woman inside. The two cops waded slowly through the room, bent heads swinging as they searched the floor. The curly-haired cop turned to me and lifted his eyebrows.

"The body?"

Tight-lipped, I crossed in front of him and led them down

the hall. I stopped by the study door and flicked my finger toward it. He saw the feet stretched bare across the doorway and froze. The woman cop looked around his shoulder, shook her head, and stepped back. The curly-haired cop elbowed the door completely open, crabbed around the feet of the body, and crouched by the head. He pursed his lips and stretched his right hand across his chest and felt for a pulse on Johnson's neck.

"He seems dead enough," he said, wiping his hand on his trouser leg. "Go ahead and call it in."

The woman cop backed out of the hall. The curly-haired cop stood up. He pulled out his notebook again and turned a slow circle, examining the room, until his eyes fell on me.

"Did you touch the body?" he asked.

"On the neck, like you did. Also on the back of the head."

He jotted my reply in his notebook.

"What else did you touch?"

"The sliding glass door. When I found the body, I used a handkerchief to pick up the phone and call it in."

"What were you doing here?"

He wrote slowly, so I talked slowly. When he finished, he flapped the notebook closed and told me to wait in the back-yard until someone came by to get a full statement.

I sat in a chaise longue on the back porch, with a view into the house. Within the half hour a couple of plainclothes from Homicide arrived, poking their long noses into the family room. They stared my way for a moment, then ignored me. A forensics man dusted for prints. A photographer crouched, and the hall burst into a split second of light. Out of a second burst, the shape of a man emerged, sweeping through the family room and out the sliding glass door. He was short, with bristly black hair and a nose like a crow's beak. He pointed at me with a crooked finger. I stood.

"You Marston?" he said in a dry voice.

I handed him my business card and watched him peer at it. He pocketed the card and asked the same questions the curly-haired cop had. I responded with the truth, when and where I could.

He flicked his finger at my chest.

"Most people would have walked away at the front door, but you came around back here and broke in. Maybe you were looking for something. Maybe you didn't much care if he was home or not."

"If you want to play a game of maybes, maybe I thought he was sitting in the backyard, getting a fog tan. Or maybe I thought he just didn't want to talk to visitors."

"And maybe you're handing me a line of bullshit."

He pulled out my card and squinted at it.

"Just what is it that you do? I don't get it from this card."

"I help companies with their security problems."

"You got an investigator's license?"

I handed it to him. He copied the number down on his note pad and returned it.

"You here in relation to a case?"

"Ever hear of Jack Carlisle?"

He shook his head. "Tell me."

I gave him the short version of the story.

"You ever been a cop?" he said with another finger flick at my chest.

"Not as a civilian."

"Fuckin' amateur," he muttered. "Why'd you want to talk to this guy?"

"He managed the hotel where Mr. Carlisle spent his last night."

"You got any reason to believe this is related?"

"Nothing that would impress a crack investigator like yourself."

"Try me," he deadpanned.

"Seems a little coincidental," I offered.

His crow face smirked.

"It's all a goddamn conspiracy, right? Let me tell you something. We get a couple of these crash-and-bash-type killings a year. It comes with the fancy furniture and cars. You got 'em, somebody else wants 'em, and if you're unlucky enough to be around when they take 'em, they knock you over the head."

"They were pretty thorough for thieves."

"People that got money sometimes hide it in strange places. There are enough Krugerrands hidden in this county to finance the national debt. I've seen houses torn up worse than this."

"You're the expert."

"Damn right I am," he croaked, and gave me the thumb. "I may have some other questions to ask you later, but why don't you get lost until then."

"My pleasure," I said, and it was.

From a gas station phone booth on Sir Francis Drake Boulevard I called the number the voice had left on Johnson's answering machine. It was a hair-cutting salon. The receptionist put me through to Sharon, and I booked an appointment for a trim, letting it drop that I had been referred by Jim Johnson.

With the last of my change, I dialed the hotel and gave Mankewitz the police version of Johnson's death. He was properly horrified. I told him I'd keep in touch.

The salon was sandwiched between a Chinese restaurant

and a photocopying shop in one of those instant mini-malls
that seem to spring up on every suburban street corner in
California. The interior was all hard surfaces: chrome, glass,
porcelain, and vinyl. A tall blonde with a wave of curls wider
than her shoulders introduced herself as Sharon and led me
to a chair in a corner of the shop. The chair was backed into
a sink. Settling into the chair, I lowered the back of my head
over the sink and tried to relax while she tucked a towel
around my neck.

"Are you a friend of Jim's?" she asked, her voice distant,
as though her mind were communicating through a million
leagues of interstellar space.

The water hissed through the hose behind me and splashed
into the sink. A jet of water streamed through my hair.

"I know him well enough to get the idea you're his friend."

I heard her laugh softly. All I could see of her was ten
bright pink and absurdly long nails. I closed my eyes. The
muscles in my neck and shoulders loosened as she worked
the conditioner in. My mind began to wander. I remembered
my first haircuts, when my father took me to see an old man
with tufts of hair splaying from his nostrils, who scraped an
electric razor around my skull like a lumberjack with a buzz
saw and an acre of forest to clear. I had a theory that long
hair came into style because of barbers like him, and went
back out again because of women like Sharon.

I felt a sharp tug on my hair as she pressed the water out.
Then I stood up with the towel draping my head and followed
her to a swivel chair in front of a mirror. I looked dashing.
A cross between an Arab sheik and a wet English sheep dog.

The stylist measured out my hair with a comb and began
to snip at the ends. I watched her face while she worked. It
was a fresh young face. Her eyes squinted in simple concen-

tration. The image of her lover's pale and twisted face flitted through my head. I chased it away.

"How long have you known Jim?"

She paused over her scissors. "About three months."

"I used to work for the company that owns his hotel. I've heard good things about him."

"From people in the company?"

I caught her eyes in the mirror. She hid a pleased smile behind her scissors. I nodded.

"He's really excited about his work. Especially lately."

"Any particular reason?"

She whispered, "I think he's going to get a big promotion."

"He deserves it. I understand he's been working on an important project."

Her scissors stopped in mid-cut. "Did he tell you about that?"

There are few projects more important than murder.

"Not in great detail, but he mentioned it."

"He doesn't like to talk about work, at least not to me. He can be a real mystery man sometimes. But he did say it was really big, now that he was in with the really important people."

"Did he mention any names? I bet I know who he was working with."

"I wouldn't remember if he did. Just some people in Los Angeles and Las Vegas."

"I didn't know the company had hotels in Vegas."

I knew they didn't.

"I wouldn't know about that," she answered, and tilted my head down to trim behind my ears. "But that's where he lived before he moved here. He told me he moved around a lot before he started to work in hotels."

With my chin pressed down against my chest, I mumbled something about there being a lot of hotels in Las Vegas.

"He never said which one, or if he did, I forgot."

She handed me a mirror and spun the chair until my back was to the wall mirror. I examined the cut and said it was fine.

"Did you happen to see Jim this weekend?" I asked.

"Sure." She smiled. "We went out for dinner and a show on Saturday."

"Was he expecting to see anyone Sunday?"

She took the twenty I handed her for the cut and locked it in a drawer.

"I think he told me he was going to stay home and work in his darkroom."

"His darkroom?" I heard my voice jump.

"Sure. Jim is a photography nut. He keeps a darkroom in his garage."

That explained why his car was parked in the driveway. I thanked her and, with a polite smile, left the shop. Once outside, my smile faded and I complimented myself with a few four-letter words. Whoever had ransacked the house likely had the brains, unlike myself, to search the garage. The crow-faced homicide man was right. I was an amateur.

Chapter
9

THREE DAYS OF MAIL and two *Wall Street Journals* were scattered on the floor beneath the office mail slot. I tossed the lot on my desk and played back the messages on Shirley. It was the usual collection of cranks and creditors, including one call from a woman claiming to have known Jack Carlisle. She left her name and the address of the Ocean Park Boxing Club. I wondered how the girlfriend of a boxer could know Carlisle and how she got my number. One of life's little mysteries. I took the number down on a memo sheet and pocketed it.

I directed Hal to a file on detective agencies. Several from Las Vegas were listed, with an asterisk in the margin next to a number for Discovery Detectives. I had met one of the firm's principals at an electronic security trade show. The name in the file was Bill Pollock. From what I recalled, he seemed competent enough. I dialed the number. After a few hints he remembered who I was. I told him I needed an identity tracked down, and it took me less than a minute to tell him everything I knew about Jim Johnson. Pollock promised to put it on the front burner if and when he received a photograph. After bickering over the fee, I wished him luck and locked the office door behind me.

The boxing club was in an old gymnasium two blocks from

the beach in the Ocean Park section of Santa Monica. A block to the south, Main Street metamorphosed into a trendy shopping mecca for the young, sandals, and BMW crowd. Ten years earlier it had catered to the young, sandals, and Volkswagen crowd. Times change. A block to the north, boutiques sprang from the ruins of archaic establishments like grocery stores and corner taverns that didn't cater to the singles trade. Main Street was a hot property. It attracted well-educated young white money. Boxing clubs do not appeal to well-educated young white money. The latest and the trendy would creep nearer, rents would rise, and someone would turn the club into a health club. The young and mon-eyed middle classes dream of doubling their biceps for those shirtless days at the beach or for the more private moments before a bedroom mirror, but never at the risk of a black eye or cut lip.

I stepped inside. The club smelled of sweat, leather, and disinfectant. The smack of leather echoed around the club walls. Two shapes danced in a ring to my left, gloved fists flicking harmlessly against opposing headgear. Alone in a corner, a heavyweight with thighs like the chest of a horse worked on his foot speed with the jump rope. I watched him until his hands and feet became a blur.

An old black man ambled across the floor with a bucket in his hand. By his thin and wiry frame I pegged him as a World War II vintage bantamweight. When he noticed me, he set the bucket down and wiped his hands on a towel draped over his shoulder.

"I'm looking for Miss Cantini," I said.

He pursed his lips and rearranged the towel on his shoulder.

"I don't know no Miss Cantini," he said slowly, then his face brightened, "unless you mean Angel over there."

He pointed to the shapes in the ring.

"I guess her name is Cantini, though nobody calls her by that around here. But she'd be the only fighter that'd answer to being called a miss."

As I watched the two shapes in the ring, it was easy to see that one was a superior boxer. The footwork was smoother, the left jab snaked out with deceptive quickness, and the right hook compensated in accuracy what it lacked in power. Then I noticed the breasts.

"That's Miss Cantini?" I said, and my jaw dropped so fast it needed a parachute to stop at the knees.

Half shadowing her face, the bulky leather headgear hid her hair, and her lips were distorted by a mouthpiece.

"We call her Angel," the old bantamweight said with a grin. "She's the Southern California Women's Boxing Champ. She takes off that headgear, you'll see she's the prettiest fighter since Muhammad Ali, but not that you'd want to mess with her, no, sir. Most of the boxers around here won't even get in the ring with her, she's so good. Not that they'd be afraid of getting hurt. Just embarrassed at getting whupped by a woman."

The woman the bantamweight called Angel pinned her opponent to the ropes and finished with a flurry to his midsection. A man hunched over a three-legged stool in a corner called time. She dropped her gloves, spat out her mouthpiece, and gave her opponent a loud kiss on the cheek—a reward for staying in the ring when the sensible thing would have been to dive through the ropes.

The old bantamweight nudged me in the ribs. "You know why they call her Angel?"

I shook my head.

"Looks like an angel, hurts like the devil," he said, and laughed. "You like that? I made it up myself."

When she stripped off the headgear, a shoulder-length mane of hair, the dark curls streaked with sweat, shook free. The old bantamweight chuckled and bent to pick up his bucket.

"You wanna talk with her, go right ahead. She won't bite, unless you're fool enough to step into the ring with her."

He laughed again and, with one shoulder bent from the weight of the bucket, ambled away.

As I circled the ring, Angel peeled the gloves from her taped hands, climbed through the ropes, and strode to the speed bag. Her hands danced, and the speed bag cracked percussively against the headboard. Arms across my chest, I watched from a couple of paces to her side. Her eyes swung my way once, then shifted back without a hitch in the rhythm of the bag. Her features were not angelic, though the face could have inspired Rodin to sculpt her as an archangel fired with pride and determination before the fall. Sweat glowed like a patina on her bronze skin. Her cheekbones were wide and strong, and stretched below deep-set eyes. The nostrils flared, as though fire-breathing, and a small bump below the bridge of her nose gave slight evidence to the punch that had broken it. Her full mouth was a promise, and the grim set of it a threat.

"Are you Miss Cantini?" I asked.

Her fists double-timed the speed bag, and I thought that with one last powerful slap against the headboard it would burst.

"I'm Paul Marston. You left a message on my machine."

She wiped her forehead with the back of her arm, then thrust her right hand toward mine. I took it. The grip was strong, but not boastful.

"Nice of you to stop by. Want to hold the heavy bag for me?" she said, and brushed past without waiting for an answer.

I followed her to the heavy bag.

"I heard you were investigating the plane crash that killed Jack," she said, and motioned me to take a position behind the bag.

"Ever held one of these before?"

I nodded.

"How did you get my name?" I asked.

"From a friend of Jack's. What's his name?—Bates. With an ad agency."

She positioned her feet a half-arm's length from the bag, and jolted it with a few testing hooks.

"Don't let it swing so much. Put your shoulder into it. Got a watch?"

I nodded again.

"Good. Give me sixty seconds, then call time."

The bag jerked back against my shoulder as she peppered it with a combination of jabs and hooks. I held my breath, and pinned my eyes to the second hand on my watch.

"How do you know Jack?" I called out at the thirty-second mark.

"I signed a contract with him two years ago," she answered, and slid in to work the middle of the bag with a series of uppercuts.

"I didn't know Jack was interested in the fight game."

"He wasn't."

A right hook smacked canvas a few inches from my ear.

"He was interested in me," she said.

I called out time and stepped from behind the bag.

"Were you going out with him?"

"We went out a few times in the beginning, before the contract was signed," she said, catching her breath, then looked up, voicing my thought before I had finished thinking it. "But it wasn't a romantic relationship. He was married and, from what I'd heard, had a few girlfriends on the side. I didn't want to be a preliminary to the main event."

"That doesn't tell me why he bought your contract."

Absently, she swung a soft hook into the heavy bag and watched it inscribe an arc on its chain.

"In case you haven't noticed, I'm not an average woman."

"All my woman friends are professional fighters, one way or another," I joked.

She ignored me.

"I always thought of Jack as a collector. Not that he was mean or petty about it. He just liked to collect woman friends. I was unusual. Like an albino panther or something. When he knew that romance wasn't possible, he had to find some other way to collect me, so he bought my contract."

"It was all business for you."

"No," she said softly, "I liked him. It just wasn't possible."

I thought that maybe she wasn't as tough as she appeared. Her gloves snapped together, and the small trace of softness in her eyes hardened like water on ice.

"It's time to work again," she commanded.

I put my shoulder to the bag and kept my eyes to the watch. "When did you see him last?"

"A couple of weeks ago," she answered, then I held on. The bag shuddered, and I could feel the punches through the canvas. She wasn't working out now. She was trying to kill the bag. The gloves whipped into the bag with a cracking staccato. I heard her shoes squeaking along the gym floor as she weaved in, then the blows falling in sharply timed clusters punctuated by the jarring pop of her best shot. I wondered whose face she had put on the bag. Maybe it was something faceless. The old bantamweight shouted encouragement from the corner. I forgot the time.

When the combinations lost their crispness and she began

to push her punches, I knew she had tired and called time. Letting the bag swing free, I helped her remove her gloves. A fierce exaltation glowed in her dark eyes. Whoever or whatever she had pinned to the bag had been thrashed. When I asked her if she felt better, she nodded and smiled and allowed me to lead her to the water cooler in the corner.

Angel leaned against the wall while I soaked a towel and wiped the sweat from her brow. Her eyes were glazed, and her breath came heavily. A bomb wouldn't have made her blink. Good athletes reach a kind of euphoria after a concentrated effort. She was there. In a moment she snapped the towel out of my hand and grinned.

"You trying to be my trainer or something?" she said, and buried her face in the towel.

"Maybe you were a little bit in love with Jack Carlisle," I suggested.

Her eyes peered over the towel at me, startled.

"What makes you say that?"

"When they lose something, some people cry. Others get mad and hit things. I don't think you're the crying type."

She shrugged. "Call it a crush, if you want. Like I said before, it wasn't possible."

"Sometimes dreams aren't."

"Then they should be forgotten," she said tersely, and turned her back to fill a paper cup from the cooler.

"What am I doing here, Miss Cantini? I admit it's interesting that Jack owned a fighter, but somehow I doubt that you know anything relevant to his death."

She drained the cup and leveled her eyes on me.

"I thought you might need some help." She reached out and felt the biceps of my right arm, her smile impish. "You look like you could use some muscle."

I laughed. There was little else I could do when more or

less called a wimp by a woman who could probably take me
two falls out of three. Or three out of three.

"Exactly what are you proposing?" I asked.

"That we be partners," she answered, crushing the paper
cup and tossing it into a basket next to the cooler.

"You like to start high, don't you?"

"I'll take what I can get. It should have occurred to you that
when Jack died, I lost my financial backing. I need a job."

"Why this?"

"It beats mud-wrestling." She cracked a smile, then thought
about it.

"I'm the Women's Boxing Champ, I've held a karate title,
and what I make from purses won't pay my rent. People
don't flock to see a woman fight, no matter how good, unless
it's a joke, like foxy boxing. I have too much pride in what
I do for that."

"So you think, Why not detective work? Right?"

"Right."

"Lots of action, car chases, gunplay, duking it out with
the bad guys. Right?"

"Right."

"Sorry. I work the suit and tie trade. Most of the time
I sit around in cars, watching and waiting for things to
happen that usually don't. If you want excitement, this
isn't it."

"I don't care. Just think about giving me the job."

"I don't know if you have the qualifications."

"I can wait around and be bored as well as anyone. If
something happens to come up, I can take care of myself."

"But can you type?" I joked.

She snapped a left jab that fell a quarter inch short of my
nose.

"So you don't have a sense of humor," I said. "It's not

required for the job, though sometimes it helps in personal relationships."

"Oh, I have a sense of humor all right," she said, smiling. "If I didn't, I wouldn't have missed with that jab. So do I get the job?"

"I run a pretty low-rent operation. If you're really serious about this, you might try some of the larger agencies."

"I'd rather work with you."

"I'm flattered, but why?"

"You tell lousy jokes. Plus that guy Bates said you were okay."

"If you see him, tell him if he doesn't keep his mouth shut about what I'm working on, your first assignment will be to go shut his mouth."

"He'd probably like that," she said.

"You're right. He would. I'll call you in a couple of days and let you know what I think."

I told her to leave her home phone number on my answering machine, and as I walked away, her fists began to work to the rhythm of the speed bag like a snare drum.

I hit a photo-processing lab on Cotner, then delivered four copies of Johnson's portrait to the Federal Express office in Santa Monica. As I drove, I toyed with the idea of hiring Angel Cantini. I needed someone to help with the details. There was a local agency I used when I needed help with surveillance. They were expensive, and the people sent were moonlighters who fell asleep as often as not. Angel Cantini couldn't be any worse, and with a little experience wouldn't have any trouble handling the work. And she'd be cheaper. The only problem with Angel was her relationship to Jack Carlisle. She had a personal interest. I didn't know if I could trust her to step back if I told her to. I didn't know if I could trust myself.

Chapter
10

THE PACIFIC COAST HIGHWAY CUTS through the beach community of Malibu like a set of train tracks separating the wealthy from the merely rich, who have to live with the sight of the highway spoiling their ocean views. Between the ocean cliffs and hillsides, Malibu stretches into flatlands where no one wants to live. From the flatlands you can't see the water at all. The Malibu Sheriff Station stands in the middle of the flatlands.

At the front desk I asked the deputy on duty where I could find the person in charge of the Topanga Canyon plane-crash site. The lack of an ocean view had made him surly.

"We don't handle that," he said flatly.

"Who does?"

"The FAA," he answered, and gave me the top of his head as he returned to marking up a few carbons.

"Try the National Transportation Safety Board," I suggested.

He looked up and growled, "Same thing."

I parked my elbows on the desk like I wasn't planning to go away any time soon.

"They told me you would be the ones to make a sweep of the crash area, picking up personal effects."

"Who told you?"

"The NTSB."

His eyelids fluttered as he puzzled it through.

"Personal effects?" he murmured, then nodded as he caught on to something he understood. "Those are picked up by the coroner's office."

"They're only interested in items connected to the body, like wallets and rings," I suggested.

"So what?"

"So what about other items, such as suitcases, or maybe a coffee thermos?"

"The FAA would pick that up on their walk through," he answered, and tried to dismiss me with a quick nod of his head.

"You mean the NTSB," I corrected.

The tiny veins in his face flushed red, and he bobbed his head once.

"They seem to think you handled that."

"If you got all the answers, what are you bothering to ask me for?" he groused.

"I didn't have anything better to do, so I figured why not come down here and give you a hard time?"

The deputy had a tough choice between shooting me on the spot or letting me bother someone higher up the ladder. I lived long enough to be ushered into the sheriff's office. He was a broad-shouldered man with a tanned face, salt-and-pepper hair, and understanding brown eyes. The name on the desk plaque read Bernie Kohl. His smile was serene. He asked what he could do for me. I wondered if he had spent too much time in the sun or just studied Zen.

I asked him if any of his men had searched the crash site.

"What would they want to do that for?"

"To collect evidence in a potential murder case," I suggested.

" 'Other sins only speak; murder shrieks out,' " he mused.

"I beg your pardon?"

"John Webster, in *The Duchess of Malfi*."

"Don't tell me," I said, "the real sheriff is on sabbatical and you're an out-of-work English professor filling in until his return."

His smile remained serene. "M.A., English Literature, at Northwestern University, 1966. Due to the high unemployment rate among my peers, I doubled in Police Science."

"I bet you quote a mean Miranda."

"I'm particularly fond of the line: 'You have the right to remain silent.' It's one of the classic lines in modern literature, and its message is one by which most of us could profit."

"And here I thought you were kidding. You really are an out-of-work English professor."

Kohl's hands fluttered in a show of modesty. "Although it's not your intent, you flatter me. I'm just a humble public servant."

His hands dropped to the table. They were tanned at the back, but the palms were soft and pink. Kohl cleared his throat.

"To answer your question, we would make a sweep of the area in the event of a murder investigation. If there is no evidence of foul play, we allow the NTSB to conduct the investigation as they see fit."

"How do you know whether the crash is an accident or murder?"

His hands floated palms up. "The NTSB makes a ruling."

"But the NTSB requires two months to make a determination of cause."

"If there was evidence of foul play, we would investigate," he calmly repeated.

"Like if the plane was shot down by an antiaircraft gun?"

"That's a little dramatic, don't you think?" His eyes were mildly reproving. "You must understand there are jurisdictional problems at issue here."

"Name them."

Sheriff Kohl leaned back in his chair and contemplated the parking lot out his window.

"First, there is no evidence, that has been presented to me at least, and second, if there was a criminal act, which I remind you has not been established, it is unclear who has jurisdiction. The act could have occurred in San Francisco, or over any one of five counties between here and San Francisco. That is why it is in everyone's best interest to let the NTSB handle this."

"Including the murderer's."

"For a town full of celebrities, Malibu is a nice, quiet place," Kohl said, kicking his feet up on the desk. "I like quiet places. You're in such a hurry to make something out of this plane crash, go right ahead."

"But don't expect any help from you, right?"

"You'd be wise to remember the words of Titus: 'Patience is the best remedy for every trouble.' "

"Sheriff, it's been a pleasure," I said, and stood.

"Glad to be of help," he returned.

On my way out I quoted Marx: " 'I never forget a face; but in your case, I'll make an exception.' "

Groucho Marx.

The dry wheat grass, knee-high and beginning to brown, parted and snapped beneath my feet as I strode through the field where the plane had gone down. A shell of earth and blackened stubble marked the plane's impact. The plane was gone—hauled away, I presumed, by the NTSB. I paced away from the shell, my eyes reaping through the wheat grass. A black shoe, splattered with dust, stood with its toe pointed toward the road. A twisted shirt and pair of pants sprawled in the grass. The thermos was not where I recalled it had been.

I worked farther out, parting the grass with my feet. Dividing the circle around the impact point into pie-shaped wedges, I searched the entire area. I found an anthill but not much else. The thermos was gone.

A hundred yards across the field, an old house hid in a stand of oaks. I hiked to it, climbed up to the porch, and rapped my knuckles against the screen door. Inside, above the roar of a Janis Joplin record, I heard someone stumble, and a slurred voice hollered at me to go away. I rapped again. My knock was answered by a late-thirties man with the beard, long hair, and stoned eyes of someone trapped by a time warp in the 1960s. A pint of Southern Comfort dangled in his left hand. A credible witness if I ever saw one.

"Wha' da fuh y'wan?"

He spoke like he had a mouth full of marbles. His red-rimmed eyes were nervous until I showed him the ten-spot in the palm of my hand. He smiled around crooked teeth.

"Y'sellin' money, man? Far out. I'll take some."

He stepped out onto the porch. The screen door banged shut. I closed the bill in my fist. The smile sank back into his mouth.

I asked, "Did you see the airplane crash last week?"

When he laughed, his voice started low and rode a twisted staircase to the high notes, then cracked and fell into a cough.

"Yeah. Wow. Lotta noise. Lotta people. Cops 'n' stuff. Fire 'n' a fire truck. I heard three people bit the big one on 'at. Whad else ya wanna know 'bout it?"

"After the cops cleared everybody away, did you see anybody looking for something around the plane? That afternoon or the next day."

"Sure. Lotta cops 'n' a lotta kids, 'n' maybe someone else. That bill in yer hand fer me?"

"If you tell me something that makes sense."

"You shoulda come by 'fore I got to smokin' 'n' drinkin'. Take me days to make sense now."

He laughed again, but lost his balance and tottered back on his heels. Though he seemed about to fall, he didn't step back, and instead planted his heels and wildly swung his arms, as if he stood on the edge of a cliff and it would be death to fall. He fell anyway. His head cracked on the screen. He laughed again and took a swig of Comfort to steady himself.

"Southin Comfort. Ju know this was Janz Joplin's drink? I saw her in concert. Wow. Number one on my highlight film, man. Best night of my life, man."

"Wonderful. Who did you see at the plane crash?"

"Oh, yeah. I saw someone. A tall blond guy. Looked like he shoulda been on some soap opera, y'know, fluffy hair 'n' muscles. Had one of them furrin cars, y'know, a BMW a coupla years old. Silver. I got this window out back, and I sit and look out it a lot, spacin' on stuff. He come by after the cops cleared out, 'bout three. I figured him fer a souvenir hunter."

"Did he find anything?"

"Don't know. Told ya I was spacin' out. Went inta this kinda Buddhist-like trance, and when I got back, he'd gone."

I handed him the ten. The pint of Southern Comfort slipped from his hand and rolled onto the porch when he tried to stuff the ten into his shirt pocket. He sat down hard on the steps.

"Shit," he said. "Trouble in paradise."

Chapter
11

GEORGE WENTWORTH AGREED TO TALK with me within the hour when I called from my apartment in Santa Monica. I ate something squalid out of a can, showered off the Topanga dust, and pointed the Mustang south toward Marina del Rey.

The Wentworths lived in a Spanish-style two-story on the Marina. It wasn't a big money area like Beverly Hills, but it looked like a seven-figure house to me. I parked my four-figure Ford at the curb of a cul-de-sac and followed a wandering front walk hedged with flowering peonies. The door opened to a silver-haired man in his early fifties. He was a big man, about my height, but wider at the shoulders and through the middle. His blue leisure suit was topped with a gold scarf at the throat. His face, tanned and oiled like calf-skin, was beginning to lose its handsomeness with age and too many of the highballs like the one curled in his left hand.

We exchanged names, and he asked me what my poison was.

"A beer, thanks," I answered, and followed his broad sauntering back into the hall.

He ducked behind a doorway. I heard a refrigerator door open and shut. His voice boomed out in the hall.

"I hope Bud is to your liking, 'cause it's all I carry here."

"Bud is fine."

"Good!" he bellowed, and, lumbering into the hall, handed me a frosted mug with a two-inch head.

"I carry Bud because I own a couple of thousand shares in Anheuser Busch. It gives me what you might call a personal interest, as long as I don't drink up my own profits!"

His laugh was oversized. Show time. I saluted him with the mug.

"Come on into the living room, and let me introduce you to my wife." He drained his highball, and led me into a room that aspired to Old World charm. It succeeded with the Old World, but missed on the charm. Eighteenth-century end tables with delicate, fluted legs, an armoire trimmed with a chorus of hand-carved cherubs, Chinese vases, Persian rugs, and dark portraits of unknown royalty congregated in a baroque clutter of polished wood, porcelain, silver, and gilt. The room looked like a museum exhibit of the way nobility lived two hundred years ago. At the far end, reclining in a floral-print chair by a window that overlooked the bobbing marina lights, a woman turned her head halfway toward me. She wore a silver evening dress, with a single strand of black pearls set against the pale skin of her neck. The hair was her daughter's shade of strawberry-blond, streaked with silver at the temples.

When George introduced us, Madeline Wentworth said in a voice as thin and cutting as piano wire, "I don't approve of my daughter's hiring you. It is not in keeping with her character to resort to the services of a cheap detective."

"I don't know much about your daughter's character," I responded, "but I can set you straight about me. I'm not a cheap detective. I always tip at least five percent, and I never make my date pay for more than her fair share."

George snickered into his highball. Madeline cut him with a look.

"Please escort Mr. Marston to your study, Georgie. I will join you there later," she said, and dismissed us with a wave of the royal hand.

George Wentworth winked and led me down a hallway past the dining room into a sunken room that looked like a set designer's idea of a captain's cabin. A fishing net studded with cork floats hung from the oak-paneled walls. Miniature models of three-masted sailing ships cruised inside a glass trophy case. In the corner the helm of an old sailing vessel had been converted into a wet bar, with the wheel doubling as a soft drink and seltzer dispenser, and a pair of miniature rudders controlling the draft beer spigots.

"Don't mind Maddy," George said as he squeezed behind the helm. "Her opinions run a little strong, something she inherited from the old man. But if you stick to your guns, you'll get along fine. She likes a man with a firm backbone. Lord knows she does."

He raised his eyes to the heavens, as though her insistence on strength were his albatross, and rolled two great swallows of Scotch down his throat to ease the burden.

"Thanks for the tip," I said, and with my eye on a nautical chart of Santa Monica Bay, asked, "Are you a sailor, Mr. Wentworth?"

"With a little more daylight, you could look out the window there and see my ship, the *Inside Straight*, anchored in her slip."

I took his hint and looked out at the marina. In the window's reflection, I watched him rapidly drain his Scotch and water and pour another. More of a boater, I thought—one of those guys who drives an oversized upholstered bathtub around the marina a couple of times a week, one hand draped on the wheel and the other steering a Scotch.

"I suppose if we have to put up with this, we can get it

done as quickly as possible," Madeline Wentworth announced at the top of the steps.

George gave her his arm, and with slightly drunken care ushered her into a leather armchair. I sat in a deck chair on the other side of an oak sea chest. Adjusting the hem of her dress with an annoyed flick of her wrist, she said: "Keeping in mind that we have the right to refuse to answer any of your questions, what is it you want to know?"

I knew better than to try to ask anything of her, and addressed myself to her husband.

"You were in San Francisco with Jack Carlisle the day before he died. Why?"

George smiled easily, like a kid who has a well-rehearsed answer.

"Madeline and I have quite a few shares of Western Shores stock."

Madeline snapped, "And we'd have more than quite a few if you hadn't talked me into selling some off."

George shook his head as though slapped. "What do you want me to do, make money or make your father happy?"

A smile wrapped around her teeth like clear plastic. "I'm sorry, dear. Please continue."

His mouth opened as if to speak, hesitated, and sipped at his Scotch instead. I tried another question.

"TransNational was prepared to make a take-over bid on the eve of Jack's death. How would the board have voted?"

"You can never tell about these things," he said with a cautious glance at his wife. "The board had a lot of faith in Jack, but Henry Howard is a real powerhouse. He could have twisted a few arms to get the votes he needed to block the move at board level. If TransNational then decided to try for an unfriendly take-over, the vote would have gone to the stockholders."

"How would you have voted?"

George swirled the ice around his glass while money fluttered over the booze in his eyes.

"We would have realized a thirty percent appreciation in the cash value of our stock as the deal was structured."

Madeline slapped the leather arm of her chair. "We would not have voted for the take-over unless my father had agreed it was in the best interests of the company."

Rising from his chair, George strode with tipsy integrity to the helm.

I said to Madeline, "If you weren't interested in the deal, why did you send your husband up to San Francisco?"

"I did not send him up to San Francisco. It was his idea."

"Did you send him up to spy for Henry Howard?"

"That's ridiculous!" she snapped.

"Then why did he attend the meeting?"

"Working for my daughter does not give you the right to slander me."

"Now, Maddy, the man has a right to his questions. After all, he is acting as Leslie's agent," George called from the helm.

Straightening, Madeline peered across the room. Her voice was a singsong. "You aren't having another one, are you, dear?"

"Just a half measure to keep my hand in the pot," he sang back and, carefully measuring his distances, steered the drink back to his chair.

His head weaved as he spoke. "Our Western Shores stock is in Maddy's name, but I act as her financial adviser. I knew about her feelings in this. We all felt bad about it. But I thought it best to make the trip to represent her interests. I didn't know what the outcome would be, and it seemed wise to cover our bets."

"I heard that you and Henry Howard didn't get along. That you were bitter about being excluded from the family business."

"We had some disagreements years ago, which Leslie must have told you about. Water under the bridge. As a matter of fact, I'll be rejoining the company next week."

Madeline's voice was a sharp rebuke: "I don't think that's a subject that needs to be discussed here."

"I'll talk about it if I want to, dammit," George insisted.

Madeline sighed and twirled her black pearls.

"I'm to be the director of new business opportunities."

I congratulated him. Madeline forced a gracious smile and said, "We're very pleased. The company is in a crisis. Jack fulfilled his duties as chief operating officer well, until this fiasco at the end. But the deal that Jack was trying to put together is dead. We want to do all we can to help pull the company through its current difficulty."

It is unwise to be allied to a dead leader in a dead cause. I had few doubts that the Wentworths were willing participants in the TransNational deal, but there was little profit in that now. The King is dead. Long live the King.

"You realize that this job offer smells of a buy-out and gives you a motive."

"Motive? For what?" he asked.

"Murder."

"But it was an accident."

"I'm going to prove it was murder."

Madeline shot out of her chair and shouted, "I see what you're trying to do. You want to turn Jack's death into some big mystery and drag us all into the dirt, while you milk my daughter of her money and make a name for yourself. Jack's death was an accident. If you try to turn it into something else, you're going to make some very powerful enemies."

I looked up at her for a couple of seconds, counting the times someone had told me I'd never work in this town again. Turning to George, I softly said, "What do you think?"

"I want this man out of my house, now!" Madeline cried. I thought maybe she'd try stamping her foot and holding her breath, but George got the message and rose wearily from his chair.

"I think I should escort you to your car, Mr. Marston."

I followed him outside. When he saw the car I drove, his estimation of me dropped, but I was used to that. He decided to level with me anyway.

"You're wrong about the murder motive. Sure, the job offer is a buy-out. The old man is buying our loyalty, but hell, I should have had a say in running the company years ago."

"Tell me why that isn't a motive for murder."

"Because I was in on the ground floor of Jack's deal. If the acquisition went through, there would have been a re-structuring of the board of directors. With Jack's sponsorship, you can bet I'd be sitting on it. Hell, if I wanted to kill someone, it would be the old man."

"Does your wife know this?"

George smiled. "Sure. She wants to kill him too."

Chapter
12

OVER THE NEXT TWO DAYS Chris Manly's silver BMW led me through the life of an unemployed actor on a trust fund. I spent my mornings at a health spa, my lunches on Melrose Avenue, and my afternoons at the tennis courts. Evenings I attended a method actor's workshop and listened to beautiful people scream and sob as if they had real problems. Those who did not have problems invented some. Remember the little dog that died when you were six years old. Your upper-middle-class parents never really loved you, so cry about it now. Stanislavsky filtered through the ozone of American pop psychology. The good ones managed to stay in character. The bad ones needed a couch and some guy with a goatee taking notes in a little black book.

After I tucked Manly in bed on the second evening, I swung by my office to poke through the day's mail. Shirley had recorded a Las Vegas call, from Pollock. He left an after-hours number, and I dialed it. A woman picked up on the other end. When I asked for Pollock, her shrill voice rang out over the kids screaming in the background. Pollock told them to shut up, then answered.

"We pinned an I.D. on this Jim Johnson guy of yours. Hold on a minute," he said, then dropped the phone to shuffle papers and tell the kids to shut up again.

"His name here was Jim Stanley, but he could have had a string of a.k.a.'s dating back to previous addresses. He was picked up on a blackmailing charge about three years ago, but the complainant dropped charges and the case never went to court. He left town about a year ago. Previous addresses drew a blank, but we think he blew in from back East somewhere."

"Did you get a fix on his employment?"

"Sure did. He was an assistant manager for the Desert Sun Hotel and Casino. No problems there. People we talked to said he was a model employee."

"You know the town better than I do. Who owns the Desert Sun?"

Pollock paused.

"I don't know for sure, but I seem to recall it's held by American Sun."

"The name fits."

"We picked up something else that's real interesting but haven't been able to do anything with it."

"What's that?"

"Johnson-Stanley had a wife here. They divorced two years ago. She's a cocktail waitress in one of the clubs."

"What's the problem? Ex-wives love to talk about bad husbands."

"Not this one. You seem to be a pretty persuasive guy. Maybe you'd have better luck."

I thought about it for three seconds and told Pollock that I'd fly in the next day.

"Don't bother to rent a car. I'll pick you up at the airport," Pollock said, and when I hung up, I called Angel Cantini.

She was waiting for me at a corner table at the Rose Café when I backed through the door, lugging a Haliburton case loaded with camera equipment. I almost didn't recognize her without the gym shorts. She wore a tight-waisted blue dress that left no doubt about her more than ample gender.

I said, "You look great."

"I had a dinner date. It wasn't easy convincing my boyfriend I had a job appointment with a guy this time of night, so I hope your offer is serious."

Her dark hair curled like steam around her face. A trace of light-blue shadow deepened her eyes. Something like memory and desire mingled in my guts.

"The offer is serious."

"My boyfriend thought it was a come-on."

"There's a rule I try never to break, and that's to date the women I work with. If you have a hopeless crush on me, now's the time to admit it."

"I like my men with a little more muscle." She smirked.

"And I like my women with strong minds and soft bodies, not the other way around."

Her eyes turned angry. "I'm not soft in the head. Just because I'm a good athlete doesn't mean I don't have a brain. That's a stereotype that should have gone out with Primo Carnera."

"Muscles and strength don't always go hand in hand either. Take your muscle boy off the steroids for a week, and his biceps will flatten out like a tire with a fast leak."

Surprise raised her voice an octave.

"How did you know my boyfriend was a body-builder?"

"It fits. His name is Tiny, and he hangs around the beach a lot, oiling his muscles and being ogled at by the girls."

She laughed. I liked it when she laughed. She sipped an espresso and puzzled over the employment forms I handed her.

"This doesn't tell me what my salary is," she said.

"You don't get a salary. You get an hourly wage."

"How much?"

"Eight dollars an hour, plus expenses."

"I could make more than that waiting tables."

"I'm not hiring any waitresses right now. Maybe you should ask the manager here for a job," I said, and handed her my pen. She grabbed it, and for a moment I thought she might stab me with the ball-point. She signed her name instead.

Over coffee I gave her the short course on surveillance, showed her how to work the camera, and told her what I knew about Chris Manly. We left the café about midnight. Later, staring into the ceiling from my bed, I caught myself thinking about Angel. It didn't help me sleep.

Chapter
13

POLLOCK WAS LEANING OVER THE RAILING at the end of the exit ramp, sucking on a cigarette, when I entered the terminal. At six foot two and two-hundred-fifty pounds he was afraid of getting lost in the crowd, so Pollock sported an eye-jarring ensemble that clashed lime-green slacks against a blue checked shirt and a canary-yellow sports coat. You'd have to be color-blind to miss him. I elbowed through the crowd and met him with a handshake.

"Follow me," he grunted. "I got a car parked in the lot."

His jowls shook when he walked, and he licked his lips against the desert heat like a giant Saint Bernard. People moved out of his way, afraid that someone that big and badly dressed either couldn't or wouldn't stop. I followed in his wake. In the lot, he pointed out a light-green Chevy sedan. The windows had been left rolled up, and when I opened the door, my eyebrows were seared by a blast of hot air. I rolled the window down.

"How was the flight?" he asked.

It was ritual conversation.

"Fine. I spent more time on the freeway than in the air."

"Ain't that the truth," he said, and put the Chevy into drive. "Roll up your window. This thing's got air conditioning."

I rolled the window up. A stream of lukewarm air pushed eddies of dust from the vent. Pollock steered onto the highway heading north to Las Vegas, his shoulders slumped, and his beefy hands cupping the bottom of the wheel. I made small talk.

"How's business?"

"Busy. Real busy. The runaway season is starting up. Always happens when spring is around the corner. Kids get hung up here on their way to L.A., y' know."

"I'm flattered."

His eyes jerked my way. "Why's that?"

"Getting the V.I.P. treatment with you so busy. I could have rented a car and found Johnson's ex-wife without much trouble."

Pollock's throat rumbled as he cleared it. "Well, that's something we gotta talk about."

"What's there to talk about?"

His face flushed. Tiny crimson veins popped out of his skin like worms.

He said, "There are some people who want to know what you want with this Johnson guy."

"Tell them it's none of their business."

"These aren't the kind of people you want to say that to."

"Maybe you should tell me who these guys are."

His smile was embarrassed, and it worked like a cinch tightening the knot in my stomach.

"Johnson's former employers."

"American Sun?"

He shrugged, then dared a look at me and nodded. The air in the car was beginning to foul. I rolled the window down.

"Hey, you're screwin' up the air conditioning," Pollock whined.

I watched him for a minute. He kept his eyes on the road. Drops of sweat leaked out of the skin on his forehead and upper lip.

I said, "I'll decide what to do about these people of yours after I meet Johnson's ex."

"There is no ex-wife," he said, and his fat tongue rolled over his upper lip.

I felt stupid. Like a fish must feel the moment the hook sets and a tender little morsel turns to steel and pain.

"How long have you been American Sun's boy?" I asked.

"It seemed like the easiest way to arrange a meeting. I didn't think you'd come otherwise."

I didn't have anything to say to him. His eyes shifted between me and the road. Maybe he thought I'd try to punch him. I was thinking about it. Pollock tightened his grip on the wheel, his knuckles whitening, and leaned away from me, against the door. The highway stretched flat and hot. He was panting. The heat was beginning to hang the flesh on his face like meat on a rack. He wiped his forehead with the back of his hand, looked at me, then at the road, and as I wasn't saying anything, and neither was the road, he filled the silence with a whining voice.

"This is a company town, and in a company town you don't fuck with the company. What do you know about this town? You don't live here. If you don't want to meet these guys, take a taxi back to the airport. But if I were you, I'd meet them. These guys are out of your league. I've been in business for twenty years, and hell, they're out of my league."

"What are they going to do, break my legs?" I said only half in jest.

"Sure they'll break your legs, and that's just for starters. Then they'll put a line into the credit agencies and give you a long list of nonpayments. You got any loans? They'll all come due. You'll find a note under your office door that your lease is getting yanked. Some ugly rumors will make the rounds with your clients. By the time your business goes down the toilet, you'll think a broken leg is a cakewalk."

Pollock eased the Chevy against the curbfront of a broken-down office building near the warehouse district. It wasn't corporate headquarters. I followed him inside. The bulletin board directory on the wall was blank. Whoever rented here didn't want to advertise. I couldn't blame them. The building maintenance had been left to the rats. We climbed scuffed stairs to the third floor.

"I've got to search you," Pollock wheezed, and wiped his face with a handkerchief.

"You're a regular guy Friday. Do they send you out for coffee and sandwiches too?"

He placed his huge hands on my shoulders, turned me around, and pushed my arms up at the sides. There was muscle under that fat. He was strong.

"It's okay to be a wise guy with me, because maybe you think I deserve it," he said as his hands traveled lightly across my coat. "But don't try it with this guy. He'll cram it all back down your throat, and then some."

Pollock shoved open the door. I stepped inside. A bald-headed man with a ruddy face looked up from his desk.

"Mr. Marston. Nice of you to drop by," he said, and rolled his chair back from the desk.

Standing, he looked like a little bull. Not any taller than five foot nine. Most of his weight was in the chest and shoulders, which stretched the seams of a yellow polo shirt. The shirt contrasted sportily with his blue slacks and striped belt. Maybe he had a golf game scheduled after our appointment. Nothing like a round of golf after a hard day of twisting arms and busting heads. His eyes shifted from me to Pollock. The door closed behind me. The little bull stuck his hand out, and I took it. His hand was small and hard.

"I didn't catch the name," I said.

"Sam Rossi," he answered, and clapped his hands together. "What can I get you? You thirsty?"

I told him I wasn't, and wandered over to the sun-faded curtains. It was all bright sun, warehouse roofs, and flat desert outside.

I said, "I'm good with titles. Let me guess. VP of Extortion?"

His smile was fast and humorless.

"Don't tax my patience, Mr. Marston."

He pointed to a seat in front of his desk. I sat, and admired the pre-sixties commercial ghetto decor. Torn wallpaper. Once-white paint flaking off the ceiling. A dead beige carpet that looked like a lawn that somebody forgot to water. If I was killed here, no one would care. Or bother with the stain.

"Am I getting the back-door treatment, or do you decorate all of your offices like this?"

"These offices are only temporary," he said, and leaning back in his chair, looked at me over the steeple of his finger tops. "If we can do business together, maybe I can show you around corporate headquarters. We have a beautiful building downtown."

"What kind of business do you have in mind?"

"We're currently considering a number of options." His eyes suddenly fixed on mine with a false but intense sincerity. "I heard that you did wonders with the security systems at Western Shores. We have a dozen hotels that could use a security overhaul. A consultant like yourself, trained in the latest systems—why, hell, we could keep you busy for a year, easy."

"I understood you had a more immediate problem."

"Nothing very important. We heard you were interested in a former employee of ours."

Rossi shuffled through a note pad in a show of forgetting the name. He tore out a slip of paper and read, "Jim Stanley."

"I knew him as Jim Johnson."

Rossi crumpled the slip of paper, let it fall onto his desk, then brushed it aside with the back of his hand. "We're strongly suggesting they aren't the same guy."

"The photo and work record match."

"Maybe they just look alike."

"Sure. Maybe they're identical twins, separated at birth but living incredibly parallel lives. Let me see Jim Stanley out of a casket, and I'll believe you."

He cocked a finger at me and asked, "Why are you trying to stir things up?"

"I want to see what floats to the surface."

"Maybe you won't like what you find. Who you working for?"

"Sorry. That's proprietary."

"You should rethink your answer."

"It wouldn't change it."

He laughed from nowhere. The laugh bounced around the room and landed back in his mouth with a crazy grin.

"I like the Boy Scout role. But don't think you can ride very far on it. We're both big boys. I'm offering you a two-month retainer to study the security system of our Bermuda property. It will require that you stay at the property during the term of the retainer."

"Sounds tempting, but I'll pass."

His hands came palms down on the desk with a slap. I tried not to jump.

"You don't understand, do you? I'm bending over backward to make this an easy deal for you to accept."

"You're a swell guy, Sam," I said. "You lure me here under a false promise, making sure Pollock lets me know what a bunch of big shots you are and how I'll have unpleasant things happen to me if I don't go along. So you showed me the whip. Now the carrot, an all-expense paid exile in Bermuda. The Las Vegas Chamber of Commerce should give you a medal you're so swell. Why don't you try being straight with me? I know it goes against the grain, but give it a try."

"Drop the Johnson investigation," he said flatly.

"Why do you want me to drop it?"

"It's bad publicity."

"If you had a couple of goons break Johnson's head in, then I can see your point."

Rossi stopped breathing for about twenty seconds. A little man was waving a red flag inside his dark eyes. Mayhem.

"That's exactly the kind of crap I don't want to hear from you or anybody else," he snapped, jabbing the air with a stubby finger. "This company has spent a fortune on public relations, and all it takes is one asshole like you to screw it up."

"From what I've heard about your company, I wonder why you even bother with public relations."

Rossi laughed softly, but his eyes went dangerously opaque. His right hand reached into a drawer. When I saw the gun slant out in his hand, I knew that I was going to be fool enough to die if he was fool enough to pull the trigger. Metal clicked on metal, and flame shot out of the barrel.

I blew it out. His laugh bounced around the room again, and he pointed the barrel to the ceiling, pulled the trigger, and lit a fat cigar with the flame.

"Cute, isn't it?" he mumbled in a cloud of smoke. "My brother-in-law gave it to me."

The adrenaline was pumping through me like a one-hundred-volt current. It took all I had to keep from going through the ceiling.

"Real funny guy, your brother-in-law."

"If I hear even a rumor that you're going to drag this company into the mud, the next thing that's pointed at your head won't be a joke."

It occurred to me that Rossi might be a little crazy. The problem with crazy people is that they don't play by the same rules as everyone else. The little regulator in their brains that sorts out right from wrong is in permanent short circuit. No matter how hard you're willing to push, they're willing to push harder, past the point where pushing makes any sense. I stepped back far enough to make my exit speech.

"I don't give a damn about you or your company. People smarter than I have tried to put you out of business before, and I don't think my luck would be any better," I said, and opened the door. "But if you had a hand in killing Jack Carlisle, the only business you'll be running is the cigarette concession in San Quentin."

I shut the door behind me and galloped down the steps into the bright Las Vegas sun. Pollock was gone. I walked. I didn't think Rossi would try to cash in my life insurance policy yet, but the hairs on the back of my neck tingled with each passing car. A two-mile walk later, I found a taxi.

Chapter 14

"I'VE GOT WHAT YOU WANT. You've got what I want. Come by my place at ten o'clock sharp, tonight. Don't come earlier, and don't come later. I'll be waiting."

Dial tone. I played the message again while I scanned the day's mail, my feet propped on the desk. The tone was curt, and the words clipped by an anger barely in check. I couldn't make any sense of it. The voice was George Wentworth's. I forgot about it. It was late, and I was dirty and tired. Taxi to airport. Airport to airport. Airport to car. A bubble of flesh strapped in a bubble of metal and glass: the mind fogs at traveling so far with so little effort.

I dialed Angel's apartment. No answer. I called the Ocean Park Boxing Club. Twenty rings later, an old black voice answered. I asked for Angel. She was breathing hard when she picked up.

"Angel here. Who's this?"

"This is Don King. Mike Tyson is looking for another sap to take a beating for a million bucks. Interested?"

She laughed. "Hiya, Paul."

I was disappointed. "How did you know it was me?"

"I've been hanging around the brothers all my life, pal, and your voice is strictly Wonder Bread."

"Where I grew up brothers were guys who shared the same mother. How is Mr. Manly these days?"

"Boring. He didn't move out of his apartment all day. When do I get to do something exciting?"

"Are you brave enough to venture into Marina del Rey after dark?"

"Are you crazy?" she laughed. "That place is crawling with swinging singles. I'm not that brave."

I gave her Wentworth's address and told her to meet me there at ten-fifteen. She agreed and hung up.

In a file cabinet, under "C," I kept a fresh change of clothing. A pair of jeans and a black pullover sweater. I slipped into them, hung my suit on a doorknob, and rode the elevator down to the ground floor. The security guard clutched a copy of *Argosy* in his bony fingers as he sat behind the front desk. He was a nearsighted, stoop-shouldered man with no chest and a big .38 strapped to his belt. His name was Harold Birnbaum.

"Working on anything interesting, Mr. Marston?" he said when I signed myself out on his clipboard.

Harold thought that I led an adventurous life. Compared to him, I did.

"The usual," I answered, and returned the clipboard. "You might want to keep a sharp eye out. I had an unpleasant interview today with someone who might send a few friends around to my office."

The clipboard slipped through Harold's fingers and clattered onto the floor. He scrambled for it, righted himself, and, blushing, opened the door.

"I sure will, Mr. Marston. Don't you worry about a thing."

"If someone does come, call me at my home, and call the police."

"I wouldn't let them in," he protested.

"Don't try to stop them. Just call me."

He nodded, but behind his eyes glimmered visions of bravery and daring deeds. Don Knotts at the O.K. Corral.

When I parked outside the Wentworths' Marina home at a few minutes before ten, the porch light was out and the house was dark. The curtains moved as I strolled up the walk, and the moment my thumb struck the doorbell, the door swung open, with George Wentworth behind it in the darkened hallway.

"Nice of you to invite me over," I said. "I didn't think Mrs. Wentworth was going to allow you to play with me again."

He shut the door behind me and said, "You may have me over a barrel, but I don't have to stand your smart mouth, mister. I want to finish this and get you out of my life as soon as possible."

His shoulder clipped mine when he brushed by. The house was dark. I followed his footsteps through the living room toward a small orange glow at the back of the house. There was a hate in his voice that should have been a warning. Something had made him jump, and maybe if I didn't put my foot in my mouth, he'd tell me. We took the three short stairs down to his study, dimly lit by a replica oil lamp. Avoiding my face, Wentworth stood back in the shadows and pointed to a briefcase lying on the oak chest.

"What's that supposed to be?" I asked.

"Just open the damn thing," he blurted. "It's all there."

Turning my back to him, I knelt before the briefcase and opened it. Several hundred faces of Benjamin Franklin stared back at me. Green faces. Arranged in neat stacks, like playing cards. A body rushed up fast behind me. I ducked to the left, and my arm got high enough to catch part of something hard on its way down. The rest of it caught my head, and shot my mind like a cannonball into nothingness.

I came out the other side of nothingness into pain, and wanted to crawl back into nothingness again. The air roared. My head spun a lopsided circle, like a log sucked into a vortex. I tried to ignore the slug that crawled slowly toward the back of my throat. My eyes creaked open. I wanted to vomit. I saw nothing. I tried to move and couldn't. My arms and legs were gone. The slug rolled in my mouth, and I recognized it as my tongue. The roaring in my skull retreated, then changed pitch the way an engine does. Gradually I became human.

The world rolled again, but with the methodical rhythm of the sea. Starting with the pain at the back of my head, I took inventory, feeling down my shoulders, to my arms, and located my hands. They were tied behind my back. My feet were where I had remembered leaving them, still linked to the ankles. A good sign. The ankles were connected by an extra joint, which I decided must be rope.

The darkness smelled of sweat, blood, and oak. A memory of a briefcase full of money on an oak chest floated by. I wondered what had happened to the money, but had a good idea where the chest was. The roaring of the engines ceased. I could feel the open sea swell beneath me. The muffled squeak of a deck shoe sounded near my head. A lock clattered, and the chest snapped open. My lungs sucked in the night sea air. A hand grabbed the front of my shirt and pulled me into a sitting position.

"Where is it?" a voice hissed.

"Where's what?" I tried to say, but my tongue rolled back in my throat, and it came out as a groan.

"Where is it?" it hissed again.

My eyes cleared to the face of George Wentworth. I opened my mouth and heard something like speech drift out of it.

"The marker, dammit! Where's my marker!" Wentworth said, and shook me.

The back of my head rapped against the chest lid, setting off a small explosion in my skull. When the smoke cleared, I said, "I don't know what you're talking about."

Something distant droned in my ears. An engine. Wentworth heard it too. His grip on my shirtfront tightened.

"I don't have time to be jerked around. You'd better tell me where it is or I'll throw you in the sea right here."

"We're not out here to go night fishing. You're going to throw me in the sea no matter what I tell you."

"Talk!" he shouted, and cuffed the side of my head.

The engine was moving rapidly toward us. It had the throaty roar of a speedboat. Wentworth shoved me back into the chest and stood, gazing over the stern in the direction of the sound. It wasn't much of a chance. I wedged my legs against the back of the chest and sprang. The top of my head caught him in the ribs, driving him back against the cabin. I fell on my side and lashed out with my bound legs, turning his ankle. He was surprised more than anything and, cursing, stumbled over the chest. I wriggled as fast as I could, trying to get my feet between us. I wasn't fast enough. His foot swung forward and crushed my kidney. The next kick flattened my ear, and my brains turned to pudding. Hands grabbed my shirt and heaved. With the taste of blood in my mouth, I tumbled over the edge into the sea.

The first shock of cold seawater pumped adrenaline through my veins. My body went as rigid as steel. I sank. In panic I churned against the ropes. They held fast. The indigo darkness pressed in from everywhere. Saltwater stung my eyes closed. I lashed out in all directions. My lungs burned the last of their oxygen, sucking out the light in my head. I gave in to the darkness, and my body slackened. The thought of death swam up to greet me. It eyed me with the passionless hunger of a shark. I couldn't move. The thing nudged my shoulder. Its mouth opened, and I saw oblivion behind a jagged row of teeth. Not now, I thought. Pain. If I could feel pain, I was alive. I held on to the pain, and it slowly pulled me into consciousness. My face broke the plane of water, and I greedily swallowed the air like a man dying of thirst.

Using my bound legs like a fin, I bobbed to the surface for air between waves. Paul Marston, the human cork. Wentworth's boat, the *Inside Straight*, drifted aimlessly fifty yards distant.

The seawater loosened the rope. One of my hands slipped free, and I stripped the rope from my legs. A searchlight clicked on aboard the *Inside Straight* and pointed my way. I ducked beneath the waves as it passed over me. When I resurfaced, I heard a woman's voice call my name. I answered, and the spotlight found me. I swam toward it. Angel's face, worried and beautiful, stared down at me from the railing. I grabbed onto the stepladder and rested for a moment before climbing aboard. When she knew that I was in one piece, her face turned impish.

"Lordy, lordy, if it ain't a real live merman."

"If you think I'm a merman, honey, have I got a surprise for you from the waist down."

I gave her my hand and she pulled me up. It was suddenly very cold.

"Where's Wentworth?" I asked.

"Resting," she said, and pointed toward the stern.

My legs were rubbery, but I managed to guide them along

the deck. Wentworth was stretched flat on the rear deck. A purplish bruise swelled below his left eye.

"A right hook?" I guessed, and Angel nodded.

"I set him up with a left hook to his midsection, then put him away with a right cross."

"Thanks for showing up. What tipped you?" I said, and opened the door to the cabin.

I found a change of clothing in the closet. Angel leaned against the doorway and talked.

"He was going through your car when I pulled up, then I saw him dragging a chest out to his yacht. It took me a couple of minutes to figure it out, and by the time I decided it just might be you in that chest, he was shoving off."

My hands shook when I fumbled with the shirt. I told myself it was only the cold, but it was more than that. My head was splitting, and I was scared. It made me angry to see my hands shake like that.

"So I ran down to the dock and found a speedboat. I'd hot-wired a car before and didn't think it would be much different. I was just glad the thing had enough gas in it."

I stripped off my shirt. Angel whistled. I turned on her sharply.

"Do me a favor and get the hell out of here."

Her face went confused.

"What's the matter with you?"

"I'm not used to being rescued by women," I said, and shut the door in her face.

"I'll let you drown next time," she called back; then I heard her footsteps clomp away on the deck.

I was too angry to be grateful. Angry with myself. For being scared. For turning my back on Wentworth and nearly getting myself killed. I struggled with the pants. They were several sizes too large. I tied them on with a piece of rope. Then I felt ridiculous. Hell, I was happy to be alive. Opening the cabin door, I called to Angel, "How about a cup of coffee?"

She was leaning against the railing, her arms hugged across her chest. Pushing off, she walked toward me, her head down. At the doorway, when she looked up, I saw the bitterness.

"Thanks, partner," I said softly.

My mind sorted through a dozen apologies, but I said nothing else. It was enough. She understood.

Wentworth's eyes were wide open and terrified when I got around to him. I pulled him up onto a seat cushion, and the words tumbled out.

"The money is yours, all of it, and more if you want. I've got more. I don't know what came over me, I swear to you. I didn't mean for you to go over the side like that. When I heard the speedboat, I lost my head. I was trying to scare you, that's all."

I gave him the stop sign and said, "Maybe you should start at the beginning and tell me what this is all about."

"Like I said, I was just trying to scare you. I panicked—"

I interrupted him again. "What was the money for?"

Doubt shaded the terror in his eyes. "Why, for my marker, of course."

"What marker?"

"Oh, Christ! Don't you know?" he gasped, and when his head fell back, I thought he'd fainted.

Angel brought the coffee, and after I untied his hands, I gave him some. When he saw Angel, his hand went to the bruise under his eye.

"Your friend there is a real knockout. Where did she learn to punch like that?"

"Looks like an angel, hurts like the devil," I said.

Wentworth sipped the coffee. He grimaced and handed the cup back to me.

"In the cabinet above the sink there's a bottle of Scotch. Do you mind?"

I nodded to Angel, and she went to get it.

"I feel positively awful about this. I thought you were sent by San Francisco," he said, and took a long slug out of the bottle of Glenlivet Angel handed him.

"Tell me about it."

He took another slug of Scotch and offered me some. I shook my head. He shrugged and talked.

"About a year ago, when I was up at the Bayshore, I thought I'd get together a little card game to pass the time. I mentioned it to the hotel manager, an accommodating gentleman named Jim Johnson. He'd set me up with a couple of players before when I stayed there, and I'd won a little change. Playing with other hotel guests, you know, out-of-town businessmen, a tourist here and there. It didn't look any different to me this time.

"I started off ahead, and as I was feeling pretty good, put a couple of drinks under my belt. Then I hit a streak of bad luck. These guys were high rollers, and by this time we were playing for big money. I had a couple more drinks, and they must have been loaded with triple shots, because I went into a blackout."

He chased a chagrined smile with a slug of Scotch.

"Didn't remember a damn thing when I woke up. Felt like hell, though. Johnson came into my room and told me that the other players were furious, because I gambled away a lot more money than I was carrying, but that it was all right, because he had covered my bets. Then he showed me my marker. It was for a hundred thousand. Needless to say, I didn't have that kind of money, at least not to put my hands on."

"I didn't think you were strapped for cash," I said.

He laughed bitterly.

"My wife's a millionaire. I don't have a cent of my own. Funny, isn't it?"

He gave me a conspiratorial wink, then put down another ounce of Scotch. The harmless drunk in him, the one I had trusted enough to turn my back on, gained momentum.

"You see, I drink a little too much, and I gamble. Makes me a poor business risk."

"So they gave you easy monthly payments with no down payment," I said.

"At ten points a month. I figured I was set up, but there wasn't anything I could do about it."

"Why not go to the cops, or just tell them to shove it?"

His face reddened. Hugging the bottle, he turned and looked out over the sea.

"You see, that wasn't all. They had photographs. Myself and some broad. Johnson said she was under eighteen. Maybe she was. Hell, I don't remember. I made a few threats, but when he showed me those pictures, I knew they had me. He threatened to show them to my wife if I didn't pay. So I paid. Then I heard Johnson was killed in a burglary, and I thought I was off the hook. That's when I got the phone call."

"Who was it?"

"He didn't say. He told me that you were working with him, though. Offered to sell my marker back to me for twenty-five cents on the dollar. You were to make the collection."

He laughed as though it were a fine joke.

"Only you didn't want to play anymore," I guessed. "So

you planned on sapping me, getting the marker for free, then giving me a burial at sea. When San Francisco calls, you tell them that you gave me the money and have your marker to prove it. San Francisco thinks I've grabbed the cash for myself and taken off for Mexico.''

Wentworth cleared his throat, shrugged, tossed his hands up, did everything but say ''yes.'' Angel stirred at my side. When I looked over at her, she was glowering at George Wentworth.

''I can't believe this guy,'' she said. ''He's too chicken to admit he got a little carried away on a business trip, so he tries to kill you over what's gotta be grocery money to his wife. I mean, she's a millionaire, right?''

''I did it for Leslie, too,'' Wentworth protested. ''Not just for myself. You were supposed to be working for her. I didn't want to see her get sucked into the same trap that I was in.''

Angel grabbed the rope off the deck. ''I say we keelhaul him. What do you say?''

''Jesus Christ,'' Wentworth moaned.

''I say we all go home,'' I said, and tossed the keys in his startled lap.

''The man just tried to kill you,'' Angel cried.

''Sure, but he did it for all the wrong reasons,'' I answered, and fled back to the warmth of the cabin.

Five minutes later Angel tired of standing guard over George Wentworth and joined me. She prowled about the cabin, her long and muscled legs balanced exquisitely against the rolling of the sea. Her eyes would roam the corners, peering into cabinets, then hit mine and bounce away. I was about to tell her to sit down when she turned to me and complained.

''It doesn't make any sense. Why would San Francisco say you were with them?''

"One good reason George here just demonstrated. It could get me killed. Or he tells his daughter and gets me pulled off the case."

"Do you know who San Francisco is?" Angel asked.

"I have a couple of guesses. All of them bad news."

The seas calmed when we entered the marina. A few ideas tumbled through my head. I went up top to watch George Wentworth guide us up to the slip. He gave me one slow, long backward glance, then turned his head forward again.

"You were Johnson's eyes and ears on the TransNational deal, weren't you?" I said.

Wentworth didn't take his eyes off the helm.

"You told him when you were meeting, who you were meeting with, and what happened."

Wentworth nodded, and said, "I fell behind on my payments. He threatened to send a few of his friends over to review my finances, but then backed off and said he'd let me off the hook for a month if I supplied him with a little information. I didn't think it would work out like it did."

"Jack would feel better knowing that, I'm sure. You could have sold him out for less."

Wentworth's aim was off target. We hit the dock with a thud and bounced away. He gunned the right engine in reverse, eased them both forward, and the boat swung around to rest in the slip.

"Who was Johnson working for?" I asked.

Wentworth cut the engines and sat down heavily in a deck chair.

"He never told me," Wentworth said. "But I've given it some thought, and I can think of only one person. The old man."

Henry Howard.

Chapter
15

I GREW UP AROUND GUNS. On my sixth birthday, when I expressed an interest in the shotgun he was cleaning, my grandfather took me to the edge of the pond that stretched just off the porch of his summer cabin and, finding a suitable stump, set a tin can atop it. He stood me at a distance of twenty-five yards, facing the stump, with the pond behind it, and showed me how to hold the shotgun; to wedge the stock firmly into my shoulder, with my cheek resting lightly above it, and my right elbow bent ninety degrees from my body; to breath in slowly, hold the breath for a quarter of a second; and, when the aim steadied, to squeeze the trigger gently. I did so, and the kick of the gun sprawled me on my butt.

"Too much gun and too little boy," he said, and, with the shotgun perched on his shoulder, left me to contemplate a bruised shoulder and dusty hindquarters. He returned with something more my size—a single-shot, bolt-action, .22-caliber rifle.

I spent ten more summers at that cabin before my grandfather died, and they sold the cabin. He was a crack shot up until his eightieth birthday when his eyesight failed him and he had to rely on me to tell him on which side of the blind the ducks were flying. The shooting was only a part of it, though, and during those ten summers I was initiated into the mysteries of sportsmanship. I learned that you split the day's harvest fifty-fifty, no matter who shot what; you compliment the other fellow's shot, but never your own; and if you are a better shot than your partner, you let him take the first shot.

I learned the most important lesson when, at the age of seven, I displayed on the porch a porcupine I had shot at the far end of the pond. Later that night he served it to me for dinner. The flesh was bitter. I puked possum half the night. My grandfather gave me a cup of tea to soothe my stomach and said, "Never, son, shoot what you can't or won't eat."

But then, my grandfather had never hunted or been hunted by a man. In the Marines I learned a harsher code of killing: never let anyone else take the first shot; what you shoot walks on two legs and what you eat comes out of a can.

It was this second code that preyed upon my thoughts as I opened my file cabinet and pulled out the Smith and Wesson .38. It smelled faintly of oil and cleaning fluid. When I strapped on the holster, the gun felt like a strange and deadly tumor. . The phone rang. It was Leslie Carlisle. She said she was in trouble.

The maid answered my knock and, with a shy smile on her plump brown face, let me in. In her white uniform she looked like a dumpling with feet. Her English was little better than my Spanish, but good enough to let me know that I should follow. We wound through the kitchen, out a pair of sliding glass doors, and down a flagstone path that was cut into the side of a hill and was flanked with terraced rosebushes. The path turned from flagstone to poolside concrete at the bottom. At the far end of the pool, doubly shaded by three towering palms and a bright red umbrella, sat Leslie Carlisle.

She was dressed for business, not mourning, in a crisp gray suit and white silk blouse. *The Harvard Business Review* was spread on the table before her, and a glass of mineral water sparkled in her right hand as she flipped the pages with her left. When she heard our footsteps, she stood. Her eyes focused sharply on my face.

"Did you run into a door?" she asked.

I had forgotten about the heel mark above my left eye.

"I ran into your father," I said, and told her the story. She had asked me not to spare the sordid details, so I didn't. Her face turned to marble when I mentioned the underage girl. She sat down heavily, crossed her arms, and stared in the direction of the pool.

When I finished, and she didn't move or speak, I wandered to the edge of the pool to give her time to work it through. The winter sun skipped like silver coins on the water. The maid padded down the path, carrying a tray with a bottle of mineral water and two glasses, and set it on the table. I pulled up a deck chair. Averting her face, Leslie Carlisle groped for a pair of sunglasses and shielded her eyes.

"It is unbearable that a stranger should know all my family's dirty secrets," she said in a tight voice. "You must find us dreadful."

"I've never met a person who didn't have something to be ashamed of, something that would destroy him if it ever came to light. A person wants the world to think he's better, even if he thinks the worst of himself. Imagine the shame a priest must feel when he masturbates, and the terror of being caught at it."

I could feel her eyes under the sunglasses.

"You have a wicked mind," she said, and stiffly tried to smile. "Perhaps that explains your attractiveness. I don't think you're jaded. Not yet. You're still fascinated by the dirty little lives you poke your nose into, and that makes you interesting."

There was nothing I could say to that. Bearers of bad news are supposed to be beheaded, and I was instead the object of a discreet seduction. She poured the mineral water and handed me a glass. Her hand was trembling. She must have realized how vulnerable she suddenly was, because she straightened and regained the hauteur that is the birthright of an heiress.

"I'm sorry that Father behaved badly to you. I suppose some sort of bonus is in order."

"The standard fee for attempts on my life is two grand, unless the attempt is a success, in which case I charge five grand, plus funeral expenses."

"I'm not in the mood for jokes."

"Tough. Your father tried to kill me. Money won't make any of us forget that, and I'm not the kind of guy who can be bought off like the maid who bears a seven-pound gift from the master of the house. Try having a real conscience, not one minted from the family bank. You'll find people like you better, starting with yourself."

She leaned back in the deck chair, her face coloring like the roses above the pool. Something wet trickled from behind her sunglasses and tracked down her cheek. The back of her hand made a quick swipe at it. She took a deep breath. "Okay. I apologize for my father and for my whole fucking family."

She emphasized the point with a hearty blow into her handkerchief.

"Apology accepted," I said. "Before we insult each other any more, maybe you could mention why you called me over."

She nodded and, sipping her mineral water, leaned back

into the sun again. Her strawberry-blond hair glowed in the sunlight.

"I received a phone call this morning from someone claiming to have compromising photographs of my husband and his secretary. Maybe it's the same person who set you up with Father. He threatened to release them to the *National Enquirer* unless I paid him fifty thousand dollars in cash."

"To the *National Enquirer*?"

Her voice was straight and firm. "That's what he said."

I laughed. Her head tilted to the side, and a crease formed between her eyebrows.

"I'm glad you find this comical. Perhaps you could explain the humor of it."

"It wouldn't be printed. I doubt the editors have heard of your husband, and I don't imagine too many *National Enquirer* readers follow *The Wall Street Journal*. It means we're dealing with amateurs."

"Amateurs or not, the photographs are an embarrassment."

"Describe the voice."

She shrugged. "It was a male voice. What is there to describe?"

"Did he have an accent?"

"No."

"Young or old?"

She trapped her lower lip between two sharp little teeth and thought for a moment.

"Young. Under thirty, I believe."

"Was there any static on the line, or was it a local call?"

"I don't think it was local, but the line was reasonably clear. Something else. There was a woman's voice in the background, and I heard him say, 'Shut up, Karen.' "

"Karen?"

"Karen, Sharon, Erin. He must have placed his hand over the receiver, because his voice lost its clarity at that point."

His mind had lost its clarity as well.

"Describe how you are to transfer the money to them."

"I'm to put the money in a satchel and leave it in locker number 455 at the Los Angeles International Airport on Tuesday."

That was two days ahead. When I told her I'd take care of it before then, she proclaimed me her hero and wilted demurely in my powerful embrace, overcome with gratitude. Sure.

"That's what I pay you for," she said.

The sun was out when I flew into San Francisco, and the city, with its light blue bay and dark blue ocean, the orange of the Golden Gate and greens of the Presidio sparkled in the setting sun like a jeweled city, like a city crafted by Fabergé. Even Alcatraz, a jagged gray stone set in the bay, is beautiful by air. When the sun shines in San Francisco, it is the most beautiful city on earth.

The city was less beautiful at freeway level. As it approached Van Ness Avenue, the Bayshore Freeway turned to glue. Rush hour. The cars lurched and stopped, sometimes nearing ten miles per hour, but most often wedged into an unmoving grid of cars as solidly as pieces in a jigsaw puzzle.

At the first off-ramp, I bullied my way off the freeway and wound through surface streets to the Bayshore Hotel. I registered, dropped my overnight case in the room, and went down to the bar for a drink. An hour later the sun had set and the freeway cleared. I followed it north to the suburbs, in San Rafael.

Hair stylist Sharon Gleck lived in a stucco apartment building on Du Bois Street, flanked by the freeway on one side and a strip-mall on the other. I followed a concrete path through a crab-grass lawn, entered the central courtyard, and climbed a set of stairs to apartment 16. I rang the bell and stepped back a foot, waiting to see who might greet me. The door cracked open, held in check by a thin security chain lock. A pair of young male eyes looked me over.

"What the fuck do you want?" he whined.

I didn't waste time. Leading with my shoulder, I sprang forward and hit the door with my full weight. The man and the door were flung back, the chain lock yanking out of the wood with a snap. His mouth slack and his small eyes crinkled with disbelief, the man bounced off the wall behind the door and threw an overhand right. I blunted it with my forearm and gutted him with an uppercut. The air rushed out of him, and he doubled over. His arms reached out and caught my coat, then he charged, trying to wrestle me to the floor. I gave him a two-handed pull-down punch in his lower back, kidney high. He yelped, twisted, and fell to the floor. I stepped around him and shut the front door.

Sharon Gleck raced out of a back bedroom. Her hair was in curlers, and immodest flesh spilled from her open blue bathrobe. When Sharon saw me, she bolted, and I didn't think it was because I had caught her in curlers. I found her in the kitchen, her pink nails clutched around the handle of a knife still stuck in the butcher block. My hand clamped onto her wrist, and I spun her around. She shrieked. I dragged her arm into the living room and shoved her onto the couch. I had trouble recognizing her as the gentle soul who had cut my hair. She looked as though she wanted to cut my throat.

The man was crawling along the floor with a bad case of the dry heaves. He was tall and thin, about twenty-two years old, and dressed rockabilly style, with blue jeans, a black leather jacket, and a white T-shirt. His hair was thin and greased back into a ducktail. I picked him up by the collar and hoisted him onto the couch. He didn't resist.

"You have something that doesn't belong to you," I said. "I'm here to collect it before you get yourselves seriously hurt."

Sharon's eyes shifted away. Her voice was adolescent and sullen.

"I don't know what you're talking about."

"Maybe your boyfriend does."

"He's not my boyfriend," she said.

"Who is he then?"

"He's my brother. Ray."

Ray looked up. His breath was coming back to him in thin gasps. Water streamed out of his glazed eyes. I pushed his head back on the couch.

"You're going to piss blood for a week, Ray. Do you want an emergency trip to the dentist too?"

"Don't you threaten my brother!" Sharon said, and tried to stand.

I pushed her back down again.

"Blackmail is a felony offense. I haven't called the cops. Yet. Give me any trouble and I can guarantee you a couple of years in jail."

Sharon crossed her arms and pinned her eyes to the floor. "Okay. Just don't hurt my brother," she said.

Ray looked at her with pain and gratitude. I don't think he wanted to be hit again.

"The photographs," I said.

Sharon nodded and, with a tired caution, answered, "You have to let me up. They're in the back bedroom."

I stepped back and drew open my sports coat to let her notice the gun under my arm. The last thing I wanted to see was a revolver in her hand when she came back. She understood.

"I don't even know how to shoot a gun," she said, and slipped off the couch.

She disappeared down the hall. Ray piped up.

"You caught me off guard, or I'd a' broke you in two. It's not fair, catching me off guard like that."

"That's what Custer said at the Little Big Horn, but they scalped him all the same."

"So who gives a fuck about Custer?" Ray said.

Now that he could breathe, he was getting bolder.

"I'm going to give you two pieces of advice, and I don't expect you to listen to either of them," I said. "If you want to keep on being a hood, learn to fight and learn to play solitaire."

"I can fight. You just caught me off guard, and now you got a gun, and I can't go up against a gun, now can I?" he said with a crooked smile.

I smiled back.

"But why should I learn solitaire?"

"Because you're stupid. Stupid hoods get caught and thrown in jail. Solitaire will help you pass the time."

His mouth opened and snapped shut. He gave me his tough look, the one that made the high school kids tremble.

"Ha, ha. Very funny. Why don't you take your gun off and say that."

"I promised your sister I wouldn't hurt you."

His face reddened. I could read his eyes. He was working up the courage to jump me. Ray wasn't dangerous. He didn't have enough brains and hadn't learned to compensate for it. In another twenty years, after a lifetime of losing, he might learn a craftiness that would substitute for brains. More likely he would die in an alley, and die stupidly.

His sister walked into the room, carrying a shoe box.

"Tell your brother to relax a little bit, or I'll fix his overbite."

Sharon set the shoe box down on the coffee table and sat next to her brother, grabbing his hand. He pulled it away.

"Ray, things are bad enough without any more trouble."

"He called me stupid." Ray pouted.

"Was this blackmail scheme your idea?" I asked him.

He nodded.

"Learn solitaire," I repeated, and opened the shoe box.

Inside there was a folder of negatives and photographs, and a cassette tape.

"How did this come into your possession?" I asked.

"Jim had me open a safe-deposit box because he needed someplace to store things. For tax purposes, he said. When he died, I got curious and opened it. This is what I found."

There were several sets of photographs, all along the same general theme. Most of the photographs were obviously shot through a two-way mirror in one of the rooms at the Bayshore. I shuffled the ones of Jack Carlisle and Valerie Rogers to the back of the deck, mindful of the dead's right to privacy. The negatives of George Wentworth and a busty young girl were there. So was an interesting set of photographs depicting Chris Manly and a young boy. I didn't find George Wentworth's marker.

"Is this all of it?" I asked.

"You won't hear from us again. It was a stupid idea," Sharon said with an angry look at her brother. "We thought it would be a fast way to make some money. I wanted to open my own shop."

"When did you call George Wentworth?"

"Who?" Sharon said.

I showed her the photograph.

"We didn't know who that was. I don't know who most of those people are. I recognized Jack Carlisle, but that was all. His wife was the only person we called."

Chapter
16

AT MIDNIGHT THE LOBBY of the Bayshore Hotel was empty. The piano bar was in full swing, with a guy the lobby billboard identified as Diamond Danny at the keys warming up for a Las Vegas lounge act with an audience of six tired-eyed salesmen from Cincinnati. Behind the registration desk stood a beautiful woman with skin the color of creamed coffee. I asked her if Joe Mankewitz had been in today.

"He was still here when I came on at eight," she said, her smile dazzling. "But I think he left a few hours ago."

"Did you see him leave?"

"No, but there's nothing to keep him here this late that I know of. I could check his office if you like."

I told her I'd like that, and watched her hips swing through the back door. She returned thirty seconds later.

"His door's locked, and the light is out, so I'd guess he's gone home. Could I tell him you called?"

I declined and walked across the lobby to the elevator. Mank would know that I was back in San Francisco, and that would make him a curious man. Having a master passkey, he could enter any room he wanted. I knew of a good reason why he would want to visit mine. One of the rooms in the Bayshore was equipped with a two-way mirror, something that could fool a guest, or a maid, but not the head security man. Mankewitz knew about the mirror, knew about John-son, and unless he was a total fool, was part of the blackmail scheme. It was my guess that he had pegged me as the bag-man to George Wentworth. That hadn't worked. He would try something more direct this time.

I didn't try to keep my entrance a secret. I rattled the key in the lock, and gave the knob a sharp turn. My gun was out and cocked at my ear. The door was mounted on a self-closing hinge. When I stepped into the room, I flicked on the light, and held the door open with my foot. If Mank was in the room, he would wait until the door closed before making his move. My eyes tracked along the closed bathroom door, over the bed, across the side wall, and stopped at the curtain. A pair of brown wing tips poked out of the corner, and the curtain bulged slightly above them. It was an old trick, and I couldn't believe Mank was that stupid.

Picking up an ashtray from the dresser, I let the door swing closed, and as I moved left, threw the ashtray at the bulge in the curtain. It smacked the bulge dead center and dropped onto the carpet. According to the trick, Mank should have leaped up from behind the bed, or out of the closet, or fallen from the ceiling. Nothing happened. With one eye on the center of the room, I slid open the closet. It was empty. I left the bathroom door closed, and crabbed around the bed.

Mank was stretched on the carpet between the bed and the sliding glass door, a revolver in his hand and a bullet hole in his head. I knelt over him and examined the wound. There were powder marks on his right temple, and the hole was small and symmetrical. The carpet at his head was soaked. A towel was bunched over his hip. I picked it up at the corner. There was a blackened hole in it, and it was stained with blood. The killer had wrapped his gun in the towel, forced Mank down, and shot him point-blank. The towel would blunt the noise and catch the blood when it spurted out of the wound. Very neat, clean, and professional.

I called the woman at the desk and told her to notify the police. I stripped off my holster and set my gun on the dresser so the police wouldn't shoot me when they walked in. Then I leaned back on the far side of the bed, away from poor dead Mank, and waited.

The first two men who walked through the door wore the blue-black SFPD uniform. They looked at the gun on the dresser, dead Mank on the floor, added two plus two, and cuffed my hands behind my back. While they were puzzling over my identification and permits, two homicide investigators waltzed in, smelling of cigarettes, sweat, and coffee. Smiling and nodding, they listened to my story, then asked me to tell it again. I was a hit. They asked me to tell the story six or seven times over the next five hours. When they discovered that I had found another body only a week earlier, they gave me a free tour of the city jail and a bed for the night in a holding cell. I wasn't thrown down a flight of stairs, and no one questioned me with the help of a taser gun, but it wasn't quite the same as being given a key to the city. In the morning, when they had verified that I was who I was, that my permits were in order, and that I lived more or less with respect to the laws of society, I was released. They kept the gun.

With a half hour of airplane sleep, I drove to my Santa Monica apartment, showered, and selected an IBM-blue suit from the closet. Under it I wore a pinpoint oxford cloth white shirt and a dark blue tie with a gold clip. The suit was like a thousand other suits. It was a uniform, as regimented as a Marine's parade dress. Success and conformity. If there was a day when I needed to follow the codes of power dressing, this was it.

I made another stop at the office. In the file cabinet, with the records of my employment with Western Shores, I found a tag with my name, the company name, and "all area access" stamped on it. I pocketed it and drove to Pasadena.

Corporate headquarters for Western Shores was a low Spanish-style building half hidden by trees off Marengo Avenue, south of a modern middle-class residential tract that had none of the grace or money of Old Pasadena. The front lobby was indistinguishable from the countless other corporate holding tanks I've had the misfortune of visiting: commercial brown carpeting, vinyl chairs backed against the walls, twenty-four-by-thirty-six-inch product shots hung with precision and absolutely no imagination, and a long guest registration desk barring entry to the sacred halls beyond. I gave my business card to the woman at the desk, who was one of those chosen more for her hair style than her brains, and asked her to give it to Bill Henry, the man who had replaced me as director of corporate security.

"Do you have an appointment?" she asked with an empty sweetness.

"No."

"I'm sorry, but Mr. Henry does not usually see anyone without an appointment."

"He'll see me," I answered.

She frowned in uncertainty, momentarily overcome by the responsibilities of her job. What if I had a bomb in my back pocket and was determined to detonate it once inside? Worse yet, what if I was a salesman?

"May I ask what this is regarding?" she cleverly asked.

"Bill will know."

The receptionist nodded. When in doubt, punt. She read my name into the phone, waited for a moment, then hung up. Her smile was sunny. I was one of the chosen. I belonged.

"If you care to be seated, he can see you in five minutes," she said.

I picked up a magazine titled *Modern Appliance Manufacturing*, which detailed the exciting world of designing, tooling, and assembling dishwashers and trash compactors. Heady stuff. The five minutes accelerated into ten. The door behind the receptionist opened, and a thirty-five-year-old woman, with black hair pinned behind her neck, a floral print blouse and yellow skirt, gave me a nod. I followed her down a series of corridors bustling with young executives and secretaries who looked as if they were engaged in very important business, then waited by a closed oak door with Bill Henry's name on it while his secretary announced my arrival.

With a curt "Mr. Henry will see you now," the secretary held the door open for me. Bill Henry stood, and we shook hands over an immaculate desktop. He was a career officer who had served in Korea and Vietnam before retiring to find better wages in the private sector. Henry kept himself fit. His spine, stiff and straight as a two-by-four, carried shoulders that never moved out of square. His hair was steel-gray, shorn to the skull at the sides with a short crew cut at the top. The only ground he surrendered to age was a pair of thin steel-rimmed glasses. He was fifteen years my senior. I had held his job before him. His manner was polite, but his eyes were guarded with pride and rivalry. His right hand turning palm up, he gestured for me to sit.

"You've been screwed," I said, and tossed an envelope on his desk.

Henry scowled and spilled its contents. Five photographs depicting sexual fun and games stared face up from the desktop. His sharply disapproving eyes dissected the photographs, then snapped shut when he recognized the face of Jack Carlisle.

"One of our hotels?" he asked in a voice faint with doom.

"The Bayshore in San Francisco."

"Was this Mankewitz's doing?"

"Mankewitz and Jim Johnson. Johnson ran the show, but Mank knew about it. Both were lining their pockets."

Henry slid the photographs into the envelope. His fingers handled each by the edge, very carefully, as though the images of sexual contact could stain. Outrage strengthened his voice.

"These photographs could do serious damage to this company from both the inside and out. Hell, you have a photograph of the former chief operating officer playing horsey with his secretary. The press would kill us if they heard about a blackmail scheme like this."

"Front-page headlines," I said.

"The photographs and negatives have to be destroyed," he said, simple as a command, and handed the envelope to me.

"Evidence in a murder investigation can't be destroyed."

"You mean Johnson and Mankewitz's murders."

"No. Jack Carlisle's murder."

Bill Henry's eyebrows twisted together. "What evidence do you have that he was murdered?"

"I'd rather not go into that. What I need from you is the name of the person who recommended Johnson to the company."

"That is privileged information." Henry balked. "I can't do that without an express order from the senior vice-president or the CEO."

"I said you've been screwed, Bill, and I meant it. These

photographs and the story behind them mean your walking papers here, and if the story leaks to the business community, you'll have to live on your army retirement pay or find another profession. You hired a man with a public record as a blackmailer."

"I'm not an incompetent, dammit. I had to play office politics."

"Excuses won't play on your résumé. Johnson ran an operation under your nose which compromised the former COO of the company and one of the principal shareholders. If that story gets around, you won't be able to get a job as a security guard at K Mart."

His hands flat on his desk, Henry stared silently forward. A drop of sweat slid down the side of his shorn skull and pooled at the rim of his eyeglasses. His eyes rose and penetrated mine, trying to judge my character.

"You're the only person who could leak that story," he said.

I nodded.

"Would you do that to me?"

I nodded again.

"In the Marines I got into the habit of taking a man at his word," he mused. "It's not the same in civilian life. If you turn your back on a man in this company, you get backshot."

He rapped his knuckles on the desk and came to his decision.

"Do I have your word that this story won't be spread?"

I nodded.

"Mr. Jim Johnson was hired on the basis of strong personal recommendation from Ted Dantly. I was told that a background check would be unnecessary."

"Who's Ted Dantly?"

"A hotshot. Vice-president of finance."

Finance is no longer the realm of bean counters with beady eyes and calculators. Power is where the money is, and the money is in finance. It is a given in the corporate world that manufacturing fears sales, sales fears marketing, marketing fears corporate, and everybody fears finance.

Every office operates under an unwritten code of furniture language. The size and placement of a secretary's desk depends on the importance of the executive. Ted Dantly's secretary had a desk that could land an airplane, and it was placed like a blockade in front of his door. The secretary behind the desk was equally imposing. She wore a business suit that followed her figure like a straitjacket, and her expression reminded me of the gargoyles guarding Notre Dame.

"I don't believe you have an appointment?" she said, flicking the corner of my card with her fingernail.

"That's correct."

"I'm sorry, but Mr. Dantly doesn't see anyone without an appointment. If you were to call this afternoon, I could perhaps schedule you in next week."

"The world could end before then," I said.

"I'm sorry, but that's the best we can do," she answered with a sweet twinkling of teeth and a get-the-hell-out-of-here message behind the eyes.

I asked for a slip of notepaper. She handed me one that bore the inscription "Message From:." I wrote something on it, folded it twice, and set it on her desk.

"Give this to Mr. Dantly with my card. I'll wait."

Again the brush-off smile. "Mr. Dantly is in a meeting and cannot be disturbed."

"I'll wait."

"It may be quite some time before I can give this to him."

"You needn't worry. I brought a tent and camp stove in case I have to wait overnight."

With an oppressed sigh, she set the note on the corner of her desk and turned away. I sat in a chair against the wall and watched the executive foot traffic in the adjacent corridor. The secretary forgot about me. I counted ties. Blue. Gray. Brown. Paisley.

Someone left Dantly's office, and the man himself appeared at the door. He looked like an advertising agency's concept of the ideal senior executive. Tall, trim, fit. His hair was black, gray at the temples, and styled short, each hair swept up and back in a side part as rigid and immaculate as sculpture. The eyes were dark, knifing out from a face as crisply tailored as his Italian suit. His secretary approached. In the distracted gesture of a man busy with important work, he held his hand out to the side to receive the paper, without bothering to acknowledge the person who handed it to him. His eyes touched down on the note. He frowned and looked at my card. The secretary said something, and he looked up, spotting me. I waved. The secretary nodded at something he said and closed the door behind him. Her expression was friendly when she approached to say that Mr. Dantly could "fit me in." I had been elected to the Pantheon.

Ted Dantly did not stand or offer his hand when I was allowed entrance into his office. My feet trod on gold carpeting. Antique lithographs of coal-powered trains were hung along the walls with the precision and predictability of mathematics. The office was four times the size of Bill Henry's. A red velvet Victorian-era armchair sat in the corner, with a view of a tree-lined courtyard. Two burgundy leather chairs faced Dantly's desk. I sat in one of them. Dantly reclined in an overstuffed swiveler. "I have another appointment in five minutes, so let's cut the crap and get to the bottom line," he commanded.

"The bottom line," I said, "is murder."

Dantly cleared his throat, read my note again, and tossed it on the desk. "You wrote that I'm about to be questioned by the police. Whose murder are we talking about?"

"Five murders in fact. Jack Carlisle, Valerie Rogers, Henry Wallace, Jim Johnson, and Joe Mankewitz."

"I was under the impression that the first three persons you mentioned died by accident, and that the other two were unrelated victims of circumstance."

"There's a strong possibility that all five murders are connected," I said, and knew it was the wrong thing to say the moment the words left my mouth.

"Strong possibility? According to who? You?"

Contempt edged his voice. He paused, waiting for an answer, and when I didn't benefit him with one, he went on the attack.

"I've heard all about you, Mr. Marston, and what you're trying to do to this company."

"What have you heard?"

Dantly straightened and punctuated his remarks with a cutting sweep of his hand.

"That you have some wild idea about a conspiracy and have the annoying habit of accusing employees of this company without the benefit of fact. Out of respect to the person who has hired you, I won't throw you out of the building."

"How do you know who hired me?"

"We're running a major corporation here. There is little we don't know about what impacts our business."

His voice was soft and expertly controlled. The use of the royal "we" was calculated to inspire fear. He hadn't risen to the top of his company by being easily intimidated. He knew his power politics.

"It's obvious that the police don't share your alleged conspiracy theory, or they would have been through this company with a fine-tooth comb. Do you think you're smarter than the police?"

"You gave your personal recommendation for employment to a man who had a record as a blackmailer and who worked for a company with mob connections. Why?"

The question stunned him.

"Who are you talking about?" he stammered.

"Your friend. Jim Johnson."

"He's not my friend. I didn't know him before he came to this company," Dantly said sharply, regaining his balance.

"Then why did you personally recommend him?"

"I didn't."

"It's written in his employment file."

"Who gave you access to his file?" he demanded.

"That's not important. What will you tell the police when they ask?"

"None of your damn business!" he shouted, and stood, his chair skittering away behind him.

"This interview is over."

I pushed myself out of the chair and, with a sad, pity-the-poor-bastard shake of my head, reached for the door.

"Wait!" he called, and when I turned to look at him, the look on his face was one of fear. "I'll tell you what I'll tell the police. I gave my recommendation on the personal request of another officer of the company."

"Who?"

"It will take a subpoena to get the name from me."

"When the subpoena comes, I suggest you be prepared to prove it with documentation of the request. Without it, no one will believe you. You have been set up. From how high you fall and how hard you hit depends on facts as interpreted by the court, which has little or nothing to do with the truth."

"The company will stand by me," he maintained.

Men have hung by similar words, I thought, and shut the door behind me.

In the corridor I pinned the "all area access" tag on my lapel and toured the building. If you look like you know what you're doing and keep moving, you can go almost anywhere within most corporate facilities. When I had finished with the first building, I crossed an open space and scouted the manufacturing facility. It was a long, high-ceiling building where a thousand brown-skinned people skillfully assembled dishwashing machines. The parts were manufactured in the Far East, shipped to Pasadena, and assembled with a proud "Made in U.S.A." stamp prominently displayed.

At six o'clock I returned to the white-collar building and entered the restroom. I found a comfortable seat and daw-dled away another hour. By seven o'clock the corridors had emptied of all but the industrious few who still sat slumped in their cubicles, mesmerized by the glow of computer ter-minals and dreams of promotion. Dantly was not one of them, and the gargoyle who guarded his office had slunk away for the night. Her desk was unlocked. Dantly's ap-pointment calendar was in the upper right-hand drawer. He had taken two trips to San Francisco during the month of January, the last concluding two weeks before Carlisle's death.

Chapter
17

GRETA GARBO WAS ON CABLE, playing Mata Hari in her usual melancholic style. She makes a decent living at it until, in grand Hollywood tradition, she falls in love with a dashing enemy aviator. He is blinded in an airplane crash after Mata Hari is foolish enough, before making love to him, to insist on blowing out the candle in the shrine to the Virgin Mary which had been given to him by his mother as a safeguard from evil. The final scene is heartrending. The blind aviator visits Mata Hari in her prison cell on the morning of the execution, convinced by the softhearted authorities that she is in a health clinic about to undergo a minor operation (I suspect there was some brain damage to the poor fellow as well), and rhapsodizes about how they will live happily ever after. Then she is shot by a firing squad, and the movie is over. The movie is a little ridiculous, and wonderfully sad, hinging on the idea of dying for love, and by the time "The End" flashed across the screen, I was misty-eyed and in my cups from mixing Greta Garbo with Murphy's Irish Whiskey.

Then I saw love again, from a meaner angle, when I spilled Johnson's blackmail photographs onto the kitchen table. No romantic lighting and dreamy soft focus. Hard and clear and ugly, with flaccid bodies and drunken faces. The lone cassette skittered onto the floor. I palmed it, carried it across to the tape deck, and plugged it in. Something that sounded like feedback blared from the speakers. I flipped it over and tried the B side. It was blank.

I slept.

In the morning I drove to Hollywood to look up Wiz. He had a real name, like everybody else, but most people called him Wiz. The name had been given him by a director who had been amazed by the man's ability in motion picture sound. Wiz was a renegade eccentric with stringy hair, a sparse gray beard, and skin that never saw the light of day. That morning he sported a red bandanna and a T-shirt that read "Fuck 'em if they can't take a joke." Whenever I saw him, the scent of marijuana was in the air, and I suspected that he must have been taking something else because when he spoke the words tumbled out of him like change in a Vegas jackpot. He was strange even by the warped standards of Hollywood, but he was the best there was at weaving the thousand sounds on a motion picture soundtrack into a musical whole.

Hunched over the main mixing panel in the darkened studio, Wiz glanced over his shoulder when I walked in, and he remembered who I was.

"I thought you might want a break from the usual movie crap you work on," I said, handing him the cassette tape.

"What's on it?" he asked.

"I hoped you could tell me."

Wiz nodded and kept an eye on the loop of film rolling on the screen above us. It was a scene from some gangster movie, and his fingers played across the endless switches, knobs, and dials with the skill of a concert pianist, bringing up the flick of a match for one shot, dropping a footstep on the next, notching and tweaking each voice until it sang with its own resonance. When the film had finished its loop, Wiz pressed a switch and spoke into a microphone. The screen went dark.

"A twenty-five-million-dollar gangster movie," he said. "Can you believe spending that kind of bread on a gangster movie? After Coppola, what have these clowns got to say?"

Wiz pedaled back in his chair, dropped the cassette into a nearby deck, slipped it into gear and, with a quick one-two motion, swung to the side and plugged the deck into the sound system. The studio vibrated with a steady hum. Wiz listened carefully for thirty seconds. It was loud. My skull was vibrating with the harmonics. Wiz didn't seem to mind.

"That's some buzz all right. It sounds like an overlay of frequencies, probably 30 Hz, definitely 60 Hz, which usually means the sound recordist like an idiot was running his machine on AC, and it sounds like 120 Hz, or somewhere around there. My ears aren't as good as they used to be, so you can probably hear it better than I can, but it does sound like the frequencies are masking some other sound. God knows what it is until we clean up the signal a little bit."

Wiz hit the stop button.

"When do you need this back?" he asked.

"As soon as I can get it. A few acquaintances have turned up dead, and who knows but what I might be next."

"Maybe tomorrow if I can get to it tonight. You said your life is in danger?"

I said that I thought so.

"What's your life compared to a twenty-five-million-dollar gangster movie?" he said, and with a twist of his eyebrows: "That's Hollywood, baby. See you tomorrow."

He pressed a button. The film began to roll, and his hands danced across the console.

Angel had left a 9:00 A.M. message with Shirley. Manly had packed his gear into his silver BMW and was heading south, with Angel in pursuit and promising to call at the next stop.

Waiting is not one of the things I do naturally well, and though I've had more experience than most in the art of doing nothing, I've never mastered it. I tried to work on Hal and tried to read the *Journal*, but wasn't much good at either. Angel called about noon.

"Where are you?" I asked.

"San Diego."

"Wonderful. Mind telling me where in San Diego?"

"At a Denny's off Interstate 5, south of Highway 94. Manly stopped for lunch. He's having a hamburger."

"Anyone there with him?"

"No."

"Did he make any calls?"

"I told you, he's eating a hamburger."

"You don't drive from Hollywood to a San Diego Denny's just to get a burger."

"Well, that's what he's doing," she insisted.

"Could be one last American meal before the border. You have to find a way to keep him stateside."

"Okay."

I liked the way she said, "Okay," as though it would be as easy as walking to the corner market for a bottle of milk.

"If you have to leave, call me at the pay phone where you are now. I'll be waiting there for you."

She said that was fine, and we hung up.

Traffic along Interstate 5 was light, and with one eye on the road and the other in the rearview, I kept my foot heavy on the accelerator and took the one hundred thirty miles in just over one and a half hours. I didn't see either Angel's or

Manly's car in the lot at Denny's. A quick tour of the restaurant yielded nothing but strange faces. I camped by the pay phones, drinking coffee and sticking a fork into a lump of something red advertised as cherry pie. I didn't wait long. The phone rang, and I answered it to Angel telling me that she and Manly were shacked up at the Notell Motel south of San Diego.

They changed the sheets every hour at the Notell Motel. The marquee advertised privacy, water beds, mirrored ceilings, and XXX movies. Noon was the rush hour, when the registered guests forwent lunch and ate each other. I was relieved when Angel answered the door fully clothed. Her mouth turned impishly at the corner.

"Hiya, sailor. Wanna date?" she said, shutting the door behind me.

The room was done in by a dreadful bordello decor. Manly was bound and gagged on the bed. Both head and footboards were mirrored, as were the ceiling and the closet doors beyond the bed. The walls were papered in red velvet. The bedstead and dresser were plywood-stained dark mahogany, with little gilt knobs. Westernized illustrations from the Kama Sutra littered the walls, giving pointers to those not susceptible to slipped disks. The television was thankfully blank.

"Why this place?" I asked.

"Where else could I bring a bound-and-gagged man and not raise an eyebrow?" she answered with a big, healthy smile.

I looked down at Chris Manly. His eyes were terrified.

"All we lack are the whips and chains," I said.

"You have to call room service for those," Angel answered. "But I don't think our friend here is still in the mood."

I knelt next to him on the water bed and said, "I'm going to remove your gag. If you scream, I'll do things to your face that will leave you doing character bits for life. Understand?"

Manly nodded rapidly. I removed the gag. His chest heaved with quick gulps of air.

"Where were you going, Chris?"

Automatic response: "San Diego."

"Bullshit. You were heading for Mexico. Why?"

He glanced rapidly around the room. I was on one side of him, Angel on the other.

"I needed to get away," he stammered.

I flipped a photograph out of my pocket and held it in front of his nose. He closed his eyes tightly and mumbled one of the more common profanities, which appropriately matched the content of the photo. I tossed the photograph to Angel. She glanced at it and said, "No wonder he wasn't interested in me. I'm the wrong sex."

"He swings both ways. Anything with a bank account, right, Chris?"

"Where did you get that?" he said with a violent shake of his blond curls.

"You know where I got it. The Jim Johnson collection."

"It's a fake, a trick photograph."

I showed him another one.

"Is this another fake? What's that thing in your mouth, a popsicle?"

Manly tried to jerk upright and clobber me with his bound fists. The water bed sloshed beneath us like the sea in a gale. I shoved him back down and held him there by the throat until both he and the bed quieted.

"You flew up to San Francisco with Valerie Rogers," I guessed, "and while she was out with the boss, you had a little party of your own. A couple of weeks later these photographs show up. Johnson doesn't want anything at first. Just to let you know he's got them."

"I thought you said you were a reporter," he gasped when I let go. "What are you putting the squeeze on me for?"

"I'm a reporter of sorts, but not for the mass media. I work private."

"A detective?"

"Bingo," Angel said.

"But we're not putting the squeeze on you," I added.

"What do you call this?" he said, holding up his bound hands.

"Angel, what would you call it?"

"Not sure. Rope, I think," she said, and gave the knot a yank, tightening it.

"Don't touch me, you dike," Manly hissed.

It was the wrong thing to say. I dipped my shoulder between them as Angel lunged, and I slapped Manly, hard.

"Don't hit me!" he wailed.

Angel bounced off my shoulder lightly, and said, regaining her balance, "Yeah, you bully. Let me hit him instead."

"Apologize," I ordered, and slapped him again.

"I'm sorry. Christ, what do you want?"

"A trade. The photographs for the thermos."

"What thermos?" he said.

I slugged him just below where the ribcage joins. He doubled over on his side. Angel winced. Fun work, beating up a bound guy half out of his mind with fear. Maybe I'd try old women and children next. When Manly began to breathe again, I rolled him over on his back.

"The evening of the crash, you went out to Topanga Canyon and picked something up. My guess is a thermos."

"You guess wrong. I was home all night, waiting for Val."

"You screwed up, Chris. People notice you. Call it your star quality. Someone saw you nosing around the crash."

"How could someone see me if I was home all evening?" he repeated.

"Jim Johnson asked you to do a favor for him. He asked you to go to the site of a small plane crash in Topanga Canyon and look for a thermos. If you found it, he'd return the photographs."

Manly slammed his eyes shut and made a grinding noise with his teeth.

"Did you know that your girlfriend had been on that plane when you went out to get the thermos?" I pressed, and forced his eyes open with my thumbs. "Did you know that they had just zipped her into a body bag? Maybe you helped set her up. Maybe you helped murder her."

He started to sob. I didn't want him to get sentimental, and slapped him twice.

"I didn't know!" he cried, afraid. "Johnson told me to look for the thermos, but I didn't find anything. I didn't know Val had been on the plane. Not until later."

"We know you found the thermos," I repeated.

Manly shook his head.

"What are you afraid of?" Angel asked softly. "Johnson and Mankewitz are dead. We have the photographs. So why do you lie?"

"Johnson said he had mob connections," Manly blurted.

"If they knew about you, do you really believe you'd still be alive?" I asked.

Manly thought about that, then something other than fear stirred behind his eyes.

"I need money," he said.

I stood up and walked away from the bed.

"Angel, move his nose three inches to the left."

"Let me untie him first."

"No. Hit him like he is."

She hesitated. I motioned with my eyes to go ahead. She leaned over with a shrug and grabbed him by the shirtfront. Manly twisted his face wildly from side to side.

"Topanga Canyon! It's buried by the creek," he cried.

"Tell us about it," I suggested.

"I didn't know Val was on the plane. I swear to God I didn't know that. Johnson told me to find the thermos. He said it was important, but didn't tell me why. He promised to return the photographs, but the photographs were only part of it. If I didn't do what he said, he told me he'd send somebody by to break my face. So I did what he told me to do. I went out to the canyon, found the thermos, and buried it."

I nodded, and Angel released him. It was good that she hadn't wanted to hit him, but would have. She turned her head away and grimaced. I didn't know whether she was disgusted with Manly, with me, or with herself. Maybe she was a little disgusted with all of us.

Manly drove my car, and Angel followed in hers. He kept it at fifty-five and leaned as far away from me as he could while staying in the car. His lips puffed out in a tough-guy pout. I let him sulk in peace. As we passed San Clemente, I asked, "How did she get you?"

Manly didn't answer until a half dozen miles slid past the windshield and the silence and his need to perform overwhelmed him.

"My car overheated south of San Diego," he said. "She must have emptied the radiator. I didn't know that, of course. I pulled off the freeway, steam pouring from the hood, thinking my luck had really gone sour. I don't know a damn thing about cars. Then this chick pulls in behind me, says her brother is a car mechanic, and looks under the hood."

"I think she pulled one of your hoses while you were having lunch," I said.

Manly shrugged. "I didn't suspect a thing. I mean, here's this good-looking chick, really well built, and she's stopped to help. That's all. Then she points something out in the engine, and I leaned over to take a look. Wham! She brings the hood down on my head and it's lights out on Broadway."

"Embarrassed?"

"She's a chick, right? Men aren't supposed to be taken like that by a girl."

"The times, they are a-changin'," I said.

He gave me a funny look.

We reached Topanga Canyon at twilight. A hundred yards west of the crash site, Manly slid the Mustang to the side of the road, with Angel picking up our dust. We stepped out. The air smelled fresh—not like Los Angeles air, but sweet, full of living things. Manly pointed down at the dry Topanga Creek bottom and said, "It's buried beneath the rocks down there."

"We'll wait while you find it," I said.

Angel stood at my shoulder while Manly scrambled in the riverbed below. There was doubt in her eyes, doubt about me.

"It's not my style to hit men who are tied up," she said.

I nodded and watched Manly, not looking at her.

"You looked like you enjoyed it a little," she added.

There was nothing to say to that.

"Would you beat him, tied up like that, if he hadn't told you about the thermos?"

"Yes. And if that hadn't worked, I would have tried hanging him."

"The ends justify the means?" she said.

It was an accusation and not a question.

"The ends never justify the means. You do what you have to do and try to live with yourself after. If you can't, you're in the wrong job."

Stones clattered below. Manly lifted the thermos above his head and scrambled up the bank. I took it from him. Aphrodite rising from the sea, and a silver cap.

I told Angel to meet me at the office after dropping Manly off, and I spun away, wanting to smash something.

Chapter 18

THE DOOR TO THE OFFICE BUILDING was locked. I rang the buzzer and waited for Harold to let me in. His shoulders straightened when he saw me, and he tossed off a quick salute. I asked him how he was.

"Fine, real fine," he said, and rattling the keys, gave the lock a turn. "I've been keeping an eye on your office, and everything's been nice and quiet."

I thanked him and told him that a woman would be by in an hour or so. He shot me a conspiratorial wink and opened the door. I could have told him it was more complicated than that, but I kept my mouth shut. Harold had his own ideas about my sex life, and it wasn't his fault that I couldn't live up to them.

The thermos tucked under my arm, I unlocked the door to my office, swung it open, and, flicking the light switch, stepped inside. The bone behind my ear was prodded by something small, round, and deadly. The door slammed shut. A white guy sat on the edge of my desk. He was big and dressed tough in a blue demin jacket turned up at the collar. A scar cut diagonally across both lips, and a two-day stubble blackened his jaw. I was given a shove from behind, and the guy with the gun stepped around me. He was a Chicano, short, but tightly muscled along the neck and shoulders. His arms were dotted with crude, homemade tattoos. The one on his forearm, a half-coiled snake, told me he had done time in the Chino penitentiary.

"We'd just about given up waiting for you, chump," the white guy said.

His grin opened a row of dirty, broken teeth, and a mouth that looked like something left in the back of a refrigerator. I asked him the name of his dentist. Unwise. Five knuckles spun my jaw around. A sense of humor in a hood is a rare commodity.

"Maybe you should keep your mouth shut, asshole," he said, and cocked his arm back to hit me again.

I cradled the thermos in the crook of my arm and waited to roll with the punch. His fist hovered next to his ear but didn't fire.

"Wait a minute," he said, dropping his fist. "We don't want to break anything valuable, do we?"

The white guy stretched his hand out. I gave him the thermos. All solicitude and concern, he set the thermos down carefully on the desk, then pivoted on his left foot and drove a right into my gut. His aim was low, and I took the punch well below the ribs, on the band of muscles stretching across the stomach. I pretended it was a great punch and doubled over.

"A friend of ours told you to stay away from San Francisco, and seeing as you didn't, he asked us to stop by and remind you again," the white guy said when I straightened.

The Chicano sat back against the desk, holding the .38 in a relaxed grip.

"I'll tell him you did a great job. You can run along and collect your paycheck."

I ducked his left but caught a looping right with the side of my head. I went down on one knee. The white guy stepped around to the side and lodged the tip of his boot into my midsection. It was a good shot. While I fought for breath, he palmed an ashtray from my desk and slammed it over my right eye. The glass shattered on my skull. Several seconds stretched past. The room seemed absolutely silent and still. Then someone laughed, and the laugh was slow. The white guy was walking toward me, slowly, as though the air had thickened to the density of water. He was looking at the Chicano while walking toward me. Something warm flowed down my face. The Chicano was laughing, his hand floating up to holster the pistol. The white guy's head was turning toward me. He was still smiling. His head was turning from right to left. It seemed incredibly easy.

My legs steadied, coiled, and I rolled out of the silence and slowness with a right cross. I saw his eyes widen as he turned into it, then he went down like water over Niagara. On the follow-through, I planted my right foot and turned with it, driving my left foot forward. The Chicano was moving faster now, scrambling to pull the gun from his holster. The instep caught him across the bridge of his nose, and he fell back against the desk, his legs sprawling open. I chopped at the spot between his legs, which brought his face back up in a hurry. I knocked it down again, and he rolled off the side of the desk. There was a heavy step behind me, and I twisted to the side. A fist bounced off my hip. The white guy lunged, setting his left foot firmly to power an overhand right. I ducked and met his forward knee with my heel and all my weight behind it. The joint snapped under him, and with a scream he toppled to the floor. The scream continued as he writhed on the carpet, and I stopped it with a fifty-yard punt to his midsection. No air, no voice. I stepped around the white guy and looked down at the Chicano. He wasn't moving. There was blood on my shoes, arms, and hands. All of it mine. I pulled the Chicano's gun from his holster and shoved it under my belt. I opened the door to the hallway and dragged him out by his heels. The white guy was sitting upright, his face pale. I touched the barrel of the gun to his forehead, and the last ounce of blood drained from his face.

"You can tell Rossi that I got his message. You can tell him that you beat the crap out of me. Now get out of here."

He crawled out, and I shut the door behind him.

I had to do something about the blood, but couldn't remember where I kept the tissues, or if I even had any. In desperation I grabbed the latest bill from the phone company, the one that said past due in large red letters, and pressed it against the cut above my eye. It almost worked. I knew that I should have gone to a doctor, but my eyes closed instead, and I had begun to whirl down a velvety black vortex when a knock at the door roused me. I got up to answer it. It was Angel.

"What the hell happened to you?" she asked, and steered me back to the chair.

"I just went fifteen rounds with Mohammad Ali in his prime. You'll read about it in the morning papers."

Angel propped my head back, peeled away the tissues, and with deft, practiced fingers, probed the cut.

"Sorry, pal, but you need some stitches. About five would do it, I think. I'm a pretty good cut man, but this is emergency-room size."

I locked the office door behind us, greatly disappointed that my two assailants had crawled down the back stairs before Angel arrived. We rode the elevator down.

"If I take any more blows to the head this week," I said, "I'll end up on a street corner wandering in circles and talking to space aliens."

Angel didn't laugh. "Then maybe you should learn some self-defense. If I taught you a little karate, you'd be able to take better care of yourself in a fight."

I didn't talk to her for two days after that one.

It was a slow night for emergencies. I was admitted, stitched, and billed in two hours. A cab took me home. The cut was swathed in a bandage that wrapped twice around my head. I looked like a refugee from a budget mummy flick. With the aid of a pair of scissors, I stripped the bandages off. My hair was matted with dried blood. I hid my ruined clothes in a sack and did the best I could with my hair under the shower. Thus refreshed, I lifted a bottle of Murphy's from the bar and drank to another day, another dollar.

The 1944 version of *Sherlock Holmes and the Spider Woman* was on the cable. I felt I could use a few pointers. Before I could settle comfortably into it, a knock sounded at the door. With the Chicano's .38 in the pocket of my robe, I checked the peephole. It was Leslie Carlisle, making a midnight call, dressed in blue jeans, a gray silk shirt, and a strand of pearls laid by milk-fed oysters. I let her in.

"What happened to your face?" she asked, stepping through the doorway.

"I called some guy in a bar a pansy. How was I to know he was Lyle Alzado?"

"Who's Lyle Alzado?"

"Forget it," I said, and let her lead me onto the couch.

She sat on the arm, and her fingers gently probed the skin around the stitches.

"Will it leave a scar?" she asked.

"I hadn't thought about it."

"Scars can be very sexy."

There was an unhealthy interest in her eyes.

"They've never done much for me. What are you doing here?"

"You haven't called for two days. I wanted to know what you've been doing."

"At one o'clock in the morning?"

She turned my face toward her, and the look in her blue eyes stirred the blood below my belt.

"You're asking questions a gentleman needn't ask," she said.

After we kissed, I lifted her up and carried her to the bedroom.

"Are you sure you have enough strength for this?" she asked, her voice low and lazy.

"I'll let you do most of the work," I said, and shut the door behind us.

After we had finished, Leslie sat up and lit a cigarette.

"What have you learned the past few days?" she said.

"Sorry," I said. "I don't screw when I work, and I don't work when I screw."

She laughed. "You're telling me. I've seen potatoes with more energy."

"Ouch. Excuse me while my male ego crawls into a corner and dies."

"I should think that my frequent gasps and moans indicated what I thought of your performance."

"Those? I thought you just suffered from asthma."

She laughed, and then it was like a wall dropped. Her face blanked, and with one arm across her breasts, and her cigarette hand braced in the air, she stared silently into the corner of the room. I left her alone. The cigarette burned nearly to the filter before she blinked out of it and said,

"You're the first man I've been with since . . ." Then another moment of silence. "You know, since Jack."

"Do you feel guilty about it?"

"I don't know what I feel. Let's not talk about it," she said, and stabbed out her cigarette.

"Don't tell me you're the type that suffers from postcoital depression," I said.

She shrugged and rolled on her side, facing me. A sliver of light from the hall fell across one of her small breasts, illuminating the nipple, then slid upward along her neck and ended in an arrow at her temple. I followed the path with my lips.

"There's only one cure for postcoital depression," I said when I reached her mouth.

"What's that?"

I raised one of my eyebrows.

In the morning, when I woke, she had gone.

Chapter
19

THOMPSON WASN'T IN HIS OFFICE when I dropped the thermos off at the NTSB for analysis. I dashed off a note on government stationery and swore his secretary to a solemn oath to get it to him the moment he returned. When I asked her how long it normally required to process lab tests, she consulted her daily desk calendar, complained about the crowded work schedule, and suggested I call back toward the end of the decade.

Wiz's nose was buried in the labyrinthine bowels of his sound console when I found him, a flathead screwdriver in one hand and a soldering gun in the other. He jumped at the sound of my voice.

"Shit," he said, "I thought you were one of the union guys. They catch me repairing equipment instead of calling 'em in, they cut off my right arm and stake it to the union contract."

He hadn't changed clothes. His T-shirt didn't look slept in. It looked lived and died in.

"Didn't you get home last night?" I asked.

"Home? Hell, no. They lock me in here at night to make sure I get the mix done on schedule, just because I disappeared for a few days the last time they let me out."

Wiz soldered a connection in the console, then eased it shut. It was close to pitch-dark in the studio. He moved by touch and memory.

"That was some tape you left," he said. "Somebody went to a lot of effort to hide what was on there, though to listen to it, I don't know why. It seemed innocent enough to me. Of course, I didn't think they had anything on Nixon, either."

He slid one of the sound pots up, flicked a switch, then rolled over to the cassette deck.

"It was easy to notch out the three main frequencies laid over the tape, but those frequencies resonated some harmonics that were hell to clean up. Then when I had a clean signal, I couldn't figure out what I was listening to, until it occurred to me that it had been recorded at way below normal speed. I played around with that for a while, until a couple of voices emerged from the sound envelope, but it still didn't make any sense, because the voices had been recorded in reverse. I rerecorded the voices on a new tape, speeding it up and turning them around again."

He pressed the play button. A telephone conversation between two men boomed from the speakers.

I got the medication you sent, said the first voice.

I recognized the voice immediately. It was Jim Johnson. *There was a set of instructions. Did you receive that as well?* said a second voice.

Sure did. The instructions are perfectly clear. Are you certain the dosage is adequate?

Enough to kill a horse.

There was laughter.

You can expect visitors this weekend, continued the second voice. *Do you foresee any complications?*

None from my end. How about yours?

It's all systems go down here. Let's hope the project will be a success.

No reason it shouldn't be. The plan looks good on paper. Now it's just a question of execution. It's been a pleasure doing business with you, Mr. Dantly.

Click. Dial tone. End of tape.

"Make any sense to you?" Wiz asked.

"More than I could hope for," I answered.

I took Angel to dinner at a Thai restaurant in Hollywood, across from the Capitol Records building. We ordered chicken coconut soup, glass noodles with shrimp and ground peanuts, and a pompano fish smothered in hot red curry sauce. I warned Angel to watch out for the finger-sized green peppers floating in the soup.

"I'm Italian. I eat peppers all the time," she said, and ate one to show off.

I pulled out my watch, and timed her. At five seconds, her skin turned the first of six shades of pink; at ten seconds, beads of sweat popped out over her brow; and at the quarter-minute mark, her eyes glazed over and she began to lose consciousness. I thought I might have to throw her on the floor and perform CPR on the spot, but with two glasses of water and both our beers, her vital signs stabilized.

After dinner I handed her a pair of headphones and played the Dantly tape. She listened quietly and, when it was over, said, "That clinches it. When do we turn this guy in?"

"We don't."

"Why the hell not?"

"Because I don't think it ends with him. He was working with Johnson, but somebody else was pulling the strings."

"He was one of the top guys in the company, right?"

"Right."

"Then if he bumps off Carlisle, he could be next in line for Carlisle's job."

"He couldn't take the chance. They could just as easily bring someone else in from outside the company, or Henry Howard could take control, which is what happened."

"He had to have a motive," she repeated.

"You have the motive right. He wants to run the company. But killing your competitor to get a big promotion went out with Macbeth. He wouldn't be stupid enough to murder Carlisle without some assurance that he was going to be the next president."

"Then he was double-crossed, because he killed Jack and still isn't president."

"The company is still in turmoil. Maybe when things settle down a bit, Henry Howard will resign. Or maybe it is a double cross. The only way to find out is to stir things up a bit more."

"If you stir things up anymore, it's likely to get hotter than that pepper I ate."

Angel smiled and looked at the spot over my eye. "How's your head?"

"It only hurts when I look in the mirror."

"I'm sorry for that crack I made about teaching you self-defense."

"So am I," I answered.

"What do I know? Maybe he had a gun."

"Maybe."

"Are you still mad?" she asked.

"Yes," I said, and paid the bill.

Dantly's two-story neocolonial was mid-block on Beechwood Drive in Brentwood. The community security service drove down Beechwood every hour on routine patrol. Angel and

I watched Dantly's house in half-hour shifts. Angel took the first shift, parking three houses south of Dantly's. I drove to a phone booth at a corner gas station on San Vicente and dialed Dantly's number. When he picked up, I hit the play button on my cassette deck.

"Who is this? What's going on?" he shouted at hearing his voice played back at him.

Midway through the conversation, he understood, exhaled a brief profanity, and was silent. The conversation ended. I turned off the deck.

"What do you want? Who are you?" he whispered.

I hung up.

At the end of Angel's first shift, I coasted to the curb up the street from her car, north of Dantly's house. I slid over to the passenger side, as though waiting for the driver to return. A few minutes later the headlights of Angel's red pickup lit, and she pulled away from the curb. I turned the radio to the local jazz station and counted the high C's. When I tired of C's, I tried F sharps. On the list of exciting ways to pass time, stake-out duty ranks with watching slugs mate. Angel's pickup appeared on the opposite side of the street, a few spaces down from where she had parked before. I waited five minutes, then turned the ignition over and drove to the corner of Beechwood and San Vicente and waited some more. Exciting.

We pulled four shifts each before Dantly jumped. I was parked on San Vicente, facing west, watching the fog roll in and worrying about visibility, when Dantly's Mercedes 280 SL ripped around the corner, followed at a discreet distance by Angel's pickup. Dantly headed west into the fog bank, then turned south on Ocean Avenue. I lost his taillights in the fog, but knew he wasn't more than a hundred yards in front of Angel. Suddenly the Mercedes appeared on my

right, backing into a space on Ocean by the entrance to the
Santa Monica Pier. Angel's brake lights flashed in front of
me, and I swung around her, turning left onto Colorado, left
again to Second Street, and a final left into the McDonald's
parking lot. I killed the engine and was out the door before
the Mustang stopped rolling.

When I reached the corner of Colorado and Ocean, Dantly
was gone. I crossed against the light, passing under the neon
sign that arched over the mouth of the pier. I walked fast.
The railing was to my right, and below it the sand stretched
darkly into mist. The fog wrapped around the pier like cold
smoke, dimming the gaily painted arcade shops, boarded up
for the night. As the rapid heel-toe click of my footsteps
swept past the carousel, I glimpsed behind a glass facade the
upthrust necks of intricately carved wooden horses, dark and
riderless in the winter night.

Strange footsteps sounded ahead of me. I slowed and turned
to the rail. An old man, his hand cupped around a briar pipe,
walked past, led by a lean gray whippet on the end of a leash.
I waited for him to go by, then, turning my coat collar up,
walked slowly toward the end of the pier. There was a four-
foot surf breaking, and as it crashed against the supports,
the vibrations shot through the pier and up my legs. Near
the end of the pier the surf was loud and constant. The urban
night noises, the honking horns, raised voices, motorcycles,
and airplanes overhead were swallowed by the din of it, like
light enveloped by fog.

A red barn-shaped building, bearing the worn white letters
"Sinbad," loomed where the wooden planks dropped off to
the sea. Against the railing on the far side, the vague shape
of a human shadow moved. The harbor master's office squatted a dozen paces ahead. I took cover behind it. My eyes
tried to cut through the fog. I heard nothing but the surf

below. I contemplated moving closer in, fearing my eyes had
played a trick on me and that I had staked out a trash can.
A small gust of wind thinned the fog momentarily, and the
figure separated into two very human forms hunched over
the rail. The fog rolled back in, thicker than before, and I
lost them completely. A voice carried for a moment above
the surf, in a short, low outburst. The pier trembled and
groaned as a large wave rolled by, then quieted. High heels
clicked sharply on the wooden planks, approaching from the
direction of the two figures. A face cleaved through the fog
and was gone. A feminine face. Strawberry-blond hair. For
a brief instant I saw eyes the color of sapphires sparkling in
the dull night.

The fallback was Angel's apartment, near the corner of
Rose and Pacific in Venice. I stopped by my apartment first
and packed a change of clothing into an overnight bag. In
the bedroom closet, behind a row of old coats, my grandfather's collection of hunting guns stood wrapped in their
leather cases. A Winchester .3030, a .306 with scope, and
three shotguns; an over and under .16 gauge, a .20-gauge
pump action, and a twin-barrel .410. I selected the .306 and
the .410 shotgun. The .410 was a small-gauge, lightweight
gun with a small pellet spread. It was a marksman's gun.
Most hunters like a shotgun with a larger pattern, which has
a better chance of bringing down something on the wing. I
chose the .410 because it was light enough to shoot with one
hand, and my target wasn't going to be wearing wings.

I stashed the guns in the trunk of the Ford and drove to
Rose and Pacific. I carried the overnight bag to Angel's
second-floor walk-up and rang the bell. It opened immediately.

"I'm glad you decided to show up. You had me worried,"
she said, letting me in.

"I'm touched by your concern." My voice was more flip than it should have been.

"So screw you. The next time I think you're out bleeding to death, I'll read a magazine or something."

The phrasing was unusual, but her point was clear, as was the pissed look she gave me. I pointed at my overnight bag.

"I won't be able to use my apartment for a couple of days, so I stopped to pick up a few things I'll need."

"What's wrong with your apartment?"

"I have the feeling the boogey man will be hiding under my bed one of these nights."

She laughed and asked if I wanted a drink. I said I'd have a beer and, while she went to get it, I looked around. Her apartment wasn't what I had imagined it to be. I didn't see any barbells, and a framed poster of Arnold Schwarzenegger was noticeably absent. The apartment was small, with one bedroom and a living room shoulder-to-shoulder with a cramped kitchen. There was a rattan-style couch and coffee table in the living room, flanked by two deck chairs and a dozen potted plants. Against the far wall there was a small black-and-white television, a bargain stereo, and a trophy case.

"I saw you walking onto the pier, so I took the park," Angel said.

She handed me the beer. It was a light something that tasted like it would be good for your hair, but not to drink. I put down two sips and set it aside.

"I didn't see anyone except a few bums. The fog was pretty thick, so I could have missed him, but I don't think so. You have any luck?"

"I found him at the end of the pier. I don't know how lucky that was, when I think about it," I said.

"Do you mind if I put some music on?" she suddenly asked.

I said I wouldn't, but expected something dreadful and aerobic. She put on a recording of a Bach concerto. Surprising woman.

"So who did he meet?" she asked, and sat on the couch.

"Leslie Carlisle."

Angel whistled softly and began cracking the knuckles of her left hand, one by one.

"Madam client. This is pretty serious, isn't it?"

"Damn serious."

"She has her husband murdered and then hires you to expose it. Doesn't make much sense," she said.

"No, it doesn't," I said.

She moved the knuckle-cracking exercise to her right hand.

"And stop that. You're making me nervous."

"Stop what?" she asked, oblivious.

"Cracking your knuckles."

"Shut up and leave me alone," she said easily. "Any other ideas?"

"Dozens, and all of them as bad as the first."

"Nothing you can do about it tonight," she said, and telling me to make myself comfortable, disappeared into the bedroom.

I make myself comfortable by snooping around. It's a personality defect that helps me be good at what I do for a living. I checked the kitchen cabinets for liquor and didn't find any. Her provisions were mostly whole-wheat natural-food fare. The dishes were mix and match from at least four different sets. I moved into the living room, looking for books, and didn't find any. I stopped at the trophy case. It was chest-high, with oak sides and a glass front. There were about a dozen trophies inside. Miniature bronze figures in clumsy action poses. Boxing. Karate. I wondered where my shooting trophies were. As a young man, I had proudly displayed them in a case like this, before I did my stint in the service and the targets turned from clay to flesh and blood. There was a thump behind me. I turned. Angel had tossed a couple of blankets on the couch.

"What are those for?" I asked.

"It's too late to get a hotel, and you can't go back to your apartment, so you sleep here tonight."

There was a light one-one-two tap at the door.

"Shit," Angel said.

I slipped the .38 out and moved behind the door.

"What are you doing with that?" she asked.

"What do you think? Ask who it is," I whispered.

"I know who it is," she said.

I shouldered the gun, but kept my hand on the butt. Angel opened the door. The guy who entered looked something like the way a brontosaur would look if it walked on two legs and had no neck. His shoulders were so massive that a mere shrug of them would have swallowed his small head. He had a broad chest and a waist that narrowed down to next to nothing, like a wedge. If you pointed his toes and gave his skull a solid rap with a mallet, he'd go so straight into the ground that you could hit a golf ball off the top of his head. Angel called him Larry. He kissed her on the mouth. With one opened eye, he spotted me and broke it off. Angel introduced us. There was a heavy dose of New York in his accent.

"Yeah. Hi. That's some cut over your eye," Larry mumbled.

"I got beat up by a couple of Girl Scouts when I refused to buy their cookies," I said.

He looked at me like I was screwy. Angel quickly asked

if he wanted a beer. He ignored her and ambled over to the kitchen to get it himself. His biceps rippled when he ripped the twist-off cap with his bare hands. Wow.

"Angel tells me you're a private dick," Larry said.

His lopsided grin told me that was his idea of a joke. I was going to have a lot of fun hating this guy. Larry drifted into the living room and pointed at his chest.

"I'm a professional trainer myself."

"There are other people who want to look like that?"

He gave me his screwy look again. Angel wedged her shoulder between us.

"Larry trains professional people, like doctors, who don't have the time to develop their own training schedule."

"Maybe I could work with you," Larry said. "If you put on a couple of inches here and there, maybe people wouldn't be so eager to push you around, and you wouldn't get hurt like that."

"If anyone gives me a hard time, I just shoot them. It's faster, and easier on the knuckles."

"Funny guy. You were just leaving, right?"

He stepped toward me. His arms hung loosely at his sides, and his chest was thrust out in the arrogant pose of a man accustomed to throwing his weight around, but not to fighting. I moved half a step to the side, ready to cut his legs out from under him if he pushed it. Angel dug her shoulder into his side and steered him toward the bedroom.

"I need to talk to you for a moment, Larry," she said.

Larry noticed the blankets. He frowned at me, scowled at the blankets, and followed Angel into the bedroom. The door shut. It was quiet for about fifteen seconds. I half-heard another thirty seconds of Larry demanding that he stay and I go. The bedroom door opened again and Larry stormed through the room. I assumed he had lost the argument. On his way out he turned to me and pointed an exquisitely muscular finger.

"If you touch her, I'll rip you apart."

I let the front of my sports coat part, revealing the butt end of the .38.

"Try it, and I'll give you a steroid injection you'll never forget."

Stalemate. He left the room an unhappy man, slamming the door hard enough to bring the roof down.

"You have a charming taste in men," I said to Angel.

She stood in the doorway to the bedroom, her head resting against the jamb. She looked tired. Maybe she was just fed up with macho nonsense.

"You didn't try very hard to like him," she said.

"He didn't give me a reason to."

I walked over to her and leaned against the other doorjamb. She looked up at me, and in her eyes I thought I saw that we both wanted the same thing. Then she looked down, and I knew that we were both afraid of the same thing as well. Timing is everything. Being alone at bedtime doesn't necessarily mean the time is right. I gave her a gentle shove backward, into the bedroom. A soft look of surprise fell across her face.

"Thanks for the bed," I said, and, feeling virtuous but more than a little regretful, shut the door between us.

Chapter
20

THE FOLLOWING MORNING I checked into the Shangrila Hotel, an Art Deco building on Ocean Avenue overlooking the Palisades. I used an alias at the desk and paid in cash. The clerk acted as if he had never seen the stuff before and asked if I wouldn't rather pay by credit card. With the cut over my eye half-healed, and a suspiciously light overnight case at my side, I looked like the type of man who would check into an exclusive hotel, run up a five-dollar room tab, and then skip. I left a fifty-dollar deposit at his insistence to cover any phone calls I might want to make, and declined the bellboy's offer to help me find my room.

It was a hundred-dollar-a-night room, with a two-hundred-dollar view of the northern coast toward Malibu. I stood at the window and got my money's worth. The phone was on the bedside table. I sat on the bed and called Thompson at the NTSB and asked if there was any word yet from the lab.

"There was a small accident with the test sample from the thermos," he said, and cleared his throat.

It was ominous.

"How small," I asked.

"Somebody put a rush tag on it by mistake."

"What does that mean?"

"I don't want to upset you, but I'm looking at the results right now," Thompson said, and laughed.

"Hold on while I pick myself off the floor from a dead faint."

"You want to know what we found?"

"Desperately."

"The sample contained substantial quantities of digitalis."

"Digi-what?"

"Digitalis. It's a medication used to treat patients with cardiac arrhythmia. In small doses it acts as a cardiac stimulant, but if the dose is large enough it can precipitate cardiac arrest."

"Did your analysis pick any of this stuff up in Valerie Rogers' system?"

"Not on the first pass, because you have to test specifically for it, and we didn't. We're checking a tissue sample this afternoon."

"I thought that she had already been buried," I said.

"She was. But I had a hunch something might come up, and I put a little of her away for a rainy day."

The thought was gruesome, but I asked him to keep me posted.

"This is your last free chat," Thompson said. "We passed this along to the FBI. A special agent by the name of Curt Heidleman is very much interested in meeting you."

"I'm not giving interviews today," I said, and, with a round of thanks, hung up.

Leslie Carlisle's red Targa Porsche was parked in the drive when I pulled to the curb of her Cheviot Hills home. I wondered how I could have missed it the night before at the pier, then recalled that there are more Porsches here than in the rest of the states combined. In Southern California people who want to be noticed drive an Oldsmobile.

While I waited in the foyer, the maid padded upstairs in her starched white skirt to inform Leslie Carlisle of my arrival. I wondered what the socially appropriate greeting was between a client and employee who had slept together, if only once, and when the client had just been witnessed at a clandestine meeting with the man who had her husband murdered. The maid motioned to me from the top of the stairs, and I followed her down the hall to a closed door. The maid's knock was acknowledged, and I was admitted.

Leslie Carlisle stood behind a black lacquer desk, framed by the picture-window view of Los Angeles in a shroud of smog. Her handshake was brisk and formal.

"I hear from you so infrequently I gather you've discovered something of importance," she said.

I placed the cassette deck on her desk. She sat down and clasped her hands beneath her chin like a poker hand. Her eyes were cautious.

"This tape was found with other materials owned by Jim Johnson," I said, and pressed the play button.

Ted Dantly's voice entered the room. Leslie winced once, when Dantly said there was enough medication to kill a horse, then listened quietly through the rest of it. I switched off the tape. She closed her eyes and massaged her temples in a small, circling movement of her fingertips.

"I'm the biggest fool the world has ever known," she whispered.

It was self-judgment and invited no reply. She stood unsteadily, her chair spinning away, and stared down at the tape player.

"Is this the only copy?" she asked.

"The original is in a safe-deposit box. This is the only copy of the original."

She turned to the window and looked absently at the city below.

"There's something you should know," she said, very softly.

I watched and waited. I had a feeling that there was a lot I should know.

"Ted Dantly called me last night. He was very upset. He insisted that we meet. Something about his phone being tapped. I thought it was all nonsense. Who would want to tap Ted's phone? But he isn't the sort of man to lose his head over nothing, so I agreed to meet him."

"Why did he call *you*?"

"Because he knew I had hired a detective," she said.

There was no hesitation in her voice. None at all. She kept her face to the window. Her face glowed in the afternoon sun.

"Where did you meet?" I asked.

"At the Santa Monica Pier."

"Why there?"

"I don't know why. He insisted."

Her head jerked to the side, and she looked at me, her face shadowed by the sun behind.

"Why are you asking me so many questions?"

"Professional habit."

"You sound as though you believe I'm guilty of something."

"What could you be guilty of?"

"If I'm guilty of anything, your questions aren't going to make me break down and confess."

Then came the look I had seen before, at our first meeting. Her eyes were hard and brilliant, and behind them moved a great amusement, as though she could look down upon the thoughts tooling in my mind, thinking them before I could. It made me uncomfortable. She said through an effortless smile, "It's ridiculous, of course, meeting on the pier, but Ted thought he was being watched. He didn't want to take any risks. He said that he knew Jack had been murdered, and was afraid that he had played an unknowing part in it."

"The tape suggests that he was an active partner."

"I know it does. He claims he was set up. I don't know what to think now."

"Who set him up?"

"He wouldn't tell me. There was this look of terror on his face. He said that if he talked, he would be killed. I know he was afraid, because I saw it in his face."

"Maybe we should talk to him about it."

"He'll just deny everything."

"The tape and thermos might convince him it's time to talk."

Leslie's eyes hit mine with a sudden intensity. "You found the thermos?"

I told her how I picked it up and what was in it. The air went out of her.

"Oh, God. Digitalis is Grandfather's heart medication."

Leslie's eyes glassed over like marbles, and her head weaved slowly from side to side. There was no focus to her. I opened the door and shouted. The maid scurried up the stairs with short, skirt-constricted steps. I told her to bring a pitcher of water and a bottle of cognac.

Leslie's voice called to me, small and scared. "Hold me."

The maid craned her neck to look inside and, startled, hurried away. Leslie stumbled from behind the desk. I went to her. She latched onto me, her head flat against my chest and her arms tightly pressed around my waist. She cried.

There wasn't much I could do except stand there and hold on. I haven't cried since the age of six. When a woman cries in front of me, things happen in my chest that I can't explain. Crying is an act more private than sex. You lose control. You admit that you've been hurt. I can't do that. I'm jealous of those who can care that much.

The maid tapped on the door. Leslie Carlisle released her grasp, sniffling and wiping at her eyes. I took the tray from the maid and shut the door with my heel. I poured a tall glass of water and a short one of cognac, and helped Leslie put them down. Her breath evened out. My insides were all balled up. I took a shot myself.

"I'm sorry," she said, dabbing here and there with a handkerchief. "But it's an awful thought. Too awful to bear."

"You knew that this was one of the possibilities from the start."

"That doesn't make it any easier. Suspicion can be shrugged off. Proof is real."

Her hands shook when she tried to pour herself another cognac. I poured it for her.

"I think it's time to go to the police with this," I said, handing her the glass.

When she looked at me, her eyes were wild. "We can't go to the police."

"Why not?"

"He's my grandfather. I can't have my own grandfather arrested."

"Your husband was only the first in a string of murders. Five people are dead because of this. It's not something you can sweep under the rug."

She thought about money, and what money can and can't buy, and drank her cognac. It relaxed her.

"Could he be convicted on the basis of what you have now?" she asked.

"Not without Dantly's testimony. The digitalis will mean little in a court of law. Anybody could get their hands on it. I suspect the contracts on Johnson and Mankewitz were put out through American Sun Corporation, and it's doubtful they will be willing to talk. There's a good case against Dantly, but if he doesn't talk, it ends with him."

"I need to discuss this with Mother." The cognac had strengthened her voice. "Can we put off the police for a day or two?"

"No," I said.

It wasn't a word she accepted. The stone-like quality of her eyes returned.

"This could kill the company. If a police investigation compromises the chairman of the board, investors will run from us like the plague. There won't be any company left."

She reached across the desk and grabbed my hand. Her grip was fierce.

"I haven't asked you for any favors. I'm not asking you to withhold evidence from the police. All I want is forty-eight hours to formulate a strategy to keep the company solvent. Tomorrow morning we'll meet with Mother, and you'll tell her what you've told me. The company must survive this."

She was persuasive.

"You have forty-eight hours," I said.

Each of those words was to cost someone a life.

Chapter
21

IAN WADDINGTON WAS WAITING for me at a corner table of Harry's Bar in Century City. Harry's Bar is fine, but if Hemingway had lived to see Century City, he would have tried to take it out with his shotgun. Waddington wore a charcoal-gray suit with maroon pin stripes, a white shirt, and a maroon silk tie pinned by a gold clip with a ruby inset. He was a short man with sandy-brown hair and features that would make him look like an apple doll in fifty years. His skin was the color of chalk. Raised in New England, he distrusted the sun and held suntanned skin as a sign of frivolity. When I first met him, shortly after he had migrated west, he said he had moved to Southern California because there was more money and less intelligence here than anywhere else in the world.

"Is this on your expense account or mine?" he asked, shaking my hand across the table.

"I paid the last time. It's your turn," I said.

"Bullshit. You've never bought in your life. But I'll buy if you have any dirt on Western Shores."

"The inquest into Carlisle's death has been picked up by the FBI," I said.

"When?"

"This morning."

Ian smiled broadly and signaled the waiter. He ordered a chicken curry something, and I had the filet of sole.

"I am not an expert in police procedure, but I would hazard a guess that they have a suspect or two in mind," Ian said, his phrasing a polite pump for information.

"No official suspects. But if they follow the map of clues, they'll bump into at least one senior officer at the company, and maybe more."

Ian extracted a felt-tip pen from his front suit coat pocket and doodled on his napkin. It was a linen napkin. A calculator came out of another pocket. He punched the buttons and frowned. Then he backed away from the table, excused himself, and disappeared for five minutes. When Ian returned, he seemed a very happy man.

"Hot tip?" I asked.

Ian nodded. The waiter uncorked a bottle of Stag's Leap Chardonnay, 1983 vintage, estate bottled. Ian swirled it, nosed it, and rolled a drop around his palate. He pronounced a favorable opinion, and the wine was poured. Ian wasn't the type to embarrass you at the dinner table.

"Western Shores has been a tough stock for most investors to predict," he said.

"But not for you."

"I've had a little help," Ian said.

He raised his glass to me. We drank. The wine was dry and had a stone-like edge. Perfect.

"The assets of Western Shores are now worth more than the cumulative value of the stock issued. I think it's going to attract a corporate raider, or maybe genuine take-over interest from an outside player. One investor in particular has picked up quite a few shares—about four percent of the total amount of stock issued."

"A raider?"

"That's the funny part. It's Richard Preston. He's been a friend of the Howard family for years, but by the way Henry Howard reacted, you'd think war was declared. Preston claims he is purchasing the stock as a trust for an unnamed beneficiary and isn't interested in contesting control of the company."

"Is that believable?"

A small smile worked its way up and down Ian's mouth. It was a bemused smile. It was a cynical smile. It was a smile that said when money is involved, you don't listen to the words, you look to the bottom line.

"Anything is possible, but Henry Howard didn't get to where he is by trusting people who have something to gain at his expense. He can't be happy with that much company stock falling into one pair of hands, no matter what the explanation."

"Is Western Shores vulnerable to a take-over move?"

"I think that when word gets around that senior officers are implicated in Carlisle's death, the stock will dip back into the twenties, and someone, whether it's Preston or some other corporate raider, will smash Henry Howard and take over Western Shores. And when that happens, I'll be able to buy a yacht from my brokerage fees."

Some people have made a hell of a lot of money by doing nothing more than being present and taking their cut when money changes hands. That was Ian Waddington. Others have lived their entire lives on the fringes of big money, but when the Banker in the Sky calculates their final net worth, it comes out on the debit side. That was me. But my conscience was clean.

Angel found me in line at the Nu-Art, a revival house that was screening *The Scarlet Empress*.

"What are you doing here?" I asked.

"I came to see a movie. Is that okay with you?"

"What about Larry?"

"He's being a jerk," she said.

"About last night?"

"He's just being a jerk in general."

"With his deltoids, he figures he doesn't need much in the way of personality."

Angel didn't laugh, but she didn't tell me to go to hell, either. When the line began to move, she slipped her arm through mine.

Directed by Josef von Sternberg, *The Scarlet Empress* stars Marlene Dietrich in the role of the top fornicating monarch of all time, Catherine the Great. Married off to the mad heir apparent to the throne of Russia, Catherine falls in love with the Captain of the Guards. Meanwhile, he's sleeping with Catherine's dragonish mother-in-law, the Queen. In revenge, Catherine sleeps with anyone and everyone in uniform, except the Captain. When the Queen expires, Catherine has her mad husband murdered, and rides into power on the broad backs of the cavalry. The film has a cast of thousands, stunning black-and-white photography, and more gargoyles in the set design than any film since *The Hunchback of Notre Dame*.

After the tail credits, we took a walk on Wilshire Avenue. I asked Angel what she thought of the movie.

"I liked the Captain of the Guards." she said.

He was tall, curly-haired, and looked like he might have the body of a power lifter under his coat of armor. She asked me what I liked about the film.

"Marlene Dietrich." I said.

Angel was incensed.

"Right. That figures. She was one of those women who wore her heart south of her belt."

"The captain didn't strike me as being any different."

"Maybe not, but at least he could admit he was in love."

"It's easy to admit love if your bread is being buttered on both sides."

"What's that supposed to mean?"

"He was two-timing her with the Queen."

"So what? She got even."

"And won the throne of Russia. It was power she wanted, not love."

"And you admire that?"

"I respect it."

"You have a warped idea about love."

"If Larry the weight lifter is any example, your ideas aren't very straight either," I said, and I must have sounded smug, because Angel pulled away and raised her voice.

"Are you being sarcastic? Because if you are, I wish you'd tell me."

"I'm being sarcastic," I said.

"You always have a flip answer, don't you? Why don't you just admit what you're really feeling?"

Her anger was contagious.

"You seem to know everything. Why don't you tell me."

"You're jealous."

The corner light was red. Angel ignored it. She flung her last words at me and darted across four lanes of traffic. At the opposite curb, she shouted, "Admit it!"

"Damn you!" I yelled, over the squeal of a blue bus breaking to the side. "I'm jealous!"

She didn't hear me. As the bus pulled away, her face was visible for a moment in one of the lit side windows, then vanished behind a black spewing of exhaust.

Chapter
22

IT WASN'T UNTIL THREE O'CLOCK that morning that I realized my subconscious had re-ordered my priorities. Mankewitz and Johnson had been murdered since Carlisle's plane went down, a couple of goons had broken into my apartment and tried to do the same to my head, I still couldn't figure out who was going to profit most by the turmoil at Western Shores, and I didn't trust my client. I had enough worries to keep me awake for a week, but the only thoughts twisting through my mind were of Angel and the unsettling emotions that surfaced whenever I thought of her. By four o'clock I concluded that I had a crush on her. By four-thirty I decided I had to put a stop to it.

When sleep finally came, it was heavy and dreamless, and I slept through an hour of jazz on my clock radio before waking to the sound of a car alarm. I pried my eyes open with three cups of coffee and called Angel. There was no answer at her apartment. I guessed that she was working out at the boxing club, and drove into Ocean Park.

It was a bad guess. The old bantamweight directed me to a gym a couple of blocks to the north, where Angel did her strength training with Nautilus machines and free weights.

A young blonde in a red leotard sat at the front desk of the Westside Athletic Club. She knew Angel by name but wouldn't let me into the gym without an escort. I volunteered her, and she agreed. As she stepped from behind the desk, I silently rehearsed what I wanted to say to Angel. I almost didn't notice that the blonde's red leotard and white tights fit her like the skin of an apple, and the difference between her attire and total nudity wasn't worth imagining. Almost didn't notice. She guided me past the aerobics floor, where a dainty redhead shouted instructions like a drill instructor to a group of sweating, panting masochists, and opened a sliding glass door that led to the weight room.

Angel was strapped into a Nautilus machine that looked like it had been imported direct from the Spanish Inquisition. She was pulling a chrome bar over her head and fighting to keep it from snapping back and ripping out the muscles and ligaments of her arms and shoulders. The chrome bar connected to chain-driven gears that moved a set of weights the size of a small refrigerator. Angel's teeth were gritted together, her blue leotard had sweated through, her face was bright red, and her fatigued muscles were trembling like a case of Parkinson's. She was having fun.

When Angel saw me, she slowly lowered the weights and moved her hands away from the chrome bar. Then she smiled, chagrined.

"I never thought I'd see you in here," she said.

The blonde in the red leotard backed away. A muscle man seated on a bench and lifting free weights almost popped his triceps when a specific part of her back nearly met him cheek to cheek. I thanked her for the escort. She turned and wove away through the machines. The muscle man sighed heavily and went back to his weights.

"Ready for a workout?" Angel asked, unstrapping the belt binding her to the Nautilus machine.

"Maybe next week," I answered.

"Come on, no pain, no gain," she chided.

I reversed the equation.

"No gain, *no pain.*"

She worked it through and gave me a long, disapproving look.

"I wanted to talk to you," I said, meeting her eyes, "and I didn't want to wait until tomorrow."

"Maybe we should step outside," she suggested, and when I agreed, led me through the weight room and out a set of sliding glass doors to the pool area. Two swimmers in caps and goggles were following the lap lanes, their arms methodically arcing from water to sky. A dozen chaise longues circled the pool and all but one were empty. At the far end of the pool, a thin man propped a reflective mirror on his chest, bronzing his chin.

"I thought about what you said last night, and decided you were right," I said, trying to be sure of myself.

"It's always nice to be right. What was I right about?"

"About me."

Angel nodded as though she understood, then stopped herself. "What about you?"

Butterflies began to queer my resolve. I pressed on.

"That I was jealous."

She smiled. "There's nothing wrong with being jealous."

"It's hard enough to do our jobs well without having to worry about our personal relationship screwing everything up. I wasn't being fair, and I apologize. It won't happen again."

"What won't happen again?"

"Scenes like last night."

"That's what you came to tell me? That you're going to stop being jealous?" she asked, and when her voice raised an octave, I couldn't tell whether it was from disbelief, scorn, or anger.

"You have your own private life, and it's not fair of me to interfere with it," I explained.

"So you're going to just suppress your feelings? Is that it?" she demanded, her eyes beginning to burn.

Angel was not one to suppress her feelings.

"If they get in the way of our working relationship, then yes, I will."

"You can't just close yourself off like that. How am I supposed to know what you're feeling? Am I supposed to be psychic?"

Faced with Angel's anger, my own anger rose unchecked.

"You don't need to know what I'm feeling."

"Yes, I do!"

"You want to know what I'm feeling?"

"Yes!" She shouted.

"I'm angry!" I shouted back.

"Why?"

"None of your damn business! You're not the only one with a private life, you know."

"Fine. Just fine. Then just close yourself off," she said bitterly, and spun away.

She moved too fast. Before I could stop her, Angel stormed into the women's locker room. Anger made me brave, but not brave enough to follow. I hung around outside the door, until a woman walked out of the locker room and gave me the kind of look reserved for perverts. I wandered back to the pool. It was the wrong direction. The sliding glass door to the weight room opened, and body builder Larry sauntered out to stop me.

"You're in the wrong place, pal, and I think I'm going to make you pay for it," he said, puffing out his chest.

Two of his body builder buddies, their bodies straight out of the Paleolithic era, squeezed through the doorway and lined up behind him. One was short, the other tall. Both were broad.

"This doesn't concern you," I said, and tried to walk away.

Larry blocked my path and shoved me back toward the pool.

"So you say. But I think it does," he said.

He stood with his knees locked and his hands half raised in fists. His body was tensed like steel and aggression glazed his eyes. I didn't want to fight him. I didn't like him, but there are a lot of people I don't like. It wasn't my job to fight him, and nobody was going to give me a medal if I won. Plus, he was big as a horse and could kill me if I made a mistake.

"I don't want to play this game, Larry, so I'm just going to walk away."

I took another step. His meaty palm splayed against my chest and pushed me two steps back. If he pushed me again, I'd be treading water.

"You're going to play the game, all right, and you're going to lose," he said.

The short body builder laughed at the remark, and Larry looked back for encouragement. I couldn't wait for another chance. When his grinning face swiveled around to me again, I popped a quick hard left that caught him flush on the nose. The jab wasn't good enough to put him down, but it made him mad. I didn't think Larry was a polished fighter, and mad was what I wanted him. His head snapped back, and he looked at me in a shock that quickly transformed to rage. He bellowed like a pricked bull, and charged me with an overhand right. I ducked under it, grabbed the shirt at his chest, turned my hip under his, and threw him as far as I could over my shoulder. It was far enough. His head cracked sharply on the concrete, and the force of his body carried him into the pool.

On the follow-through I crouched low and whirled to face Larry's two buddies. They glanced back and forth at each other, trying to decide what they were going to do. I waited for them to make up their minds. They didn't take long. Both stepped back, and the tall one held his hands chest-high with the palms out. I relaxed. Someone shouted at me from behind. I turned to the voice.

A swimmer at the opposite end of the pool shouted that a man was drowning. I looked for Larry on the surface of the water and didn't see him. He was lying on the bottom of the pool, proving muscle doesn't float. His two buddies began shouting behind me. Nobody seemed to think of moving anything except their mouths. I dove in, wrapped my arms around his chest, and hauled him to the surface.

His two buddies grabbed his arms and hoisted him from the pool. The short one bent over Larry's unconscious face, then began to hop around excitedly.

"He's not breathing," he shouted.

The tall body builder fled toward the office, shouting for help. I pulled myself from the pool, and crabbed around Larry's body. With the palm of one hand I arched his neck, and with the other I forced open his jaw. I didn't think about what I was doing. I was worried that I had killed the man. The short body builder hopped around Larry's feet, shouting at me to hurry up. I pinched Larry's nostrils together, cupped my mouth over his, and forced air into his lungs. I turned my head aside, counted, and fed him another blast.

Larry's body jerked, and a wounded gasping sound poured from his throat. I gave him another breath. He opened his eyes, and sat up coughing and spitting. He looked at me with revulsion.

"Fucking fag," he wheezed.

I stared back at him in amazement, and caught myself before I attempted to explain. Some guys are just never going to be your friend.

Chapter
23

LESSON ONE IN POWER POLITICS is to play on home turf. The sunlight beating through the curtains beyond her head, Leslie Carlisle sat behind her black lacquer desk in the upstairs study. Madeline Wentworth and I flanked each other, facing Leslie. Backlit, her expressions obscured by shadow, Leslie asked me to begin by recounting the results of the investigation. I talked briefly, recounting the facts but not the theories. Madeline watched me carefully as I spoke. A string of pearls ringed her neck. Halfway through the account, her hand rose to fondle the strand, rubbing the pearls through her fingers like a rosary. Leslie mostly looked down at her hands on the desk. She knew what I was going to say. When her eyes stirred, it was in the direction of her mother.

I stopped at Leslie Carlisle's midnight rendevous with Ted Dantly. Madeline gave her pearls a small kiss, and released them.

"I suppose you have in your possession the physical evidence mentioned in your report," she said.

"In a safe-deposit box, accessible only to me, or my lawyer, should something happen to me."

"We should be so lucky," Madeline snapped.

"He was only doing his job, Mother. A job I hired him to do."

Madeline turned to her daughter. Her voice was bitter. "You don't solve family problems by exposing them to the public. This little folly of yours is going to cost everyone pain and money."

Leslie broke the code of polite restraint. She leaned forcefully across the desk and, enraged, shouted, "Grandfather's folly cost five people their lives, including my husband's!"

The raised voice shocked Madeline into silence. She looked away from her daughter, embarrassed, and picked at her pearls. Leslie's hands were shaking.

"I admit that I am not an expert in these matters, but the evidence seems circumstantial to me," Madeline said.

Her voice was soft. She glanced up with a conciliatory smile.

"Circumstantial. That's the correct word, is it not? It proves nothing outright."

She looked to me for guidance.

I said, "Jack Carlisle was murdered. Ted Dantly was involved. Henry Howard is implicated, but nothing is proved against him. The police will likely consider him a top suspect, depending on what Dantly says."

"Have you been to the police?" Madeline asked, shocked.

"Not yet. At the request of Mrs. Carlisle, I'm waiting until tomorrow."

"What will you tell them?"

"What I've told you."

"Dear God, that could ruin us all." She sniffed.

After tomorrow that wouldn't be my worry. Madeline leaned heavily against the chair, shielding her eyes as she added the losses in her head.

"We have to plan for the contingency that Grandfather will be seriously implicated in this affair," Leslie said.

She was all business. The rage was gone. Her face was like

a map of nowhere. No lines, no directions, nothing. Her calm voice commanded the room.

"It's quite possible that Grandfather is innocent. The evidence could be misleading. The company will maintain his innocence until proved otherwise in a court of law. You and I will go on record as supporting him. Nevertheless, his leadership has been badly compromised."

Madeline listened carefully, then asked, "What are you proposing?"

"Grandfather will have to be removed as president and chief executive officer."

Madeline's laugh was short and brutal. "Short of dynamite, how do you propose to do that?"

"Grandfather is not the man he once was. Even if we assume he is innocent, his inability to overcome investor disapproval proves that he is slipping. His sale of the company's resort properties is sheer folly. The company is no longer under the pressure of a hostile take-over. There was no reason to sell off our crown jewels, unless it is part of a deal Grandfather made with American Sun."

Madeline squirmed in her chair, and when she cocked her head to look at her daughter, there was a new appreciation in her eyes. "Even so, he won't go willingly."

"He will have to be forced out. Between the two of us, we can do it. Tens of thousands of shares have changed hands in recent weeks. These new investors will welcome a change in leadership in the hope that they can turn a short-term profit."

The minds of mother and daughter began to click together. Madeline said, "A sizable number of shares have been purchased by Richard Preston. You remember him, don't you, dear? He could represent the swing vote, if we knew for whom he was purchasing the shares."

"I think I know who it is, and I think we can count on those shares siding with us," Leslie said.

"You're serious about this, aren't you?" Madeline suddenly asked.

In her mind, the deal had reached the realm of the possible. Leslie nodded. Madeline made a show of conscience, sighing heavily, then said, "If you follow through with this, I'll back you up."

Leslie extended her hand across the desk. Mother and daughter shook hands.

"That still leaves us short a chief executive officer," Madeline said.

"I will be the new president," Leslie said.

They were simple words, but they carried weight. Madeline crossed her legs, examining the curve of her high-heeled foot as she considered the proposition.

"The board would never accept it. They'll want to choose someone from among themselves," she said.

Confidence in her squared shoulders and measured voice, Leslie answered, "When Grandfather realizes that he will have to resign, he'll do the one thing that will ensure his legacy—appoint a successor. The successor will be someone from the family. Jack had to marry me before Grandfather would appoint him. I'm not going to marry anyone this time. Father is no more a realistic choice than he was six years ago. I will be the only reasonable candidate."

Madeline's head rocked back, and her eyes met Leslie's with shrewd appreciation. "You've really figured all this out, haven't you?"

"The board won't like it, and one or two members are bound to resign in protest, but the rest will fall in line. We will have effective control of the company. There will be no choice and no chance involved."

"I should have named you Henrietta," Madeline said, and stood.

Madeline didn't say good-bye to me. She turned at the door and said to Leslie, "This will be a baptism of fire for you, my dear, but I want you to know that I approve."

After Madeline left, Leslie and I sat quietly in the sunlit room, each thinking totally different thoughts. When the silence became noticeable, Leslie gave me a look that meant I should dismiss myself. I didn't.

"I didn't know you were interested in running a company," I said.

"You shouldn't be surprised. It's a family trait," she answered.

"When did you come to your decision?"

"A few days ago. I've done some soul-searching lately, about what to do with my life, and I came to the conclusion that this was it."

"The timing is a little suspect."

"The timing is perfect," she said. "The company is in a crisis. I'm ready."

The tone of her voice didn't invite debate. I had performed my duty, and it was time for me to leave. She pulled out an address book and, opening it, said, "If you don't mind, I have to make a few phone calls."

"Why haven't you told me that you were sleeping with Ted Dantly?"

It was something I just said, without giving it much thought. Her eyes held mine. She read my thoughts. What I knew. What I guessed. She looked down at her hands.

"How did you find out?" she asked quietly.

"I followed Dantly to the pier that night."

"Sometimes I think you know everything." She sighed. "You're right, of course, but also wrong."

"Tell me."

"I'd rather not. It's embarrassing."

"You'll have to overcome it. The police are not going to believe your affair with Dantly is entirely coincidental."

"Why not?"

"Don't be stupid. You've had an affair with a man implicated in your husband's murder. The police will suspect that both of you hatched the plot in bed."

"I did not plot to have my husband killed."

"Glad to hear it. I'll assume you're innocent for now. The police won't be as generous."

"The police can think what they want to," she said, angry. "How am I supposed to react to this? I loved Jack. It makes me ill just to think that someone would suspect me."

I softened. "Dantly could reasonably expect that if Jack was dead, you'd marry him. He would become the logical successor not only in marriage but in running the company."

She did not answer. I was tired of trying to read through the shadows of her backlit face. I stood and closed the curtains. There was a silver lamp on her desk. I turned it on. She didn't try to stop me. She didn't notice.

"When I heard Ted's voice on that tape, I was so afraid. How do you ever know what the other person is thinking? There are people out there who look and talk just like us, people who seem absolutely unremarkable, yet they are rapists or murderers. And there is no way of knowing."

She looked to me for help. I didn't offer any. She told her story.

"Jack had I don't know how many affairs. I hoped that when we had children, he'd stop. But we never had children. It wouldn't have stopped him anyway. His affairs were a major part of his life. He wouldn't do without them. I was faithful. For a while. A year ago I met Ted. I was lonely, and he was attentive. After years of coping with Jack's affairs, my self-esteem was at an all-time low. I thought that maybe there was something wrong with me. Ted was a good-looking man, successful in his own right, and he wanted me. It was a revelation. I felt desirable. I felt that it wasn't my fault that Jack had affairs. Now, I wonder if Ted really wanted me at all. Maybe he just wanted Jack's job, and I was the means to get it."

She stared into her hands and, in a small voice, a voice strangely flat and factual, said, "If Ted did have a hand in Jack's death, then it will be twice that I've been some man's path to power. I'm not going to be the path anymore. I'm going to be the power."

Chapter
24

DONAHUE IS ON TELEVISION and all is right with the world, I thought, perched on the bed in my hotel room and eating Chinese take-out while switching between Phil Donahue and Oprah Winfrey. I couldn't decide which show I liked better. Phil roamed through his studio audience, thrusting his microphone forward to get the Woman's Opinion on the dangers of massive weight loss. Sensitive, yet masculine, with a good-hearted seriousness. Oprah looked elegant in an emerald green dress, and talked with the Countess of Something-or-other about the duties of being a socialite. Articulate and intelligent, even in the company of fools. A rare ability. I decided to watch both. Life with a capital *L* rebalanced and began to look normal again.

Maybe the world wasn't such a dangerous place after all, if, wherever you went, you could turn on a television set and find a Phil Donahue or Oprah Winfrey. Maybe I could stop by my office, pick up the phone messages, and find nothing more ominous than a two-day collection of bills piled under the mail slot. Maybe I could go home and sleep in my own bed without worrying whether or not someone would try to make that sleep permanent.

A commercial break featuring an anti-hemorrhoid product brought me to my senses, and I decided to stay where I was and phone into the office for my messages by remote. Special Agent Curt Heidleman of the FBI had called four times. With each call, his voice grew colder, indignant that I was not returning his calls. His fourth message was like a blast of Arctic air.

The final message on the machine was the one I had been waiting for: "Marston? This is Ted Dantly. I need to talk to you right away. I'll be at my office until seven. This is extremely urgent."

The machine beeped and rewound. I dialed the number for Western Shores.

"Thank God you called," Dantly said when he picked up the line.

"You wanted to talk to me. Start by telling me who you're working for," I said.

"Not over the phone. Are you crazy?"

"No. Just tired of being jerked around. You're less than twenty-four hours from needing a bail bondsman, so if you want my help, act fast."

"We have to meet in private. I'll tell you everything I know. Tonight. At the Santa Monica Pier, by the harbor office."

"That's a stupid place to meet. Suggest someplace else."

"No. It has to be at the pier. Don't ask me why. I'll tell you tonight, at midnight," he said, and hung up.

It was a setup. Somebody had decided that it was time to take me for a long walk off a short pier. I didn't know who, and I didn't know why it had taken that somebody so long to discover that I was dangerous.

It was a half hour before sunset. The golden hour. The Shangrila is a half mile north of the pier. I put on my swimming trunks.

The winter surf was choppy, like it gets in the late afternoon when the wind blows hard and cool off the surface. I waded in until the water surged around my thighs. The current was strong, pulling northwest to Malibu. The waves didn't have much form. I ducked under the last of a set, and the turbulence swirled over my back. Swimming hard, I cleared the break before the next set and swam south, against the current. It was hard work. Fighting the panic that always comes when the water is cold, I moved just fast enough to keep warm.

It took half an hour to close on the pier. Fifty yards up, I rode a wave in and sat in the white water where the surf comes skimming to an end. My lungs greedily sucked in the air, and my limbs felt tired but strangely light. I looked out to sea and thought about how I was on the edge of a great frontier, facing a thousand miles of wilderness between the eastern and western edges of the Pacific.

Then I got cold. I stood and looked up at the pier, near the harbor office, then across the beach to the Georgian Hotel on Ocean Avenue and the decrepit apartment buildings on the far side. I wanted a location with a clear view of the harbor office, where I could comfortably watch without being seen. My eyes passed over the lifeguard tower several times before it became obvious. I jogged back to the hotel.

Two hours short of midnight a blood-red moon crawled up the eastern sky. Angel and I trudged through the sand, with the moon over our shoulders. Forty pounds of cased camera equipment dragged at my arm. Angel reached the lifeguard tower first. It was a simple hut structure, propped eight feet above the sand on four-by-four beams at the corners. A wooden ladder was attached to one of the beams. Angel climbed it first. I followed, handing her the camera case. A walkway circled the hut, fronted on the outside edge by a three-foot-high rail. The door featured a simple mortise lock. I beat it in fifteen seconds, using an expired credit card. Angel slipped through the door with the case.

A custom-cut length of three-eighths-of-an-inch plywood, hinged at the top, covered the windows. The plywood was secured in place by metal latches on both sides and padlocked. Angel handed me a crowbar from the case. I worked the tip between the metal latch and the plywood and gave it a solid yank. The screws pulled out of the wood, and the latch flapped free. On summer days, the plywood swings all the way up, hooking at the top. I snapped the second latch and propped the length of plywood up and out with the crowbar, leaving a small opening that would be almost invisible from the pier.

I stepped into the darkness of the hut and shut the door behind me.

"Damn. Now I can't see anything," Angel whispered.

I told her to look in the lower right-hand corner of the suitcase for a flashlight and turn it upside down, with the lens pointed at the floor. A dim red light, just enough to work by, filtered through the hut. Angel set up the tripod and mounted the cannon-like 500-millimeter lens to the camera. The camera was loaded with high-speed black-and-white film, the kind that can take pictures inside a refrigerator with the door closed.

While Angel adjusted the angle of the lens, I wired myself for sound. If Dantly was coming to talk, I wanted it on record. A mini-cassette recorder made a small lump in the lower left-hand pocket of my sports coat. It wasn't my best coat. A small hole was cut in the back of the pocket. I threaded a lavaliere microphone about the size of a thimble through the hole and clipped it under the lapel, with the wire running inside the lining of the coat. The wire was invisible. A frisk would pick it up, but I wasn't going to let Dantly frisk me.

We were set up before eleven. It was an hour before Dantly would show. Angel and I crouched in the corner of the hut, watching the pier though the small triangle of uncovered window. I had a pair of binoculars. Angel looked though the lens of the camera.

"I can tell this is going to be boring," she said.

"So quit," I suggested.

"Do you want to get rid of me, or what?"

"Or what."

"Okay, funny man. Let's play forty questions."

"Let's not."

"Is she bigger than a breadbox?"

"Is who bigger than a breadbox?"

"Your girlfriend."

I pulled the binoculars down. Her eye was glued to the camera. I could see only the back edge of her face.

"I don't have a girlfriend," I said.

"Never?" she exclaimed.

"What do you mean, never?"

"You've never had a girlfriend?"

"I didn't say that."

"What are you, a thirty-five-year-old virgin?"

She giggled. I flicked her nearest ear with the tip of my ring finger. She gave a soft cry, then turned and slugged my shoulder. I hit her back. She put on a few boxer moves, feinting with the right and coming in with the left. I covered up and slapped the top of her head. It was as if we were kids, slugging and slapping as a way of touching each other. But we weren't kids. I grabbed her arms, and we wrestled. I was sitting on my heels. She used her thigh as leverage and toppled me. I let my momentum carry me over on top of her, and there I was. On top of her. And we weren't wrestling. I was suddenly and strongly conscious of her sex. In the dim red light her eyes looked wild. Her breath was hard and fast. I quickly rolled aside and sat up.

"We have work to do," I growled, and trained the binoculars on the pier.

Angel put her eye to the camera. There was a funny smile on her lips. She seemed pleased with herself. I was content to be in this small dark space with her, watching her between bouts with the binoculars and anticipating what it would be like when the work was done.

The foot traffic on the pier had thinned to nothing. A half hour before midnight I picked someone out walking along the north side of the pier. He was about six foot and thin. He wore a dark-blue coat, turned up at the collar to hide the lower half of his face. I didn't like the way his head kept turning. Left toward the boarded-up arcades, right to the railing, and back to the arcades. The movements were casual but practiced. With his dark coat and fluid, characterless walk, he was nearly invisible when he passed into shadow. I nudged Angel with my foot and pointed him out. She pivoted on the balls of her feet and followed him with the lens.

"He's moving too fast. I can't get a decent exposure," she said.

"Just keep the lens on him. He'll stop."

Dark Coat crossed behind the harbor master's office, and as he came out the other side near the rendezvous point with Dantly, his pace slowed. Ten yards beyond it, he stopped, leaned over the railing, and lit a cigarette.

The camera clicked four times, at a half-second exposure per frame. His face was long and thin. He had greasy black hair, thin at the top, that swept straight back from his forehead. A bony ridge jutted out where his eyebrows and forehead met, forming a hood over his eyes. The cigarette glowed on pale skin and day-old stubble. He could have been any one of a thousand guys who wander the Southern California beach at night, down on his luck, a bottle of port in his coat pocket, killing time before calling it a day and crawling into a dirty blanket in the basement of a run-down apartment building. But he wasn't. He didn't have the eyes of the drunk and dispossessed. They were hunting eyes. He smoked casually, looking at everything and nothing, and, with a good inch left on the end of it, flicked his cigarette into the sea. He strolled around the end of the pier, his hand sliding along the rail, and passed out of sight along the southern edge.

Angel sat back on her heels. "How do you know he's with Dantly?" she asked.

I looked at her. She wasn't kidding.

"The guy is straight out of the Thug of the Month Club," I said.

"He looked like just another bum to me."

I thought about it.

"I could tell you that it was the way he looked or moved, but that would be only part of it. The other part is fear. When I saw him, he scared the shit out of me."

Angel laughed at that. "Afraid? When you're down here and he's up there?"

"Yes."

She was a fearless woman, and I was talking about something she didn't understand. She knew the John Wayne image of bravery, the stand-up-in-a-hail-of-bullets-and-blast-it-out-with-the-bad-guys idea of heroism.

"I don't let fear stop me from doing what I want to do. I listen to it. Fear makes me aware of what I can't possibly know except through the hackles on the back of my neck. Fear is a tool for survival, and if you're playing games where people want to kill you, you won't last long without it."

She brooded over what I said. I watched the pier. Nothing moved on it. At a few minutes before midnight, a figure passed under the neon arch at the foot of the pier. I put my binoculars on him. It was Ted Dantly. His long gray trench coat didn't have a wrinkle. At the end of each crisply tailored cuff swung a hand gloved in calfskin. He didn't look left or right, and his pace was fast, not like that of a man out for an evening stroll, but the self-important stride of a man professionally busy.

Dantly reached the rendezvous beyond the harbor master's office precisely at midnight. His gloved hands gripped the rail. He stared straight out to sea. Angel's camera clicked.

"What do we do now?" she asked.

"We wait until they call it off, and then tail Dantly back to his place," I said.

The minutes passed. Waiting was hard on Dantly. He was not a man accustomed to waiting, standing in one spot, doing nothing. He made a project out of it. Every few minutes he'd check his watch. Then he'd take a few steps toward the end of the pier, lose courage, and return to his spot. His elbows would rest on the railing, and his hands would fold across to cup his arms as he leaned forward. The gloved fingers would begin to fidget, first tapping, then slapping lightly at the biceps. Unable to contain himself, he would push away from the railing, take four or five steps back, and stare east, down the stretch of pier toward Santa Monica. With a nervous glance over his shoulder at the Red Sinbad building across the pier, he would then step back to the railing and check his watch again, like a Judas goat tethered to a stake, panicked by the mingled scents of lion and hunters crouched in the shadows.

At one o'clock the routine changed. Dantly turned away from the railing and, facing the Sinbad building, tossed up his hands. A guy I hadn't seen before strutted from the shadows. His blond hair was long and stringy and fell over the collar of a dirty green army jacket. He stood half a head taller than Dantly. A red C-shaped scar was carved into his right cheek. Dantly was telling him something, motioning wildly with his arms.

Dark Coat appeared, coming out from behind the last arcade booth. He laid his hand on Dantly's shoulder. He said something, and Dantly calmed, his hands dropping to his sides. With an arm draped over Dantly's shoulder, Dark Coat led him back to the railing. Dantly continued to talk. Dark Coat nodded, smiled, understood. He patted Dantly on the shoulder, then looked across at the blond guy in the army jacket. An understanding flickered between them. It wasn't obvious. A look and a slight nod.

Army Jacket said something to Dantly. He answered, turning his head. Dark Coat's hand slipped off his shoulder. Dantly gave him a quick side glance, then continued talking to Army Jacket.

Dark Coat fingered something in his coat pocket.

As he spoke, Dantly gripped the railing. Army Jacket nodded, listening, but his eyes were on Dantly's hands, not on his face. Without warning, his fist curled up in a short and powerful thrust, lodging in Dantly's gut. Dantly's face compressed and he started to double over. With a quick flick of his wrists, Dark Coat snapped a cord around Dantly's throat and pulled him upright. Army Coat clamped onto his wrists and braced a shoulder against his chest.

Dantly was pinned between them. His handsome face swelled as the cord buried into his throat. Dark Coat pulled still tighter, his brow furrowed with nothing but the physical strain, like a hunter wringing the neck of a bird. Dantly's eyes bulged. His body jerked wildly. Angel cried out, and I told her to shut up and shoot. I heard the camera click. With each snap of the shutter, Dantly weakened. The jerking slowed, and his shoulders gave a final little flutter. The body went slack. Dark Coat held him up by the cord and gave it a final solid twist before lowering him gently to the pier. The cord was unstrung from his neck.

Army Jacket backpedaled and looked down the pier. There were no witnesses in that direction. Dark Coat expertly went through Dantly's pockets. He found something and put it in his own pocket. Army Jacket walked around and grabbed Dantly's legs. Dark Coat had him around the chest. Together, they lifted the body to the railing and dumped it over the edge. Dantly's body cartwheeled and hit the surf with a dull splash.

Angel stumbled away from the camera. Her foot tripped over something, and a beam of light arced across the hut. The flashlight hit the far wall and skittered to a stop. I dove for it, and tripped the switch. When I looked up, the men on the pier were gone. Angel asked if I thought they had seen it. I didn't have to answer. We both sighted them, midway down the pier. Army Jacket was running hard. Dark Coat trailed him by twenty yards, walking fast, his head twisted over his shoulder and eyes pinned to the hut.

Angel called out their progress while I rewound the film. My hands were sweating, and the rewind wheel kept slipping from my fingers. When I heard the film click past the final sprocket, I flipped the camera back open, grabbed the roll of film, and handed it to Angel. She pointed, and I followed the direction of her finger. Army Jacket had reached the set of stairs that led to the sand. His right elbow was bent ninety degrees, and his hand curled around something that could only be a gun.

"Follow me and stay exactly on my right shoulder. Not

one step ahead or behind," I said, and slipped out the door.

From Army Jacket's vantage, we would present a single profile target—hard to hit with a handgun.

I swung over the rail. Angel dropped down beside me. I gave her a half second to balance, then sprinted toward the pier. The sand pulled at my feet. It seemed as though I were barely moving, like the feeling you have in nightmares when you're running as hard as you can from a monster that is going to kill you, but your legs are like lead and you get nowhere. Several shots cracked in rapid succession. Army Jacket had an automatic. It sounded like a 9mm parabellum. I couldn't tell where the bullets went. He must have realized he was too far away, because he didn't squeeze off any more rounds until we neared the support beams beneath the pier. The bullets slapped over our heads. I dove for the safety of the sand, Angel beside me. I crawled five yards in and crouched behind a beam.

Army Jacket didn't feel as comfortable in the open when he couldn't see us, and I watched him slither across the sand to hide under the pier about forty yards east of us. He would root there for another minute or two, until Dark Coat caught up to him. They would then team up and sweep in, trapping us between them and the sea.

Angel knelt one beam over. Her breath came evenly, and she looked back at me with calm eyes. My own breath felt ragged.

"I'd never seen a man die before," she said.

It was offered as an explanation for losing her head and kicking the flashlight.

I said, "It's horrible, no matter how many times you see it."

The waves pounded into the pier behind us. Our voices didn't carry any farther than a few feet. I drew the .38, the one I had taken from the Chicano, and laid it on my lap.

"I've landed us in a big mess this time," she said.

"You certainly have, Stanley."

"What?"

"Skip it."

"I was hoping you'd tell me you had a plan."

"I have, but you won't like it," I said.

"Why not?"

"Because you're going to get very wet."

I told her to wade out until the water was chest deep and take cover behind one of the beams, holding the film high and dry over her head.

I was right. She didn't like it.

"No way. I'm not leaving you out here alone to play hero. I can take care of myself."

"Do you have a gun?"

"Of course not."

"Then shut up and do what I tell you."

I guess she didn't like my tone of voice, because she didn't move.

"You can't stop a bullet with a karate chop. If I have to shoot you in the foot to make you move, I will."

She gave me a look which I took to mean it would be my own damn fault if I got myself killed, and she wouldn't weep if I did, but she moved. She hesitated at first contact with the cold water, but plunged forward. I lost sight of her behind a beam.

On my belly, I crawled one row forward and toward the center of the pier. The position was close enough to the edge to prevent a flanking maneuver to my left. I stood with my shoulder to the beam, and pressed my cheek against the wood. It smelled of tar and salt. I had a clear view to the east and south. My body was hidden by the beam, but to keep the view I hung my face out like a tin can on a stump.

They would be moving, and I would not. If either of them was good enough to put a bullet through my head before I saw him, I wouldn't have much of a chance no matter what I did.

I sensed movement. A streak of blond between beams, near the center of the pier. Army Jacket. I didn't move. Dark Coat would be harder to spot, and he seemed the more dangerous of the two. Army Jacket crept closer, darting between beams, waiting, moving again. I didn't have a clear shot. He slipped closer, like a wary animal in a forest of wood and sand. My neck made involuntary jerking movements, trying to pull my face away before a bullet ripped it open to empty and rust. Someone else moved, outlined against the sand, ten yards to the right of Army Jacket and a few paces behind him. The figure was dark and moved fluidly, blending easily with the stripes of shadow and wood. Dark Coat.

I eased my head back and drew the gun to chest level. The next minute was the most difficult, waiting on blind faith that Army Jacket would not change direction and come at me from the left. I concentrated on my breath, slowly drawing it in and pushing it out.

Behind me, out in the water, a steady tapping gained prominence over the surf. I couldn't place it. The tapping sounded like a code. Army Jacket didn't like it. His automatic snapped one, two, three, four times ahead and to the right. Swinging out from behind the beam, I spotted a head of blond hair ten yards away. The head was turning my way. I squeezed off a round. The head went down and didn't move. A muzzle flashed down the pier, and the slug splintered wood near my face. I leaped forward and pinned myself behind the next beam.

I waited. He knew where I was. I knew where he was. The only question was what we would do about it. If he tried to move toward the ocean I would see him, but if he doubled back toward the center of the pier, I wouldn't. A minute passed. I started to get nervous. I moved my head to the left, dreading an unpleasant surprise, and saw him. He was a good thirty yards down the pier, floating away through the shadows.

When he gave no indication of doubling back, I decided he hadn't liked the odds, and I walked to the water's edge. Angel appeared from behind a wave when I called. She waded in. I found the blond in the Army Jacket. The bullet had caught him in the cheekbone, below his eye. It wasn't very pleasant, and I didn't look at it long. There wasn't any identification. I took his automatic and walked back to the water.

Angel stood in the moonlight, shivering, her arms wrapped around her chest.

"Thanks for the help. What did you tap with?" I said.

Her hand uncurled around the still dry roll of film.

"I thought it might help." she said.

I told her that it had, and wiped my prints from the .38. Thinking about the hole it had made in Army Jacket's head, a hole so small in relation to the entire organism but no less fatal, I heaved it out to the end of the pier. It clattered against a beam before dropping silently into the surf.

I gave Angel my coat and walked back to the car. As we pulled out, two police cruisers slowly circled in from Ocean Avenue. The bubble gum lights were dark. There are a hundred reports of gunfire for every one that turns up a body. Tonight the lights would spin the red and yellow colors of a jackpot.

I parked the Mustang in front of Angel's apartment. She told me to come up and hopped out before I could answer. When

I reached the stairs, her door was open. I climbed the stairs and closed the door behind me.

The kitchen table supported an unopened bottle of Jack Daniel's flanked by two glasses. A trail of wet clothes led to the bedroom. I cracked the seal on the bottle of Jack, poured two fingers, and threw it down. The bathroom pipes groaned, and water hissed on tile. The shower door clicked shut.

I refilled the glass. The whisky cut a trail down my throat. I closed my eyes and whirled in the darkness to send a bullet into Army Jacket's brain. He fell, rose, and fell again. The hole stared at me, a red, round eye in a dead host.

Dark Coat smiled.

Dantly, his arms flapping like a marionette cut suddenly loose from its strings, turned slowly in the air, his handsome head lolling back to greet the sea. The waves took him without a ripple.

Dark Coat smiled again.

The sound of water. Angel humming in the shower. I imagined her, naked, the water rolling off her skin, the steam billowing around her. My body warmed. I emptied the glass and poured another round. The pipes groaned again, and the hissing stopped. The click of the shower door sounded as loud as a gunshot.

I carried the bottle and a glass into the bedroom. It was dark. A lamp in the bathroom drew a line of shadow and light across the bed. With her foot perched on a dresser, Angel toweled an olive-brown leg. Beneath a transparent blue robe, her skin shimmered like flesh under water. Dark curls swept around her face as she turned to take the drink from my hand, and there was a look in her eyes that turned my blood inside out. She said something, and I answered, the words like stones in my mouth. When I took her in my arms, and she folded against me with suppleness and strength,

I thought one last time about Dantly and how a small and simple bullet can wreak havoc on something so large and complex as a man. And then the robe fell from Angel's shoulders and I felt her skin on mine. Then I thought of nothing at all.

Angel was not a passive woman. When desire took its hold, her body was fierce and quick, yielding now and then to a languorous stretching of muscle and skin. I tried my best to keep up. Not content to dishevel merely the bed, passion claimed a lamp, a framed Hopper poster on the far wall, and everything on the dresser, including the bottle of Jack Daniel's, which soaked into the carpet. Had I not been in good shape, I might have been another casualty. Two such nights in a row could kill a man.

When the light graded from dark to luminous blue, we began to talk. Angel's voice was lazy.

"What took you so long?"

"So long to what?" I asked.

"You know. I thought you wanted to do this a while ago. I wondered what took you so long to try."

"Why do you want to know?"

"Just answer the question."

"Okay. Ethics."

"Ethics," she repeated.

It sounded like a heavy and pretentious word.

"I wasn't sure it was the right thing to do," I said.

"Why not?"

"You work for me. It's possible that we'll hate each other in a few weeks because of this."

"What good is a sense of ethics if you never get laid?"

"Maybe I didn't want just to get laid. Maybe I had strange ideas about love and passion."

"Oh. The old-fashioned type. I like that."

She stared into my face. It was a simple act of intimacy. I felt very close to her. She snuggled in against my chest.

"I wanted to do this since the first day I met you," she said.

"You have a strange way of showing it."

"You don't know much about women, do you?"

"Absolutely nothing at all," I admitted.

Later, as I slipped into a dream, I heard Angel's voice: "I don't work for you anymore. From now on, I work with you, partner."

I smiled, and sleep followed.

Chapter
25

WHEN I AWOKE, ANGEL WAS GONE. There was a note on the kitchen table. She was on her morning run. Five miles. I took my usual morning run to the bathroom. After a shower I poked through the drawers, looking for a razor. I found one of those silly female razors that look like a flying saucer. Body builder Larry wasn't a frequent house guest. If he was, he shaved his legs and not his face.

After a breakfast of orange juice and a health food cereal that had the taste and consistency of granite, I called Shirley. The first message was from FBI agent Curt Heidleman. It hit me how badly I had screwed up. Dantly was the only direct line to whoever had pulled the strings on Carlisle's murder. Without him, I could make a case against a couple of corpses. Any further punishment of Dantly and Johnson would not come in this world. The next message was from Ian Waddington. It was before eight o'clock, but Ian was a go-getter. He could usually be found in his office at the start of the East Coast business day. I dialed the number, and Ian answered on the fifth ring.

"Hold on, I've got New York on the other line," he shouted.

"If you can reel it in, take it to a taxidermist and mount it above your fireplace."

"Oh, shut up," he said, and put me on hold.

When Ian came back on the line, we swapped information. He told me that the management of American Sun was in town to sign the papers on the Western Shores resort properties deal. I told him that Western Shores was less another executive. I asked him about the latest take-over rumors.

"Nothing has gone public yet, but I've heard that American Sun is cooling the waters by offering itself as a white knight should a hostile take-over be attempted against Western Shores."

"American Sun the white knight? Isn't that like trusting Launcelot with the keys to Lady Guinevere's chastity belt?"

"The way I look at it, they're all in bed together, and someone's going to get screwed. Richard Preston is the key. Nobody knows which way he's going to swing."

Nobody except Leslie Carlisle.

There are about twenty motels and fewer than five hotels in Pasadena. If Rossi was in town in connection with the Western Shores deal, he would be homesick for Las Vegas. He would stay in a high rise with room service. I located him at the Pasadena Hilton. The operator connected me to his room. When I heard Rossi's voice, I put on my best Texas twang and asked for Sam Rossmore of Austin Oil. Rossi told me I had the wrong party and hung up.

I left a short note for Angel, telling her where I was going, and drove to Pasadena. It was rush hour. The Santa Monica freeway bottled up at La Cienega, and from there it was stop and go—mostly stop—through downtown. After Dodger Stadium, the freeway opened up, and I thumbed my nose at the poor suckers stuck in traffic in the opposite direction. I parked across the street from the Hilton and crossed to the lobby.

The registration clerk was a small man in a small job with a big organization, the latter forming the largest part of his self-esteem. He had an annoying habit of ignoring those who needed assistance under the pretense of a more important task, such as straightening the cuffs of his uniform. I relied on the services of Abraham Lincoln to attract his attention, and told him to inform Mr. Rossi that a Mr. Marston would be waiting for him in the coffee shop.

There were few customers in the coffee shop. I found a booth near the entrance and sat on the booth side, with my back to the wall. There was a crack to my right where the seat cushions met. I slipped the 9mm automatic I had taken from Army Jacket between the cushions.

I studied the menu and had finally gotten the hang of it when Sam Rossi strode into the coffee shop, accompanied by one of his goons. Rossi was decked out in his Sunday best, a double-breasted suit one shade down from undertaker black. The goon was well-dressed for a goon, in a pair of tan slacks and a tweed sports coat buttoned above the navel. The coat was cut a half size too large to accommodate the piece he carried under his left shoulder. He was an inch short of six feet, thin, had curly red hair, and was probably selected for this detail because he could be trusted to have a decent set of table manners. Rossi called me his "old friend" and held his arms outstretched as though he expected me to jump up and hug him. I noticed he wasn't carrying a gun. Rossi introduced me to his goon, who took an interest in my suit.

"Nice threads," he said, and ran his hands lightly down my side looking for a gun.

"The clothes make the man," I said, and we all sat, as happy as can be. Rossi was beaming. I couldn't figure out why. Maybe he'd caught the latest telecast of Maharishi University on Channel 18 and converted.

"I was hoping we might run into you today," he said.

"The truth is, I'm in a bit of a jam," I said.

Rossi laughed. "That's an understatement, pal."

"I lost a key witness last night. He took a long walk off a short pier."

"Yeah. I heard about that. Tough luck."

"But just when I thought I didn't have a hope in the world, I found these great photographs."

The goon tensed when my hand dipped into my coat pocket. I slowly drew out a white envelope and tossed it to Rossi. He spilled the photographs of Dantly's murder on the table. Rossi's smile faded.

"You have a good memory for faces," I said. "I was hoping you'd be able to identify the players. Particularly the guy in the dark coat. There's not much hurry on the other guy. Saint Peter will figure out his name soon enough."

Rossi grunted. He handled each photograph by the corner, to avoid leaving a clear set of his prints. When he had finished and was satisfied that the photographs could not be argued to be anything other than what they were, Rossi folded them back into the envelope and handed it to me with a rueful smile.

"I'm sorry to say that I've never seen any of these people before in my life."

"The police keep files. Maybe they will have some ideas."

"I don't think you want to show these to the police," Rossi cautioned.

"Why not?"

"Where's the profit in it? I know a guy who would be very interested in a set of photographs like this. A collector. We might be able to work out a deal."

The waitress came by to take our order. Rossi ordered a

Bloody Mary. I had orange juice. The goon ordered steak and eggs. I didn't like the deal Rossi was hinting at.

"I want the same thing now that I wanted the last time we talked," I said. "I didn't care much for Dantly or Johnson when they were breathing, so I'm not going to get sentimental about their corpses. I want the guy who gave the order that killed Jack Carlisle. Maybe it was your boss. Carlisle was going to ruin a very profitable deal for you, and you had the opportunity and means to get rid of him. But I don't think that's the way it happened. You had a direct connection with Johnson and wouldn't have worked through Dantly. I think American Sun was performing a service for a friend. Henry Howard asked your boss if he knew of someone who could be trusted, and you recommended Johnson. When Howard decided that Johnson needed to be fired in a permanent way, you handled it for him. The same with Mankewitz and Dantly. In return, American Sun got better than average terms on the resort properties deal with Western Shores. From your standpoint, it was good business. Sooner or later it will catch up with you, but I'm not interested. I want the guy who was running Dantly. If I can't get a conviction, I want enough to put him out of power."

Rossi's smile grew as I talked, until it spread a crooked line above his entire jaw.

"You want a hell of a lot for a couple of snuff pics," Rossi said, and laughed.

There wasn't any humor in the laugh. Just ridicule. I looked at the goon. He was smiling.

"I'd be more than happy to help you get this Henry Howard guy," Rossi said. "He sounds like a real menace to society. But if I told you I had anything on him, it just wouldn't be true."

"Then I'm not interested in your collector."

"But he's still interested in you," Rossi said.

"You heard the terms," I said.

"I have something you might be very interested in. We could work a trade. By funny coincidence, I have a photograph too."

Rossi nodded to his goon. The goon palmed a photograph like it was the ace of spades and dealt it face up. It was a Polaroid. The photograph was taken from the front seat of a car looking back. Dark Coat sat in the rear seat. He held a snub-nose .38 across his lap, the barrel resting snugly against Angel's rib cage. She wore her jogging suit. Her hands were crossed behind her back, and a gag distorted her face.

"This morning, outside her place," Rossi explained. "We didn't know where you were hiding, so she looked like our next-best bet."

The goon's plate of steak and eggs arrived, and he happily attacked it with one eye on his fork and the other on me. My throat was dry, and the orange juice didn't help at all.

"How do you want to make the trade?" I asked.

"We take a drive to pick up the negatives and any other prints. When we have those, we let her go."

Rossi's voice was businesslike and his face impassive, but there was a glow in his eyes that made me think his brain was burning.

"I'll meet you here in an hour," I said, and started to slide out of the booth.

The goon unbuttoned his sports coat.

"When we go, we all go together," Rossi said.

The wood grain butt of the goon's .38 poked out of his jacket. The goon smiled. His teeth were yellow with egg yolk. I played clown.

"That's a great-looking gun."

With my left hand, I wiggled my fingers toward his pistol, while my right sought the crack between the cushions. Annoyed, the goon slapped my left hand away, and looked down to see my right, holding the automatic, pressed against his gut under the table.

"What the fuck?" he said.

Rossi couldn't see what was happening. The goon's hands came up, and Rossi said, "What the hell is going on?"

I subtracted the pistol from the goon's shoulder holster. Rossi pushed his chair back from the table. I swung the automatic around under the table and said, "Sit down or I'll blow your liver out your shoes."

Rossi sat. I waited for inspiration to tell me what to do next. The waitress dropped by the table and asked if we wanted anything else. Rossi and I were all smiles. The goon asked for more coffee, but Rossi cut him with a glance and the goon said to forget it. I asked for the check, and she left.

"We still have to make the trade," Rossi said. "So why don't you make the pickup and meet us back here."

"I'm not trading the pictures. I'm trading you," I said.

"That's ridiculous. You don't have me," Rossi argued.

I didn't say anything. Rossi flinched when I wedged the automatic against his ribs.

"No way you'd use that here," he insisted, but the confidence in his voice was waning.

I said, "I don't know what took you so long to get around to me, but now that you have, I'm living at ground zero. Think about it. I have nothing to lose. If I shoot you now, I get ten years on a second-degree charge. With a good lawyer, I might walk. If I let you live, you'll put a bullet through my skull. You're still alive because I'm going to trade you for the woman. If you don't want to cooperate, I'll kill you now and trade Carrot-top over there."

Rossi shifted his head between me and the goon. The goon wasn't offering any help. Rossi agreed. I asked him where Angel was being held.

"In Arcadia. We have a warehouse out there."

I explained how I wanted the trade set up, and I asked the goon if he understood. He did. I told the goon to take care of the check before placing the call to the warehouse, and I eased in behind Rossi. We walked out.

Rossi drove. Five miles east of Pasadena on 210, he turned to me and said, "When this trade is over, you're dead. I'm gonna do it myself, and I'm going to like doing it, one helluva lot."

"That's nice," I said.

"You want to hear how I'll do it?"

"Not particularly."

"I got a regular method with guys I don't like. I start with the kneecaps. When the legs are gone, the heart goes out of a man, because he knows that he can't get away. Then I do the elbows. Snap 'em back just like chicken wings. A guy with his knees and elbows busted, he just squirms on the ground, squealing. Then a shot in the gut. That's the funny part. Your hands want to cover up the hole, but because your elbows are broke, you can't, and it takes a long time to die with a gut wound. Funniest thing in the world."

I leveled the automatic and fired, putting a hole in the driver side door of my Mustang, an inch east of his belly. That is one of the great things about owning an old Ford. You can put a hole in it if you feel like it.

"Are you crazy?" Rossi screamed.

"Yes," I said.

He was quiet the rest of the way. We pulled off the freeway and headed east toward the San Gabriel Mountains. The land was flat and dry. The suburbs, less than two decades old, were already beginning to crumble and fade. Past the suburbs, a few isolated industrial buildings squatted in the desert. Rossi turned onto an empty side street. A faded sign read:

THE FUTURE SITE OF
VALHALLA INDUSTRIAL PARK
Opening June 1977 *** Reservations Accepted

At the end of the street, surrounded by weed-blown fields, three warehouses grouped together. The facades had been stripped of corporate markings. The eastern walls looked sand-blasted, with the aluminum siding showing through the dusty blue paint in irregular patches. Rossi parked in front of the warehouse farthest from the road. I took the keys from the ignition and directed Rossi at gunpoint to the trunk. The wind whipped at our clothes, and sand swept across the asphalt in fierce little swarms that stung my face. I opened the trunk and peeled the canvas case from the .410 shotgun. Rossi was not happy to see it.

"Oh, Christ, you're not going to need that," he said.

Half a dozen shotgun shells went into my left pocket with the goon's .38, and the 9mm automatic fit nicely into the right. With the shotgun at his back and the safety off, I marched Rossi up the short set of concrete steps to a solid steel door and told him to give a knock. He did and called his name. With my left hand on his belt, I pressed the barrel of the shotgun against Rossi's first vertebra, where the neck meets the skull. He stiffened. It gave me a small satisfaction. I was scared too.

When I gave him the instruction, he twisted the knob and pushed the door in. A foot inside the door, I pulled back on his belt and waited while the door swung shut. The warehouse

was dimly lit. I waited, sweating, until my eyes adjusted.
Tires were scattered around the warehouse, stacked six or
seven columns deep along the walls. Several of the columns
had been tipped over like tombstones in an old graveyard.
Aluminum beer cans, empty cartons, and wood crates littered the floor, showing up as small bright spots among the
blackness of the tires.

The center of the warehouse had been cleared. Two figures
stood at the far end. Angel was five feet forward of Dark
Coat. As on the night before, he had dressed for the terrain.
His sports coat was black. His slacks were black. His shirt
was black. In the dim light, and with the tires behind him,
he was no more than shadow. His right hand was extended
forward, as though in friendship. At the end of the hand was
a gun. The gun had a black barrel, and it was pointed at
Angel's back. He had given me no advantage. Rossi squirmed
against my grip on his belt.

"Come on. Let's get this over with," he said.

The hoarseness of his voice belied his brisk tone. I looked
left, where my back would be when we made the trade. A
small army could hide behind the cover presented by the
tires and stacked crates. I told Rossi to tell Dark Coat that
we were going to check out the back wall. His voice boomed
through the warehouse, ending with: "So for Chrissakes don't
do anything stupid."

Dark Coat didn't object. I wasn't concerned that he would
try something stupid. I wouldn't be fooled by something
stupid. It was the clever thing that could kill me.

I guided Rossi left, with my flank to Dark Coat, my back
to the ground I had covered, and Rossi leading the way into
the area I knew nothing about. Dark Coat shifted with us,
keeping Angel's body between him and my shotgun. I kicked
a column of tires and watched it collapse into the row. One

or two tires bounded free and rolled along the concrete until wobbling down. I steered Rossi forward and kicked over another stack. Nobody jumped out at me. Broken glass cracked under my shoes. The sound of it popped off the aluminum walls with a high-pitched whine. A forklift was parked along the far wall, a pallet still skewered on its twin prongs. It would have been excellent cover, but no one had used it.

Tightening my grip on Rossi, I marched him into the clearing and stopped twenty yards from Angel and Dark Coat. One overhead fluorescent still burned in the warehouse. It was located directly over my head. By no coincidence, the fluorescent over Dark Coat's head was shattered. Thin fragments of glass, remnants of the bulb, sparkled on the floor. He had given me no advantage. I signaled to Dark Coat and released Rossi.

A single tire marked the center of the clearing. It was to be the meeting point between Angel and Rossi. If there was going to be action, it would be after the midpoint, when Rossi stood a reasonable chance of ducking beneath a shotgun blast. Rossi began to walk. His legs were stiff as wood. I shifted my feet, keeping his body in a direct line with Dark Coat. The butt of the shotgun rested lightly beside my hip. I kept my eyes moving. I watched Dark Coat, and I watched the dark behind him.

Angel and Rossi met at the center tire. They both hesitated, acknowledged the other with a glance, and crossed the line. Angel moved with deliberate caution, aware of the gun at her back, but not going wooden with panic. Her pace was slow, and she rolled through each step, loose in the knees, coiled for sudden speed. Her eyes clicked across the warehouse like a metronome, covering my back. I looked away.

Dark Coat's left hand had moved. It was a small gesture,

easily unseen. Rossi moved a step faster. Angel's eyes stopped.
The whites showed, and the black dot in the center of her
eyes fixed at a point above me. Her mouth dropped open,
and her scream ripped through the warehouse as I whirled,
bringing the barrel of the shotgun up.

The catwalk overhead trembled, and the shape of a man
jutted out from behind a crate, his hand jumping with little
snaps of fire. I dove left and delivered both barrels sky-
ward. A sharp slap on my shoulder blade spun me face down
on the concrete. I rolled with the impact behind a column
of rubber. The figure on the catwalk spilled over the railing, and a row of tires collapsed like dominoes when his
body hit.

I snapped open the breech and dug out the spent shells.
I fumbled in my coat pocket for two fresh ones, but when I
tried to lift my left arm, the shoulder locked. There was no
pain and no feeling. I dropped the shells on the concrete
floor and reached them with my right hand. They slid easily
into the breech, and I clicked it shut. Rising to my knees, I
glanced right and saw Angel. She was crouched behind a
row of tires. Her face was tense but alert, and I knew she
was all right.

Shooting from the hip, I took out the remaining fluorescent
light overhead. Glass showered down in the darkness. The
odds had evened. I reloaded the shotgun and slid it across
to Angel. A handgun cracked three times from the other
side of the warehouse. The shooting was wild and hurried,
and on the third shot I saw the muzzle flash like a Polaroid
on Rossi's face. I cupped the last two shells in my hand,
rolling them to Angel, and brought the automatic into firing
position. When I saw the muzzle flash again, I squeezed off
a shot. Rossi cursed. I had come close enough to scare him.
I cursed because I missed.

The warehouse was airless and silent. A little light filtered in through a closed bay door across from Angel. The door was truck-sized, and motes of dust whirled in the cracks of light trickling in at its side. Angel backed away from her barricade and, using the columns of tires as cover, circled to my position. Her step was silent and quick, and she didn't draw a shot. Kneeling at my shoulder, she noticed the blood, and her mouth dropped open. I quickly set my gun barrel perpendicular to my lips. She understood.

Showing as little of my face as I could, I pushed my head out and glanced around the warehouse. Nothing moved, and no one shot at me. The bay door covered our right flank. Anyone passing the door would break the plane of light. Dark Coat was the professional. He would be the one to move, and he would come from the darkness and cover on the left. He would move quickly, silently, invisibly. Waiting for him would be as much fun as waiting for a firing squad. I handed Angel the automatic and told her to fire it in thirty seconds.

Palming the .38, I slipped back into the rows of tires along the wall, hoping that, when they heard the automatic, Dark Coat and Rossi would think that I had not moved. With each step, I kept silent count of the seconds, until I hit twenty-five. I waited. The crack of the automatic echoed against the aluminum walls. There was no return fire. Dark Coat and Rossi had gone silent. Crouching, I crept forward a few steps at a time, waiting and listening for a scuffle of shoe on glass, or the rustle of clothing brushing against itself. My back was wet and sticky. From the shoulder blade out, I couldn't feel much. The discipline was rapidly draining from my legs. My head, suddenly light, drifted away from my shoulders. I bit my cheek, hard, until I tasted blood. The pain was real. My brain sharpened. I took another few steps forward.

From behind a column of tires to the left, something moved so fleetingly that I doubted anything had moved at all. I tensed. Nothing. A shoe scraped close on my right and I jerked aside and saw Rossi moving out from behind a crate, hand thrust forward. I threw myself left as the shot burned rubber by my ear. Another shot echoed from the left, then the answering roar of Angel's shotgun. When I hit the floor, it felt as though my shoulder had been ripped out, and unconsciousness stretched like gauze over my eyes.

Six or seven shots made a dull planking sound overhead, like the sound I used to hear when I used tin cans as targets. When my eyes cleared, the forklift was in front of me. I didn't have much time. Rossi and Dark Coat had me flanked on both sides. I moved on impulse, reaching for the ignition. Angel's shotgun boomed. The ignition was a red push button mounted on a box next to the steering wheel. I pressed it, and with the first dry heaving of battery and motor, gunfire erupted on both sides, ripping into the seat. I buried my head on the floorboard and dug my thumb into the ignition. The motor turned with an electric whir. I let two wild shots fly over the hood to freeze Dark Coat for a few seconds, and looked for something heavy. A brick was wedged against one of the tires to keep the forklift from rolling. I wedged it between the floorboard and accelerator, twisted the wheel, and slapped the forklift into gear. It lurched left, drawing fire. I rolled behind a crate.

The forklift whirled drunkenly, hit a support beam, and bounced away, scattering tires and crates with its steel forks. Rossi was caught in its path, and when it hit his cover, he flushed like a quail. He moved low to the floor and at a dead run, but he was in the open and it was an easy shot. I gently squeezed the trigger, and he jerked back. He hung there, in mid-step, before Angel's shotgun splayed him sideways against a crate.

The forklift butted against the far wall, spun its wheels, and choked itself off. It was quiet again. I was tired. I wanted to close my eyes and dream of mountains and fresh air and wide open spaces where no one would shoot at me. A gust of wind rattled the aluminum bay doors. I stood and shook the lightness from my head. At the far end of the warehouse a dim green light was outlined against the dark. Exit. I wove silently through the scattered tires, suddenly thinking about deer and how I once learned to read tracks and watering holes well enough to be waiting for them when they broke out of the bush.

The exit sign was hung over a double set of doors. The doors were mounted four feet above the warehouse floor. A concrete ramp, flush with the wall, sloped up to the doors, then ended at a ninety-degree angle. With my back hugging the corner where that angle met the wall, and with the door overhead, I waited for Dark Coat. He moved so silently I almost didn't hear him. When he reached for the rail, a ring on his finger clinked softly on the metal. I whirled and aimed. His back was to me.

"Don't move," I said.

Dark Coat was a professional. He knew how to stay alive. He didn't move.

"I suppose you want me to drop the gun," he said.

It was the first time I had heard him speak. There was a measure of Texas in his slow and lazy voice. His gun clattered on the concrete. I called out an all-clear to Angel and circled the ramp. Dark Coat put his hands behind his head and waited patiently.

"You're a good shot," he said when I reached the bottom of the slope.

"You might be better. Not one in a hundred could have hit me on the move and at that distance."

His gaunt face grinned. "Didn't make it stick, though. You're still breathing."

Angel emerged from the shadows. I asked her to frisk him. She laid the shotgun against the railing. Dark Coat voluntarily spread-eagled the wall. He was clean.

"There's a phone in the office," Angel said. "I'm going to call an ambulance. You okay until then?"

I nodded. Angel picked up the shotgun and jogged back into the shadows.

"Mind if I talk?" Dark Coat asked.

His voice was calm and certain. I told him to go ahead.

"Rossi was the front man for American Sun, and I was the trigger. With Rossi gone, you've hit a dead end."

"Who was Rossi reporting to?"

"He never said. The orders probably came from the top, but you'll never prove that."

"You never heard another name?"

"Never."

"How about at Western Shores?"

"Dantly was the only name mentioned."

"Naturally. He was the hit."

"But I did hear enough to know that you've had your head up your ass from the start."

That didn't surprise me. I was familiar with the view.

"You were supposed to be the hit the other night on the pier. I was to do Dantly only if you didn't show. I like to hear a few things about the guy I'm supposed to hit, and Rossi described you as second-rate, a loudmouth who didn't know his ass from a hole in the ground. You also gotta figure that if you were on target, they'd have sent me around earlier, instead of those two jerks you busted heads with."

"It kept me awake at night, wondering why I was still alive. Why the free information?"

His eyes glittered deep in their sockets.

"Because I think I can make a deal with you. You don't have anything against me. I'm just the gun. Somebody has to pick me up and point me. We both know that guns don't kill people. People kill people."

He laughed at his joke. It was a dark and mellifluous sound, like molasses in the back of his throat.

"If you don't know any names, you can't make a deal," I said.

"Dantly gave me something before he died."

There was a twisted emphasis on the word "gave."

"I saw you going through his pockets on the pier. What did you find?"

"He said it was the key to the murder weapon."

"Do you have it on you?"

He laughed again. "Do we have a deal, or don't we?"

"Make a deal with the cops," I said.

"Can't do. If I make a deal with the cops, I sign my own contract. If I make a deal with you, I walk, and nobody knows."

I thought about it. Between the trigger and the finger that pulled it, I chose the finger. I told him it was a deal. Dark Coat carefully went to his inside coat pocket and from his wallet extracted a small brass key. He handed it to me.

"It's the key to Dantly's safe-deposit box at the Brentwood branch of the Bank of America. In the box is the Carlisle murder weapon."

I pocketed my gun.

"See you around," he said, and slipped out the door.

I found Rossi's body, twisted against the side of a crate. Nothing of interest was in his pockets. I walked back to the ramp and stretched out on the concrete. It was cool. I closed my eyes and thought about a lake I knew in Montana, where the Rockies jut into the sky at the far blue rim of the lake like the massive shoulders of God, and the scent of pine wafted through my mind, and the crisp mountain air was in my lungs, and I was there.

Chapter 26

I CAME OUT OF DARKNESS to more darkness. There was a line attached to my arm, and I traced it up to a bottle hanging on a stand overhead. I was lying on a narrow bed that was barred at the sides. A small yellow light at the end of a cord was hung over the guardrail near my right hand. I pressed it and waited. A door opened, and cold blue light streamed in. The soft squeaking of rubber-soled shoes approached the bed. My eyes tracked the sound. A figure in white leaned over me, her face in shadow. She held something small and round in her hand.

"How much is this going to cost me?" I asked.

"If you have to ask, you can't afford it," she said, and when I opened my mouth to reply, she slipped the pill down my throat and followed it with a drink of water. I slept.

When I woke again, it was painfully bright. My left shoulder felt like the forty-yard line after Super Bowl XX. My first visitor was a chubby doctor with a baby face and the bedside manner of Attila the Hun. He marched in with a small army of interns bringing up the rear. The interns formed a circling maneuver at the foot of the bed, while Attila rolled me over and attacked from the rear. Explaining the path of the bullet in great medical detail, he routed around my shoulder with professional glee and fielded questions from the interns, oblivious that his poking and prodding hurt like hell. When I complained, he remarked in a voice accustomed to ignoring other people's pain, "A little tender, are we? My advice to you is to duck next time somebody points a gun in your direction." The interns found this tremendously funny. I suggested that he missed his true calling in proctology, but I didn't get nearly as big a laugh. Attila tucked a notebook under his arm and, with his army behind him, said, "And now here are some folks I'm sure you're just dying to see."

The crowd that entered was no smaller than the crowd that had left. The first man through the door introduced himself as FBI. Everything about the man was crisp and sharp. His steps were measured and distinct, like a march, and he wore a dark blue suit that wasn't bought from the bargain rack. He hung his I.D. under my nose long enough for me to read his name—Curt Heidleman—then slipped it back into the inside breast pocket of his suit coat. His features were delicate, and the cold, clean look of him was focused in light blue eyes that reminded me of permafrost.

Heidleman's partner was two steps behind. He said his name was John Adams. He was a small, solid man with blank eyes and a thin moustache that made him look like a catfish.

Two city cops followed Adams. One was a thin black man going prematurely bald. His name was Ray Williams. I'd seen him before, but never met him. He was a homicide cop with the Santa Monica Police Department. The other cop was from Arcadia. He was a big guy with curly hair just short of regulation length. He stood off to the side of the FBI agents, smiling and nodding harmlessly when they glanced in his direction, which was seldom.

Bringing up the rear was Bernie Kohl, the Zen sheriff from Malibu. He acknowledged my wave, then stood alone in a corner, looking peaceful. The FBI agents ignored him. They ignored everyone except each other and, unfortunately, me. Adams was elected point man.

"We'd like you to answer a few questions, Mr. Marston."

"Are we all here yet?" I asked. "If we add a couple of hookers, we can have a convention."

Adams shoved his ugly face at me. "Listen up, smart ass. You're in deep shit. You can forget about your PI license. The only question is where we send you and for how long."

"That bad, huh?"

"That bad."

"Then take your FBI badge and use it as a suppository. Any talking I do will be through my lawyer."

Adams didn't appreciate the suggestion. He grabbed my shoulder and gave it a hard twist. I screamed louder than it hurt, which was pretty bad. Adams jumped back in surprise.

Heidleman's voice was cool but sharp. "Don't touch him, you idiot. We're in a hospital."

"I didn't hurt him that bad. He's just a wimp."

"I'd say he's pretty damn smart," Williams pointed out.

Attila the Doc hurried into the room, brushing the Arcadia cop aside.

"What the hell's going on here?" he bellowed.

"The guy over there tried to rip my shoulder apart."

"I never touched him." Adams sulked.

Attila cast a stern doctoral eye at so much law assembled in so little room, the medical school diploma on his office wall a crucifix against the heathen, even the FBI.

"Is that correct, gentlemen?"

"Yes," Heidleman said.

He didn't bother to clarify which statement he was referring to. Williams and Kohl stared at the floor, which was answer enough for Attila.

"This man is my patient. His shoulder is my work. You

are not to touch it or him. If pain is to be prescribed, I'll be the one to administer it. Is that clear, gentlemen?"

"The situation is in control, Doctor," Heidleman said.

"I don't give a damn whether or not it's in control. If the voices in here rise above the level of an old ladies' tea party, I'll throw you all out. Is that clear?"

"Yes. It's very clear, Doctor," Heidleman said, his mouth sculpting each word like ice.

With a terse nod Attila was gone. I felt more confident. If I screamed again, Attila would return with his scalpel and perform a mass appendectomy.

"We're going to throw the book at you for that stunt, smart ass," Adams said.

"John, I think you had better step back on this one."

"This guy's all mouth, Curt. He'll talk."

"He'll talk. But not to you," Williams said, with not much respect in his voice.

"Shut up, or we'll make you the errand boy," Adams answered.

"Take a walk, John."

"I don't have to take shit from a city cop."

"That's right. You don't," Heidleman said. "But you have to take it from me. Get moving."

Adams angrily shot his eyes around the room, no doubt wishing he was in the back room at headquarters, where a small thing like tortured screams wouldn't raise such a commotion. He moved, shouldering the Arcadia cop on his way out.

"You should send that guy back to Hoover's charm and beauty school for a refresher course," I said.

"He's a good agent," Heidleman replied.

"But a terrible human being."

Heidleman shrugged it off as unimportant. "We'd like you to explain a few things for us."

"My lawyer will make a full statement in the morning."

"Bringing in a lawyer would be unnecessary. We don't have plans to charge you with anything at this point."

"Did I hear wrong, or were you guys gloating over throwing the book at me a moment ago?"

"John was just talking tough."

"He was talking stupid," Williams said.

Heidleman glanced aside, annoyed.

"John was right. We should have made you errand boy. Why don't you go get us some coffee?"

"Get it yourself, you federal bunghole idiot," Williams said, and the Arcadia cop giggled, immediately regretting it.

Heidleman turned a look of such fury on the Arcadia cop that he shrank back, clutching his cap in his hand. Williams grinned. Santa Monica is full of contrary people. Williams was one of them.

I decided against the lawyer.

"I can't take any more of this intense grilling, guys. You've broken my spirit. I'll talk."

The bickering stopped. I told my story. I stuck to the facts and told the truth as often as possible. There were a few details that I left out, such as George Wentworth's attempt to drown me, and I did my best to protect Leslie Carlisle. Heidleman interrupted when I mentioned the taped conversation between Dantly and Johnson.

"Why the hell didn't you come forward with this tape earlier?"

"For a couple of reasons. No one was interested in what I had to say. While you were sitting on your can watching 'Dragnet' reruns, the NTSB and Bernie Kohl over there were working under the assumption that the Carlisle crash was accidental. I had to prove that a murder occurred before I could use the tape as evidence. Then all hell broke loose, and I was too busy trying to prevent Rossi from killing me to pay much attention to the finer points of the law."

"If you had bothered to tell somebody about this, maybe Dantly would still be alive."

"Rossi might still be alive as well, and you know how much I grieve his passing."

"The point is, you screwed up."

"Dantly screwed up. I just failed to save him."

"Tell us about the Dantly hit," Williams said.

I let the photographs talk for me. My clothes were bundled in a plastic bag behind the nightstand. In the coat pocket were the photographs of Dantly's murder. The cops passed them around silently. When they got to the Arcadia cop, he whistled.

"You got actual pictures of this guy getting snuffed? That's some detective work."

Heidleman didn't agree. "Standard snoop stuff. All private dicks carry a camera, hoping to catch a little graft here and there."

Williams pulled out a cigarette and lit it. "Mind if I smoke?"

"If you want to die, it's your business."

"Funny guy," he said, and exhaled a ribbon of bluish smoke. "We found one of the men in these photographs beneath the pier. Shot through the head with a .38. Your work?"

I didn't see any reason for needless complication.

"Doesn't sound like me. I always use poison arrows."

"I'll wait for a serious answer."

"This is the first I've heard of it. We took off after Dantly was dumped over the edge."

Williams stared at me for several seconds. I tried to look innocent.

"We'll see what the girl says," he said.

"You can probably reach her through my office."

"Her most recent address is the Arcadia Police Station."

"On what charge?"

The Arcadia cop cleared his throat and spoke too loudly. "We have her in protective custody. She was found at the scene of a double homicide, carrying a shotgun."

"Unless you have a special set of laws in Arcadia, that's not a crime."

"No, but killing someone is," Heidleman said.

"She was kidnapped, and I gave her the shotgun to defend herself. You'd rather I gave her a slingshot?"

"She was due to be released this morning," Heidleman said.

"So I'll talk to her at your office," Williams said. "If she corroborates, fine. Maybe the guy was bumped off by his partner. It doesn't make much sense, but as long as you stay cooperative, that's the way I'll write it up. I don't give much of a damn about who killed him, but if you start screwin' us around, I'll give a damn real quick."

"Cooperative, hell," Heidleman said. "He's already destroyed what chance there was to close this."

"How so?" Williams challenged.

"Dantly is dead. You can't get a confession from a dead man. He was the mastermind. Working with the mob, he arranged the Carlisle crash, then had those two guys up north murdered to cover his tracks. When Sherlock Holmes here stumbled a little too close to the truth, the mob got nervous and hit Dantly. Then the idiot guns down Sam Rossi, the only mobster we know for a fact was involved."

"There's still Henry Howard," I suggested.

"Don't tell me how to run an investigation," Heidleman snapped. "There is no evidence that he was involved in this, and if he is, he's not the type of man to confess if we ask him nice. Dantly was the key man, and he's not talking."

The party was over. Heidleman suggested that I make good use of my sudden surfeit of spare time to think up a new line of work should my PI license be revoked, which he was heartily going to recommend. Bernie Kohl turned to follow him out, but I caught his eye and he stayed behind.

"It looks like you got involved in this despite your good intentions," I said.

With a philosophical shrug he said, "In our contract with life, there are many provisions which we might not like but must adhere to."

"I'll remember that the next time the toilet backs up."

"That and to call a good plumber."

I reached over to the nightstand with my good arm and pulled the wallet from my pants' pocket.

"I'm curious how you got to be sheriff. You seem to be an odd choice for the job."

"It's easy to be a sheriff. All you need is to be a big enough fool to be elected."

"You don't seem the type to arrest anyone. Your style would be to deliver a few words of wisdom, a proverb or two, and then let them go."

I pulled a brass key out of my wallet.

"Malibu isn't Dodge City. I've found the peaceful approach works best. If I wanted to, I could arrest half the town on narcotics charges, but that would accomplish nothing. I live and let live, and Malibu remains a quiet, peaceful town."

"And you stay sheriff for another election."

"One of the benefits of the peaceful approach," he said.

I handed him the key.

"What's this?"

"The key to Ted Dantly's safe-deposit box at the Bank of America, Brentwood branch. Rossi gave it to me before he died."

Kohl turned the key over in his palm, then pocketed it. "What will I find in the box?"

"The Carlisle murder weapon, or so Dantly was reported to say before he died."

"Am I to infer that you believe what I find in the box will implicate Henry Howard?"

"You are."

"There were men in this room more capable than I of investigating this. Why did you chose me?"

"A very simple reason. You're the first cop I've met today who hasn't threatened to throw me in jail."

Kohl smiled beatifically. "I told you the peaceful approach works best."

Chapter 27

ANGEL DROPPED BY in the afternoon with an armful of red roses. When she bent over to kiss me full on the lips, smelling of some delightfully wicked perfume, the swelling in my loins reminded me that I hadn't died and gone to heaven.

"Hiya, jailbird," I said, and kissed her again.

With the IV line threatening to strangle us if passion prevailed over logistics, I reluctantly let her go.

"I've never been in jail before," Angel said.

She flipped open the water pitcher lid and tossed the roses in one by one, like darts.

"How was it?"

"It wasn't so bad. They asked me a lot of stupid questions, then stuck me in a cell with a bunch of hookers."

She looked back over her shoulder.

"You remember I was wearing my jogging suit."

I nodded.

"When I walked into the cell, one of the girls looked at me, put her hands on her hips, and said, 'Now there's an angle I never thought of. Do you get much action with that outfit, honey?' "

She laughed—a full and healthy sound.

"An honest mistake," I said. "What did you tell her?"

"I told her nothing. I punched her lights out."

She laughed again and, with one last attempt at an esthetic arrangement, gave up on the flowers. "Staying all night in a cell with so much used sex got kinda depressing. We got along fine. But it's not something I want to do again tomorrow. The first thing I did was to run home and wash the jail off me."

"I always thought that the best part about going to jail was getting out."

"Then a couple of FBI guys came to talk to me. To tell you the truth, I preferred the company of the hookers."

"Were the FBI guys rough?"

"A piece of cake. I played dumb, and they fell for it."

Angel pulled up a chair, turned it around, and draped her arms over the back.

"Don't get carried away with yourself. They listen to professional liars every day. The moment you think you have them fooled, they nail you."

"I know," she droned. "I'm overconfident. I've always been overconfident. It's the way I am."

"Overconfidence can get you killed."

"So can jaywalking, but that doesn't mean I'm going to stop."

"I was just thinking," I said, but she cut me off before I could tell her what.

"You think about everything. You should exercise your brain less and your brawn more."

"There's only one type of physical exercise I truly enjoy."

"What's that?"

"Come a little closer, and you'll find out."

She stepped up to the bed. Within a couple of minutes, we had worked up a good sweat, but when I was ready to start burning some serious calories, she slipped out of my arms.

"Hospital beds aren't my style," she said over her shoulder as she left the room. "If you want more exercise, you'll have to get it alone."

She laughed—too smugly I thought—and was gone.

I stared at the walls, growing despondent as her perfumed air dissipated in a waft of sickness and disinfectant.

"So," I said to the empty room, "it looks like it's just me and Mary Fivefingers for the next couple of days."

"Most of us get over our John Wayne complex in high school," Ian Waddington said with a critical eye on my sling. "The next time, I'd advise you to wait for the cavalry before you go in six guns a-blazing."

In lieu of flowers, and not being the sentimental type, Ian plopped a copy of *The Wall Street Journal* at the foot of the hospital bed. When he spoke, his harsh New England voice sounded like a machine gun at close quarters.

I offered him a chair.

"Who has time to sit?" he said. "I gave up lunch to come and visit you."

"And me not even a client. I'm honored."

"Don't be. Beneath this mercenary exterior beats a heart of pure avarice."

Ian spread open the *Journal* to page 3 and pointed to a one-column article. It reported that Henry Howard had stepped down from the presidency of Western Shores. Leslie Carlisle had been unanimously appointed by the board of directors as his replacement.

"I advised a bullish stand on the stock yesterday when I heard the news," Ian said, and, in a high state of pecuniary excitement, his voice went into double time. "The major brokerage houses were bailing out, selling the stock like wallpaper. Leslie Carlisle has no experience running a major corporation, and the investors were very nervous—very, very nervous—about the future prospects. Wall Street was giving her a vote of no-confidence."

"But with your generous soul, you wanted to give her a chance."

Ian's laughter rattled around the room.

"Hell, no. I was betting that the lower stock price would attract take-over interest. And it did. This morning Richard Preston sold the block of shares he'd been collecting."

"Don't tell me. To Leslie Carlisle."

Ian's face slackened with shock. "What made you say her?"

"I'd been expecting her to try to take the company private."

"It's an interesting guess, but wrong."

"Who then?" I asked.

"American Sun Corporation."

The mob was beating its tommy guns into stock-option deals. It almost sounded legitimate.

"I thought American Sun was the white knight."

"It's possible they still are. Or maybe they have a dragon under their armor."

"Do you think they'll try for a take-over?"

"It's a good fit for them. Most of their assets are in soft industries, such as gambling, resort properties and real estate. With Western Shores, they'd be able to diversify into manufacturing and take advantage of the tax benefits among other things."

"But can they do it?"

"They own over eight percent of Western Shores stock. If they want to try a take-over, they're in an excellent position to make the move. A hostile take-over would generate publicity, which they don't need, given their background. It would be better if they had a friend on the Western Shores board of directors."

"A friend, or someone who was bought off or black-mailed."

"A friend is someone you can count on to do your bidding. It doesn't matter how the friend was acquired. Do you know someone who could answer to that description at Western Shores?"

It was a question I couldn't answer from a hospital bed. For two weeks I had been investigating Henry Howard's organization and thinking about the man and his motives. It was time to meet him.

Chapter 28

"THIS TYPE OF WOUND ALWAYS REQUIRES five days of hospitalization!" Attila the Doc shouted when presented with my release papers. "If you could count any better than you can duck you'd understand that you've only been here for three days."

"I'm a precocious healer," I said.

"You're healed when I say so. Get back to bed."

I had struggled into a fresh change of clothing brought from my apartment by Angel, who stood waiting by the door. Attila glowered at her. She slunk out of the room. He turned his eye on me. I handed him a pen.

"You can sign it 'against doctor's orders' if you like," I said.

"Damn right I can," he said, and signed with an angry flourish.

I thanked him. Attila shoved the pen into my hand, ink side down, and said as he whirled out of the room, "Don't come running to me for sympathy when you fall over and die on the sidewalk."

Angel drove me to a small gun-and-ammo store in a section of town that made Beirut look like Disneyland. The storefront was built like a bunker. There were no windows and only one door. The door was solid steel and locked. I rang the bell. The proprietor's eye appeared at the grate and passed judgment: Yay or Nay. Angel and I were Yays. We waited for thirty seconds while bolts were thrown and chains unlatched. The door swung open and we stepped inside. The proprietor shut the door behind us and repeated the elaborate process of locking up. I counted fifteen locks, chains, and deadbolts. Next to the door a sign read: "In Case of Fire Prepare to Roast."

What remained of the proprietor's left leg was attached to a prosthesis that caused him to stoop awkwardly to reach the locks near the floor. His name was Harry Maxwell, and he had dealt in guns since before I'd learned to breathe. He hobbled behind the glass display case and watched carefully as Angel and I strolled through the shop. He was a cautious man. A black patch swung low over his left eye. When he propped his hands on the display case, the right one looked like a bird claw due to the absence of the ring and forefingers. His shape was small and round, like his bald head, and he had a gap-toothed smile. He looked me up and down with his right eye, and said, "You was in here just a short while back, wasn't you?"

I nodded. He tapped his forehead above the black patch with his remaining forefinger.

"You bought a Smith and Wesson blue chrome .38 with a walnut handle, if I recall."

"You recall correctly."

Harry beamed. "I never forget a gun or a face. You looking to add to your collection?"

"I'd like another Smith and Wesson .38, and a Dan Wesson .44 Magnum."

He nodded as though those were the two best guns you could buy, and propped his samples on the display case.

"Did the last one do all right by you?"

"Did until I lost it."

Harry frowned. "You should be more careful. I'm a walking example of what can happen when a gun gets in the wrong hands."

"I don't think it can do much damage where I lost it," I answered, and told him the guns on the case would do.

"You want a holster for either of those?"

"Just the .44."

He showed me a few samples. While I looked them over, Harry began to gab.

"Lost my two fingers to a .44. Some fellow had come in and pulled it on me. Shoulda seen it, but didn't. Damn thing was big as a house. I was holdin' my hands up, with my fingers spread wide, when the damn fool lost his head and started shooting. The bullet passed right between the two of them, but it was so damn big it took 'em both off at the roots. Lucky I didn't lose my damn hand."

"Now my leg, I lost that to a shotgun, twelve gauge. Got into a tussle with a young feller who come in to rob me, and he blowed the damn thing off. Lucky I didn't lose my nuts too, if you'll pardon my French, ma'am."

On my previous visit, Harry had told the same stories, but capped it off with a ribald telling of how he lost his eye.

"Tell her how you lost your eye, Harry," I suggested.

Harry's bald head colored like a rose. "I couldn't tell that tale to no woman. Too embarrassin'."

I chose a holster, and Angel helped me strap it on. Even with my arm in a sling, it made a sizable bulge under my coat. The .38 was neatly concealed in the sling, resting butt side out next to my arm. Angel and Harry took turns looking at the sling, and both agreed the .38 was invisible. I paid Harry cash and, waiting for his machinations with the door, left.

In the car Angel asked, "So what happened to his eye?"

Angel drove. I settled back and told what I could remember of Harry's story.

"As Harry tells it, he was a libertine in his younger days, drinking and gambling and whoring and being a general nuisance to society. On this particular day Harry and a buddy went to a whorehouse outside of Reno, where they'd stopped for a few days of gambling. It had been a while since Harry had had any, and to study up he had bought what he said was one of those fancy French novels. He read a story about a guy who drove all the girls wild by sucking on their toes, and though he couldn't quite understand it, figured it had to be true. He and his buddy had a few drinks and chose their girls, and this being a small whorehouse and the clientele not that particular, the four of them retired with their drinks to the same room. The first thing Harry wants to do with his whore is to show her what an experienced man he is, so after they get stark naked, he bends over and starts sucking on her toes. His buddy thought that was the funniest thing he'd ever seen—Harry licking this woman's feet and the woman bending over to see what the hell he was doing—and on the spur of the moment, the buddy goosed her with an ice cube from his drink. The woman let out a hoot, then a yell and a kick, and the last thing Harry could remember was a giant toenail coming for him like the horn of a bull."

Angel listened in silence.

"You're lying," she accused.

"I'm not lying, but Harry probably is."

It was dark when Angel turned up Loma Vista and followed it north through Beverly Hills to Trousdale Estates. She turned left on Evelyn Place, and I pointed out Henry Howard's estate as we passed it. The estate was fronted by a block wall, gated at the driveway. Angel turned around in the cul-de-sac at the end of Evelyn, backtracked, and dropped me off at the corner. I walked past the gate to the far end of a block wall partially obscured by a row of Eucalyptus trees. The wall was seven feet measuring from the ground, but smooth at the top. It was too tall to jump over, and pulling myself up it with one hand was a struggle. I almost regretted not having had Angel stay to give me a leg up. I made it on the second try and dropped easily over the other side. For the first minute I crouched motionless, listening for dogs and searching the darkness for beam detectors, infrared cameras, and other perimeter intrusion detection devices. Even in the estates of the rich, most security is focused on the home and not on the grounds. When I was satisfied that Henry Howard was no exception, I skirted the edge of the wall, and took cover behind a Eucalyptus tree.

Across the grounds rose a stark white Georgian-style mansion, with dark green trim, classical Greek colonnades, and front steps of red brick. Flanked by yellow and red roses, the drive hugged the north end of the estate, curving at the front of the house around an alabaster fountain inlaid with gold tile. Parked at the near end of the fountain was a black-and-white sheriff's patrol car, with "Malibu" lettered on the side. I crept along the edge of the trees until I had a view of the front and southern exposures of the mansion. I lay flat on my stomach behind the base of the tree and tried to feel comfortable. At a few minutes past eight, the front door swung open, and Bernie Kohl stepped out into the porch light. He said something to a man in black-and-white livery standing in the doorway, tugged on his cap, and walked to his car. When he had pulled around the drive, a small electric motor hummed, and the rolling of metal wheels sounded across the lawn. The gate creaked open and, when the patrol car had driven past, rolled shut again.

I watched and waited, noting the pattern of house lights flicking on and off over the space of two hours. At ten o'clock sharp the light in a small room at the rear southern corner of the house clicked on. It was the room that I had been waiting for, with low sash-type windows out of the reach of the house perimeter lights, and partially obscured by bushes. I waited ten minutes for whoever was in the room to settle down, then silently slid across the lawn. With the bushes as a shield, I raised my head to the side of the window and, at an oblique angle, looked inside.

The room was a study. The walls were lined with books. In the corner, beneath a Tiffany lamp, stood a tufted leather easy chair and a bronze ashtray stand. A large oak desk dominated the center of the room. The head of a roaring lion had been carved into each of the front corners of the desk, and the legs were shaped into giant paws.

Behind the desk sat what on first impression seemed a young man. His shoulders were massive and square, like a young man's, and his head towered over them stiff and sure, as though it too had been carved from oak. But the hair was shock-white. It was Henry Howard. I recognized him from the company's annual report. On the inside cover page there was a picture of him sitting on the corner of a desk, half turned toward the camera, and smiling down like a benign patriarch. Even when caught in the pose of a smile, he conveyed strength and determination. The face had aged, but not softened. He had the wrinkles, loosening skin, and white hair of an old man, but the eyes, blue and cold as sapphire, set in the snowy white of his eyebrows, were young and hungry. There was an ambition in his eyes that defied youth

At eleven o'clock Henry Howard rose from his desk and left the room. Two minutes later a servant entered and dimmed the lights. I waited for ten minutes, beginning to shiver in the chill air, before crossing the lawn and slipping back over the wall.

Chapter
29

AFTER AN EVENING WITH ANGEL, scaling my hormone count back from toxic levels, I phoned Bernie Kohl's office and made an appointment for that afternoon. We met at a delicatessen on the corner of Fourth and Wilshire in Santa Monica. I arrived first and secured a corner booth.

"The fabric of my life was soft and smooth before I met you," Bernie sighed when he sat across the table.

His Zen calm was rapidly metamorphosing into Jewish despair.

"I haven't been yelled at so loudly and frequently since my poor mother passed away, bless her cantankerous soul. If you wish to make a gift of evidence to me in the future, mail it fourth class care of general delivery, and if there's a God in heaven, he'll see that it's lost."

"That's not the proper attitude, Bernie. You can really make a name for yourself in law enforcement with this case."

He looked at me like I was crazy.

"I work in Malibu. I like peace and quiet. If I wanted to risk life and limb, I'd be a stuntman and not a cop. They get paid better."

I let him grouse over his menu for a minute, then asked, "What was in Dantly's safe-deposit box?"

"Do you know who I talked to yesterday?" Bernie shot back.

I did, but said I didn't.

"Henry Howard. He just about chewed my head off and lit the stump for a cigar. Threatened to call his mayor, his chief of police, whom he claims is practically his best friend, and both U.S. senators, to whose campaigns he contributes heavily."

"What you found in the box must have implicated him," I hinted.

"I needed a court order just to get near Dantly's box, but they wouldn't let me see it alone. Too simple. Everybody had to be in on it—a representative of the court, a bank officer, Dantly's executor and lawyer, a forensics guy from downtown. The vault was more crowded than the men's room at a beer garden."

"You at least got it open, then."

"And this morning this Curt Heidleman guy is all over my hindquarters because you gave the key evidence to me and not to him, and accuses us of being in some kind of Marxist conspiracy to freeze him out."

"So what was in the box?"

"And his partner is threatening to throw you in jail again, this time on a withholding-evidence charge."

"Bernie, what was in the box?"

"I doubt if he can make it stick, but if I were you I'd hire a good accountant, because I can guarantee your tax returns are going to be audited every year for the rest of your life."

I slammed my fist on the table. The silverware bounced high and came clattering down. All conversation in the restaurant ceased. The waitress, bustling by with a loaded tray, gave me the evil eye.

"What was in Dantly's safe-deposit box?" I whispered.

Bernie Kohl smiled beatifically.

"Why do I have the feeling you've asked that question before?"

"Okay. I admit it. You were a happy man before you met me. I've screwed up your life. I apologize."

Satisfaction shone on Kohl's tanned face.

"Apology accepted. We found a prescription bottle of digitalis capsules. The name on the label is Henry Howard's. Out of a prescription for one hundred capsules, fifty were left."

"Enough to do the job."

"So the coroner says. The prescription was filled the third of February, this year."

I counted back in my head.

"Ten days before the Carlisle crash. What did Henry Howard say about it?"

Bernie Kohl slipped a small black book out of his pocket and read his notes.

" 'This is slander, you son of a bitch. I'll have your badge for this.' "

He looked up, remembering.

"Wait a minute. That was later. He said that his prescriptions are delivered to his house every month by the pharmacy. Apparently, he takes a number of medications in addition to digitalis. He's too busy to be bothered with it, and has his maid sign for it."

"And when his old supply is exhausted, he reaches for the new, and, surprise, it isn't there."

"That's the way he told it," Kohl said. "He thought it was an oversight and ordered a new prescription after raising hell with his maid and the pharmacy, or so he says."

Kohl took a last look at his notes and signaled the waitress. A man in uniform inspires awe and respect. She hopped over and, carefully ignoring me, whom she likely thought to be an informant or a prisoner or some other lowlife, took his order.

"Assuming that Howard is lying," Kohl said when she had scurried away, "he would have received the new prescription, given it to Dantly, and claimed that it was never delivered."

"Let's assume Howard isn't lying."

"I'd rather think that he was lying," Kohl admitted. "If he's going to give me so much trouble, I'd just as soon he be guilty. Otherwise I'd have to arrest someone else whom I didn't dislike as much."

"Then think of it as just pretend."

"Okay." Kohl shrugged.

"There are at least three other ways that the prescription could have gotten to Dantly," I said. "The delivery man from the pharmacy could have removed the digitalis from the order, and the maid might not have noticed it was missing."

"The delivery man having been bought off by Dantly."

"Correct."

"Too complicated. Dantly couldn't trust him to keep his mouth shut, and at last count the delivery man was still alive."

"Or the maid may have passed it along to Dantly."

"Same criticism."

"But still it's a possibility. The house must have half a dozen servants, all of whom have access to the medicine cabinet."

"Five servants, not including the gardener," Kohl added. "During the period between the third and thirteenth of February, Howard received several guests, including eight at one sitting for a dinner party. Dantly was one of the guests at that party."

"Who were the other guests?"

"Howard refused to say. He didn't want his friends to be subjected to police intimidation."

"The household staff should be able to fill out the guest list," I suggested.

"So what?" He shrugged. "All we can really prove is that more than a dozen people had access to the prescription in addition to Henry Howard."

"But who among them would know that Henry Howard was on heart medication, and knew where to look for it?"

Kohl fingered his soup spoon, then polished it with his napkin and set it back on the table.

"No good," he pronounced. "Even if we can prove how it fell into Dantly's hands, we can't categorically prove it was the murder weapon. It's not as though we could do a ballistics test. Digitalis doesn't vary significantly from one lot to another."

"Dantly considered it evidence enough to be his life insurance policy," I said.

The waitress brought Kohl's order: lox, cream cheese, a bagel, and a bowl of matzo ball soup.

"Every now and then it's good to remember your roots," he said with a happy smile, and cradled the soup, musing for a moment, until the steam rising from the broth misted his glasses.

"You dusted the bottle for prints?"

"Of course. We lifted a clear set that matched the pharmacist, and some partials of another set. Small fingers. Probably the maid's."

"Maybe we'll get lucky, and someone will confess," I said.

Bernie gave me his most beatific smile. "Shallow men believe in luck. The wise man makes his own."

Chapter
30

IN THE AFTERNOON ANGEL AND I rented a car guaranteed to raise little attention in Beverly Hills—an emerald-green Mercedes 280 SL. I told Angel to drive by the corner of Evelyn and Loma Vista every fifteen minutes until midnight while I paid a visit to Henry Howard. I gave her my lawyer's card in the event that I didn't show up, or if she noticed me lounging in the back of a police cruiser.

At a quarter past nine o'clock I scaled the wall in the shadow of the Eucalyptus trees and dropped to the other side. I carried a small satchel, which contained a towel, a rubber-coated ball peen hammer, and a glass-cutting instrument I had developed a year ago with the help of a machine shop. I walked along the southern wall behind the cover of Eucalyptus trees and, at the point of shortest distance, crossed to the house. The study was dark. I positioned myself below the window and zipped open the satchel. The glass-cutter was built from telescoping steel frames. I attached it to the windowpane directly outside the sash-type lock and adjusted the amount of suction on the outer frame. I covered the outer frame with the towel to absorb sound and slowly marked the glass along the inner frame with the diamond-tipped cutter. When the etching was complete, I set the vacuum on the central suction cup and tapped the corners of the cut with the rubber hammer. I tightened the vacuum on the central cup, and the small rectangle of glass popped out with a crack no louder than the snap of a twig. I released the suction cups and set the glass cutter back in the satchel, with the towel and hammer.

I was gambling that the alarm system would not be activated until the house was closed for the evening. I opened the window, crawled over the sill, and shut the window behind me. I left a short note of introduction, neatly folded, on the corner of the desk, and took cover behind the bookcase at the far end of the room, nearest the window. I listened. If the system was activated, the phone would ring within two or three minutes, with the private security cops on the other end. The house was quiet. I began to relax.

At a few minutes before ten I heard the study door open, and a swath of light cut diagonally across the desk. I pinned myself against the side of the bookcase. Footsteps padded on the carpet, and the desk lamp clicked on. The footsteps retreated. The study door eased shut, and a different set of footsteps, slower and heavier, sounded on the rug. The desk chair groaned with the weight of bulk settling in. A drawer scraped open and shut. Then there were several seconds of a silence more noticeable than sound. The chair creaked again, as though tilted forward, and I heard the soft rustle of paper unfolding. Henry Howard had found my note.

Before he could stand and raise an alarm, I stepped out from behind the bookcase with my hands facing palms out, but not far from my .44, should it be required. The note had prepared him for the shock of seeing me. He turned sharply but didn't cry out or fall dead from a heart attack.

"I hope you haven't come to rob me, because I haven't a dime," he said, as though he expected me to believe it.

"If I wanted to rob you, I wouldn't bother introducing myself. I'm Paul Marston. I'm investigating the death of Jack Carlisle for your granddaughter."

"I know who you are," he growled. "How the hell did you get in here?"

"Through the window."

"There are better ways of meeting a man than breaking into his home."

"I thought I'd save time. You have the annoying habit of not returning my calls."

"You're not a man I want to talk to. Get out before I have you arrested."

He rolled back from his desk and gripped the arms of the chair with huge, clawlike hands. I crossed the room and pulled up a chair in front of his desk.

"No one knows I'm here. I have a gun, and if I have to leave in a hurry, I won't leave anything that can be traced back to me."

His grip eased. Cunning agitated his eyes. "Am I to understand that you have me under duress?"

I nodded.

"You'll have to speak up, son. Microphones can't see."

"Who said anything about microphones?"

"Anything that I say to you will be under the threat of gunpoint, and cannot be held against me in a court of law. Am I to understand that you have me under duress?"

"Yes," I said.

Henry Howard pulled a cigar out of a case on the desk, clipped the end, and settled back in his chair.

"Then you can ask your questions."

Howard struck a long wooden match and smiled privately behind the flame. Despite my gun and the threat to use it,

I knew that he was not intimidated, but chose to talk for his own reasons. Clever reasons, by the look on his face. There was no use in being timid.

"Why and how did you have Jack Carlisle killed?"

Henry Howard paused in the lighting of his cigar. His eyes glared out from his worn features like stones inlaid in old wood.

"Do you wonder why I didn't want to talk to you? Your question presupposes an answer I'm not inclined to give. I did not have Jack Carlisle killed."

"The evidence suggests you did. You had access to American Sun to hire Jim Johnson, who poisoned Carlisle with digitalis. The digitalis was transferred to Johnson through Dantly. Among Dantly's personal effects was found a half-empty prescription bottle of digitalis, filled out to you. You had the motive in wanting to regain control of your company, access to the murder weapon, and with Dantly and Johnson working as your agents, the opportunity."

Howard's face was obscured in a billowing of cigar smoke. He shook out the match and tossed it into a brass ashtray on the desk. When the smoke cleared, he said, "It all makes sense when you put it that way, but it doesn't make it any more true. It can't be proved that Carlisle was killed with the same capsules as were in my prescription, and even if you could prove it, it wouldn't establish that I gave the digitalis to Dantly. It makes just as much sense to work from the premise that he stole it."

"Dantly wouldn't kill Carlisle unless he was certain of being hired as his successor."

"Which I would never have done. Dantly was a good V.P. Finance, but I never would have let him run my company."

Howard worried the end of the cigar around the corner of his mouth, musing.

"You've heard, I suppose, that I'm out of the company. My own damn company, started from scratch forty years ago. If I had planned all this, as you suggest, I didn't do a very good job of it."

He leaned forward, pointing the tip of his cigar at my chest.

"I'm going to level with you. I don't have much else to lose, so why the hell not. It occurs to me that you could be useful. I'd like to see justice done about Jack Carlisle's death, just as long as it isn't done on me. Do it on the other bastards, like they did it on Ted Dantly."

"I'll do what I can."

"Against these sons of bitches, you can't do a damn thing, but I'll tell you anyway. Six years ago, on my seventieth birthday, I resigned the presidency of my company, which was the first major mistake I've made in forty years of business. My second was to hire Jack Carlisle as my replacement."

"The stockholders loved him," I said in his defense.

"He made money." Howard shrugged in a puff of smoke. "I'm not saying he wasn't a damn good businessman. He was. But he was reaping his profits by cannibalizing the hard industries I'd worked forty years developing, and reinvesting in cash-rich businesses. He was managing for the bottom line and losing sight of what made the company what it was in the first place. Jack wasn't that interested in my company. He wanted to make a reputation and move on to bigger things."

"You resented it."

"Damn right. I reasoned with him, but he didn't want to consider my opinions. He was going to take the company where he wanted to, and if I was in the way, he was willing to go over me. When I tried to stop him, I found that I didn't have enough leverage. The board listened to me, but Jack was a rising star, and I was a semiretired old man. So I did something about it."

"You hired Jim Johnson."

Howard reached under the left corner of his desk and pressed something. I backed my chair away. Howard pawed at the air with his hand, and told me to sit.

"You may have me at gunpoint, but damned if I'll let you keep me from my evening cognac."

I sat, but didn't quite relax.

"I knew a man in Las Vegas, Bob Gnocci, who was sympathetic to my problem. He runs a company, American Sun, which I'm sure you know about. Gnocci recommended one of his hotel management people, who turned out to be Jim Johnson. Gnocci had trained him personally, and certified that he was one hundred percent reliable."

"Then you had Ted Dantly hire him. Why did you chose Dantly?"

"He was ambitious and wouldn't ask questions."

The door to the study opened, and a gaunt figure, carrying a snifter of cognac on a silver platter, strode stiffly into the room. If he reacted to my presence, I missed it. He set the cognac down on the desk and stood crisply at attention, awaiting instructions.

"That will be all," Howard said.

"Very good, sir," the figure replied, and, walking like a man without knee joints, shut the study door behind him.

It was as though they had silently agreed that I didn't exist.

"In my years in business, when the hard decision had to be made, I made it, and let the chips fall where they may. But until this Johnson thing came along, I may have played hard, but I played honest."

Howard swirled the cognac around the rim of the glass and sipped at it.

"Who did you originally hire Johnson to blackmail?" I said.

Howard frowned and concentrated on his cognac before answering.

"Key members of the board. Those who were principal stockholders. The idea was to gain leverage against Carlisle on votes that influenced the direction of the company."

"George Wentworth was one. Who were the others?"

"They shall remain nameless. I didn't need many. The board wasn't dead set against me. Just one or two members."

"Did you try to blackmail Jack Carlisle?"

Howard laughed. It was short and brusque.

"I'm not that big a fool. He was married to my granddaughter, after all, and his philandering was both well chosen and well known."

"But he could feel the pressure coming from your direction," I said.

"He noticed that my voice carried a bit more weight in board meetings. I was able to swing a few votes my way."

"Carlisle was unhappy with the interference and went shopping for a buyer for Western Shores. You were afraid of losing control of the company and found a more permanent solution to your problem than blackmail," I suggested.

"If you're suggesting that I then arranged Carlisle's murder, no, I did not. My involvement stopped at blackmail."

"Why should it stop there? You had the setup for it and were already compromised with Las Vegas mobsters. Maybe they gave you a little push, but you gave the order."

Howard took a small pair of silver scissors from the desk drawer and reclipped the end of his cigar. As he clipped, his chin sank down on his chest and his eyelids lowered slowly, until I thought that he might be falling asleep. Then he chuckled.

"I always like to take the measure of a man I'm doing business with," he said, and relit his cigar. "You, for example, don't strike me as being corporate material. Too much of a lone wolf. One thing I've noticed about loners is that they get obsessive about things, because no one is around to check their thinking. They get so wrapped up in going after something that they don't realize they've been going after the wrong thing until after they've caught it. Right now you're on to me like a hound, and by God you're going to catch me. When you do, you'll find out I'm not the fox you thought I was."

With a grunt he leaned over and shoved a cigar box across the desk.

"Have a cigar. Might help you clear the cobwebs from your thinking. Nothing like a good cigar to help you ponder the mysteries of the business world. I suggest you put a bit of thought into Bob Gnocci's involvement in this."

I declined the cigar. "Bob Gnocci is your good friend. You tell me."

"That son of a bitch won't even return my phone calls," he said, grimacing. "Don't you think it's a bit coincidental that American Sun buys a shitload of stock in my company the day that I'm forced out of it?"

"I've heard the take-over rumors on Wall Street," I said.

"Bob Gnocci bought off Ted Dantly," Howard fumed. "You can bank on that. They conspired to kill Jack Carlisle, knowing it would create a crisis that would devalue Western Shores. They even think of a way to kill the son of a bitch that involves me. I can't fight back because my hands are tied by this blackmail thing. Gnocci promises Dantly a big promotion when they take over, and has him killed instead. When Western Shores hits bottom, its assets worth almost twice that of its stock value, he grabs it."

"Leslie Carlisle will put up a fight," I said.

The mention of his granddaughter quieted his rage. He looked almost proud.

"She's proved her blood this past week. I never thought I'd say it, but she's almost as big a bastard as her grandfather. If given half a chance, she'd give the company a good run. But the deck is stacked. The board will turn on her."

Howard's eyes darkened, and in the glow of the Tiffany desk lamp, his face hardened like polished wood.

"Bob Gnocci has them all in his pocket. The sons of bitches turned on me. They'll turn on her. There is no loyalty."

"Who are Gnocci's friends on the board?"

"My father was eighty-two when he died," he said sharply. "I have six more years left. They're all cowards and assassins. I'll start another company, by God, and run all the bastards into the ground."

I asked again about Gnocci's friends, but he didn't seem to hear me. His cigar trailed one last wisp of smoke and died. He didn't notice when I stood up. In contemplation of a world populated by bastards, assassins, and cowards, the light in his eyes had been extinguished, and his face had no more life in it than the oak lions carved in his desk.

I left by the front door.

Chapter
31

IT HAD BEEN YEARS SINCE I HAD DONE any work with a large caliber gun. In the morning, while Angel was on her five-mile run, I booked an appointment with Leslie Carlisle. When Angel returned, she talked for the first time about how Rossi's men had abducted her, and mentioned that she had never fired a pistol. We decided to give it a try, and drove to a shooting range in the San Fernando Valley. Angel practiced with the .38 while I emptied the .44. I had bought the gun because it was big and I wanted people to know that I had a big gun under my shoulder. The last thing I wanted to do was try to shoot someone with it. I wasn't much good. I fired twelve rounds, forming a pattern on the target you could drive a truck through.

Angel couldn't shoot at all. At a distance of fifty feet, the target was still a virgin after twelve rounds. We worked on her stance and form, but she still couldn't hit the target. I brought the target in, ten feet at a time, to find her range. At the distance of ten feet, she was deadly. She clustered six rounds within three inches of the bulls-eye. At distances greater than ten feet, the safest place to be was where she was aiming.

"I don't understand it," I said, taking the gun. "You're

doing everything right, but at any kind of distance you can't hit a damn thing."

Angel's face colored, and the muscles along her jaw tightened, a sure sign that she didn't want to talk about it.

I nestled the .38 in my sling and worked at finding a fast and accurate way to draw and fire. Angel watched, her arms wrapped across her chest, one leg thrust out, embarrassed but still defiant.

"You can't hit what you can't see," she finally said.

"What do you mean by that?" I asked.

She looked away, her jaw tighter than before.

"I'm nearsighted," she mumbled.

It surprised me. I told her to put on her glasses.

"I don't wear glasses," she said.

"Why the hell not?"

"Glasses are ugly," she mumbled, still not looking at me.

"The bullet hole you'll put in somebody by mistake will be a whole lot uglier."

"I don't need to carry a gun," she said. "I can take care of myself well enough without one."

"I don't understand. You put yourself in a boxing ring and risk a broken nose and loose teeth, but you won't wear glasses."

"That's right," Angel said. "You don't understand."

Angel had been reluctant to give up the Mercedes, and though I couldn't afford it, we kept it around for one more day. She drove the 405 freeway south toward Cheviot Hills, while I brooded in the passenger seat. Her control of the car was effortless, but I noticed that on the open road she squinted at the distances.

"What am I going to look for, once I'm inside?" Angel asked behind the wheel.

I wedged a roll of duct tape between my knees and tore four two-inch squares of tape. I laid the four squares directly over each other, forming one laminated square of tape about a sixteenth of an inch thick.

"Upstairs, two doors to the right of the stairs as you come up, there is a study. It has a black desk, and a row of books on the wall to your right. Search the desk for any correspondence with American Sun Corporation or Ted Dantly."

"What should I do with it if I find it?"

"Read it, then put it back where you found it. It's very important that no one know you've been there. It would also be helpful if you could remember what you've read."

"I'll remember," she said with confidence and some irritation.

"What's the tape for?"

"To keep the door from locking."

Angel parked half a block up the street and waited in the car. I stepped out into the fading February sunshine. The golden winter light cast long shadows on the street as I walked. Mine was the shadow of a tall one-armed man, sauntering over the curled brown leaves with false bravado.

I rang the front bell. Leslie Carlisle opened the door fifteen seconds later. It was the maid's day off. I was afraid it might be. Leslie wore a cobalt-blue dress, matching her eyes.

"You've been hurt," she remarked, noticing the sling.

"I found out I wasn't faster than a speeding bullet," I said, stepping just inside the doorway. "But I can still leap tall buildings."

As I spoke, my fingers pressed the laminated square of tape over the metal striker plate, where the latch clicks into the doorjamb.

"The next time I see you, I expect it will be with a broken leg," she said, and shut the door behind me.

I did not hear the lock click into place. She led me into the living room and sat on the leather sofa. I took one of the low-slung S-shaped chairs. She asked if I would like something to drink. I declined.

"This will be my final verbal report," I said. "There will be a written report sent to you in a week or so."

"You feel there's nothing else for you to do?" she asked, and began to massage her left temple, unconsciously, her fingers describing small circles.

"The police have the facts and the manpower. Most importantly, they have the will to do the job. I'd just get in the way."

"The police questioned Grandfather day before yesterday." She let loose a long, agitated sigh. "Mother and I warned him it was going to happen, but he didn't take it well."

"I don't think the police will bother him anymore," I said.

Her fingers trailed down her cheek and rested lightly on her throat. Small creases spoiled the smoothness of her brow.

"Why not?" she asked.

"There is new evidence that pretty much clears him."

Her mouth opened, then closed abruptly. She leaned back heavily and, in a sudden loss of elegance, crossed and then uncrossed her thin arms.

"I'm relieved, of course," she said, after too long a silence, "but a little confused. I thought the evidence all pointed in his direction."

"It does, and very neatly. You arranged it all with a great deal of cunning."

Her head cocked slightly to the side, as if not quite believing what she had heard, then stilled. "Nonsense. You have obviously taken a blow on your head equal to the one to your shoulder."

"I spoke with your grandfather last night. He said a curious thing. He was proud of you. He said that your ruthlessness was second only to his. I think he was wrong. You're the first person I've met without any conscience at all."

"You are accusing me not only of murder, but of criminal stupidity," she said, as though the latter were more insulting. "For God's sake, why should I hire a detective to investigate a murder that I committed?"

"The last thing I would accuse you of is stupidity. Hiring me became part of your plan, probably improvised when the police weren't showing any inclination to investigate your husband's death as a murder. Somebody had to uncover the trail of clues that led directly to Henry Howard. I happened on the scene, and I was perfect. I had known and respected Jack and could be trusted to remain loyal to his widow."

The skin around Leslie Carlisle's mouth and forehead tightened as though stretched over an angry mask. Her eyes chilled me. They were not merely angry. Her eyes were transformed, their human lights imploded to a malevolent core. The woman with whom I had worked, fought, and made love was not the woman who sat before me. What stared back at me was hard, dark, and frightening.

She leaned over, as though adjusting the hem of her dress, but continued forward and rapped sharply on the crystal coffee table. Her lips twisted to the side in a mocking smile, and she glanced back over her shoulder. Behind the couch, in the doorway to the dining room, a familiar face sighted me down the barrel of a blue-black .38.

"I missed my flight to Mexico, so I thought I'd try one more crack at you," Dark Coat said with a wry grin.

He took three cautious steps forward. I didn't move.

"With your thumb and forefinger, I want you to slowly remove the cannon from your shoulder holster and lay it on the table."

I did as directed, laying the .44 before me.

"Ma'am," Dark Coat said in gentlemanly tones, "would you please take the gun and, moving to your right, walk around the couch and hand it to me."

Leslie Carlisle lifted the gun and, circling the table as though she had a dead rat by the tail, gave it to Dark Coat. He told me to stand, remove my coat, drop it on the floor, and turn full circle. I performed all four actions with the mechanical correctness of a puppet.

"How's your shoulder?" Dark Coat asked, satisfied that I was clean.

"I have a feeling it won't be troubling me for long," I answered.

"I'm a better shot at this range," he said with a friendly smile.

The look that I had seen twice before appeared on Leslie Carlisle's face. There is nothing as deadly as intelligence. A hard, brilliant gleam showed in her eyes, as though she knew my mind and mocked it. I realized then that all else was performance except this one look of secret superiority and contempt. The contempt for all things not of herself had distilled into a single truth at the center of her being. The image she projected of herself was no more than that: an image, a deception of light and shadow, a performance.

She clasped her hands before her and bowed playfully at the waist, like an actress.

"I'll leave you to do your job," she said to Dark Coat. "I'd prefer that you not do it here, but if you must, try not to make much of a mess. It's the maid's day off."

Dark Coat checked her with a glance.

"I don't think you should go just yet."

She had turned to leave and glanced over her shoulder, with the attitude of master to servant tempered by the gun in his hand.

"We should listen to our friend's speculations," he said. "If the police question you, it would be good to know what he knows."

Leslie nodded and said, "Of course." Following his lead, she sat next to Dark Coat on the couch. He held my .44 across his lap and propped the .38 on his knee, pointed at my chest.

"Continue with your story," he directed. "Just pretend I'm not here."

I tried simultaneously to talk and think ahead. I had several options, but most seemed to end in a pine box. Leslie Carlisle listened, interested in her own cleverness, but not mine, as though the outcome were decided and held no further danger for her. Dark Coat's face was a concrete wall. I addressed myself to Leslie Carlisle.

"Your grandfather didn't know that you were sleeping with Dantly, or he would never have used him to hire Jim Johnson. When you learned that a blackmailer had been put on the company payroll, you realized there were other uses for him. With such a man, you could murder your husband and take control of Western Shores. I don't know whether you thought it up by yourself or had help from Dantly, and it doesn't matter."

"Ted was good with numbers," she said, "and even better at following orders, if you made him believe he was giving them."

"Dantly became your front man," I went on. "He made contact with Johnson, and Johnson informed American Sun. You had a meeting with American Sun, discussing your long range plans. You offered them an option on a sizable percentage of Western Shores stock, purchased at a favorable price by your agent, Richard Preston, and a seat on the board of directors. They agreed to back you up, lending you th services of Johnson, then later those of our friend here with the gun," I said with a nod to Dark Coat.

"At a dinner party hosted by Henry Howard, you excused yourself and went upstairs to his bathroom medicine cabinet and stole a new prescription bottle of digitalis, which you, being familiar with the household routines, knew would be there. You gave the digitalis to Dantly, who arranged the transfer to Johnson in San Francisco. You knew that Henry Howard would take control of the company on Jack's death, and planned to implicate him in the murder. Howard had the best motive for wanting Jack killed, the strings to pull to get the job done, and, with the prescription of digitalis, the murder weapon.

"But it didn't work the first time. You arranged your husband's death too cleverly. No one thought it was murder. Then I stumbled along to play chump investigator. I was perfect: loyal, committed, and, in retrospect, not terribly bright. You even slept with me once, to set the hook when I had reason to doubt you."

"It wasn't unpleasant," she said. "To make love with a man who was my hunter, who would kill me if he knew my secret, was incredible."

"Carlisle, Dantly, and now me. Death is your pornography. If she offers to sleep with you," I said to Dark Coat, "decline."

"Shut up and keep talking," he said.

"With Carlisle dead, and Henry Howard set to take the fall, you had to remove all trace of your involvement. Johnson was a blackmailer and couldn't be trusted. You had him killed, and the hotel security man, Joe Mankewitz."

"We thought Mankewitz would kill you first," Dark Coat said with a rich, deep laugh, "before you found out what you were supposed to find out."

"But one small thing went wrong. Johnson was a consummate blackmailer and left evidence that implicated Ted Dantly. When I started to put pressure on him, you knew he would crack. I wanted to go to the police, but you convinced me to wait. You had Dantly arrange a meeting with me, leading him to believe that I would be eliminated."

I faced Dark Coat. He listened with the savage compassion of both priest and executioner.

"Your instructions were to kill both of us," I said. "I had discovered exactly what I was intended to, and they were afraid I wouldn't stop. I didn't show up, and that left only Dantly.

"The plan can be perfect and the execution flawless, but people aren't chess pieces. They have the instinct of self-preservation. Dantly left behind something he had hoped would keep him alive: a prescription bottle of digitalis, which should have been the final nail in Henry Howard's coffin, except for one curious fact. His fingerprints weren't on it."

"The police wouldn't expect him to be so stupid as to leave a fingerprint," Leslie said.

"But you were."

"You're lying," she answered without hesitation.

"Your right thumb print is on the prescription, as big and clear as though cast in bronze. That was Dantly's insurance policy."

"This is all impossible. I told Ted to get rid of the capsules," she said.

Irritated, she began to rub her temple in small, circular motions.

"The police are testing the capsules this afternoon," I continued, "and if there is a clinical match with what was found in the thermos that Jack drank from, your rent will be paid by the state for the next fifty years."

Her temper snapped. "You're lying! Ted destroyed the capsules."

I had wanted her to come at me, putting her body between me and Dark Coat's .38. I wasn't lucky. Her spine straightened and, her chin thrusting up on a lengthening neck, she pronounced in her clear, imperious voice, "Everything will be taken care of. I am chief executive officer of Western Shores Corporation. Now"—she glanced at Dark Coat—"I want you to kill this man."

I watched Dark Coat, cognizant that my chance had already passed. His eyes were shadowed by the bridge of massive brows, and behind that shadow his judgment fell like the stroke of an ax. The corner of his mouth twitched, and with a little sigh, as close as he ever came to regret, he raised the .44 and pulled the trigger. The roar was as loud as the end of the world.

I was watching her eyes, pierced by their malice, when the gun sounded, and the top of her head disintegrated. The body jerked once, violently, and collapsed against the arm of the sofa. Blood fountained through her left temple, staining the blue of her dress a deep violet. I couldn't take my eyes off the stain. There was so much blood. It spread across her shoulders and down the side of her dress, seeping violet over her belly, like a cancer that had lived and bred inside her and was now suddenly let loose, consuming the host.

Dark Coat stepped casually away from the couch. I shut the horror away, damning it to the narrow crawl spaces that worm through the inner edges of the mind, where the random images of nightmares move. He stood about ten feet distant, the gun pointed at my chest held in a relaxed and confident hand. My shock must have been transparent, because a curious smile played across his lips.

"Stand up," he said, not at all unfriendly.

I stood and forced my mouth to move.

"Murder-suicide?"

He nodded.

"It won't fool anyone."

"I just want to keep them guessing," he said.

"Your boss has won big. He should be able to leverage his shares into control of the company now that there is no one left to run it."

"I don't know anything about the financial part. I wasn't supposed to do her unless she was blown."

"She wasn't," I said.

"What do you mean?"

"I made it all up. I lied. There were no fingerprints."

A deep laugh poured from his throat.

"I'm going to be sorry to see you go," he said. "We're a lot alike. Both hunters. You were good."

He was being careful. He liked me and wanted to do the job right. Instead of shooting from the waist, he put his eye to the sight. When the gun moved up, I prepared to drop. A soft thump sounded at the far end of the room, near the front entryway. He should have fired immediately, but hesitated and glanced to his side. Angel was streaking toward us, her body crouched low to the floor, and her long, quick strides like a cat's in a burst of terrible speed. I dropped to the floor as Dark Coat's first shot ripped through the air where my chest had been and shattered the plate-glass window behind. He whirled to face Angel as I jerked the .38 from my sling. The room shook with the percussive roar of two shots. His, the loudest, sounded first. Mine caught Dark Coat above the breastbone, shattering his neck, and he went down hard.

Angel was sprawled on the floor, her shoulder touching the baseboard of the inside wall. Blood dotted her forehead.

I crossed the room in three strides and knelt over her, my heart thrashing around in my chest. It was a cut. She moaned, and her eyes struggled open.

"I see stars," she said, and sat up.

"You're lucky you see at all, dammit," I said.

I was angry and, like a parent who has pulled a child from the path of a car, heartsick with relief. I had little right to those feelings. Angel wasn't a child. But the feelings were there.

"I must have hit the wall," she said, and tried to shake her head clear.

I sat down heavily and tossed the .38 aside. Angel read my look and smiled.

"Relax. I wanted to distract him, then get out of the way. I wasn't going to tackle him."

"You were almost killed," I shouted.

"I knew you'd get him first."

I grabbed her hand and squeezed it, hard.

"I didn't get him first. Don't have faith in me like that again. Ever. He fired two shots before I could get my gun out of the damn sling."

She returned my grip with one equally strong.

"Well, he's dead, and I'm not."

I tried to be calm.

"That's not the point. It was a stupid risk," I said, and found I was shouting again.

"I'm not going to let your ideas about femininity stop me from doing my job. That's the point," she shouted in return.

"Getting killed is not your job."

"No, but taking risks is. That's the whole idea of being equal. If I can't take risks, I can't be your partner."

"Then maybe you shouldn't be my partner!" I exploded, and immediately regretted it.

Her grip on my hand loosened.

"If that's the way you feel," she said, and backed away.

I pulled her toward me again.

"It's not the way I feel."

I ran my finger along the long, smooth line of her jaw. She watched my face warily, waiting for my understanding, as she had been waiting since the day I had met her. Though I knew what she wanted, it was not easy to give. There had always been an essential misunderstanding between what I thought and what I felt, as though my heart and brain were two men standing back to back, with the first man looking out over the ocean and perceiving the world as water, and the second man facing inland and seeing only earth. I wanted to tell her that those same qualities which she described in herself had first attracted me to her, but now that I had fallen in love, my instinct was to protect, to lessen that recklessness which I loved. And I knew that if I succeeded, I would love her less. It is not always possible—or desirable—to live easily with what is loved. So I didn't say anything. I held her in my arms, and she held me in hers, and we stayed that way for a long, long time.

FOR THE BEST IN PAPERBACKS, LOOK FOR THE

In every corner of the world, on every subject under the sun, Penguin represents quality and variety—the very best in publishing today.

For complete information about books available from Penguin—including Pelicans, Puffins, Peregrines, and Penguin Classics—and how to order them, write to us at the appropriate address below. Please note that for copyright reasons the selection of books varies from country to country.

In the United Kingdom: For a complete list of books available from Penguin in the U.K., please write to *Dept E.P., Penguin Books Ltd, Harmondsworth, Middlesex, UB7 0DA*.

In the United States: For a complete list of books available from Penguin in the U.S., please write to *Dept BA, Penguin,* Box 999, Bergenfield, New Jersey 07621-0999.

In Canada: For a complete list of books available from Penguin in Canada, please write to *Penguin Books Canada Ltd, 2801 John Street, Markham, Ontario L3R 1B4.*

In Australia: For a complete list of books available from Penguin in Australia, please write to the *Marketing Department, Penguin Books Australia Ltd, P.O. Box 257, Ringwood, Victoria 3134.*

In New Zealand: For a complete list of books available from Penguin in New Zealand, please write to the *Marketing Department, Penguin Books (NZ) Ltd, Private Bag, Takapuna, Auckland 9.*

In India: For a complete list of books available from Penguin, please write to *Penguin Overseas Ltd, 706 Eros Apartments, 56 Nehru Place, New Delhi, 110019.*

In Holland: For a complete list of books available from Penguin in Holland, please write to *Penguin Books Nederland B.V., Postbus 195, NL–1380AD Weesp, Netherlands.*

In Germany: For a complete list of books available from Penguin, please write to *Penguin Books Ltd, Friedrichstrasse 10–12, D–6000 Frankfurt Main 1, Federal Republic of Germany.*

In Spain: For a complete list of books available from Penguin in Spain, please write to *Longman Penguin España, Calle San Nicolas 15, E–28013 Madrid, Spain.*

In Japan: For a complete list of books available from Penguin in Japan, please write to *Longman Penguin Japan Co Ltd, Yamaguchi Building, 2-12-9 Kanda Jimbocho, Chiyoda-Ku, Tokyo 101, Japan.*

FOR THE BEST IN MYSTERY, LOOK FOR THE

☐ A CRIMINAL COMEDY
Julian Symons

From Julian Symons, the master of crime fiction, this is "the best of his best" (*The New Yorker*). What starts as a nasty little scandal centering on two partners in a British travel agency escalates into smuggling and murder in Italy.
220 pages   ISBN: 0-14-009621-3   **$3.50**

☐ GOOD AND DEAD
Jane Langton

Something sinister is emptying the pews at the Old West Church, and parishioner Homer Kelly knows it isn't a loss of faith. When he investigates, Homer discovers that the ways of a small New England town can be just as mysterious as the ways of God.
256 pages   ISBN: 0-14-778217-1   **$3.95**

☐ THE SHORTEST WAY TO HADES
Sarah Caudwell

Five young barristers and a wealthy family with a five-million-pound estate find the stakes are raised when one member of the family meets a suspicious death.
208 pages   ISBN: 0-14-008488-6   **$3.50**

☐ RUMPOLE OF THE BAILEY
John Mortimer

The hero of John Mortimer's mysteries is Horace Rumpole, barrister at law, sixty-eight next birthday, with an unsurpassed knowledge of blood and typewriters, a penchant for quoting poetry, and a habit of referring to his judge as "the old darling."
208 pages   ISBN: 0-14-004670-4   **$3.95**

FOR THE BEST IN MYSTERY, LOOK FOR THE

☐ **MURDOCK FOR HIRE**
Robert Ray

When he is hired to find a dead man's missing antique coin collection, private detective Matt Murdock discovers an international crime ring that is much more than a nickle-and-dime operation.

256 pages   ISBN: 0-14-010679-0   **$3.95**

☐ **BRIARPATCH**
Ross Thomas

This Edgar Award-winning thriller is the story of Benjamin Dill, who returns to the Sunbelt city of his youth to attend his sister's funeral—and find her killer.

384 pages   ISBN: 0-14-010581-6   **$3.95**

☐ **DEATH'S SAVAGE PASSION**
Orania Papazoglou

Suspense is killing Romance, and the Romance Writers of America are outraged. When a fresh, enthusiastic creator of the loathed hybrid, Romantic Suspense, arrives on the scene, someone shows her just how murderous competition can be.   180 pages   ISBN: 0-14-009967-0   **$3.50**

☐ **GOLD BY GEMINI**
Jonathan Gash

Lovejoy, the antiques dealer whom the *Chicago Sun-Times* calls "one of the most likable rogues in mystery history," searches for Roman gold coins and greedy bird-killers on the Isle of Man.

224 pages   ISBN: 0-451-82185-8   **$3.95**

☐ **REILLY: ACE OF SPIES**
Robin Bruce Lockhart

This is the incredible true story of superspy Sidney Reilly, said to be the inspiration for James Bond. Robin Bruce Lockhart's book tells the thrilling story of the British Secret Service agent's shadowy Russian past and near-legendary exploits in espionage and in love.

192 pages   ISBN: 0-14-006895-3   **$4.95**

☐ **STRANGERS ON A TRAIN**
Patricia Highsmith

Almost against his will, Guy Haines is trapped in a nightmare of shared guilt when he agrees to kill the father of the man who will kill Guy's wife. The basis for the unforgettable Hitchcock thriller.

256 pages   ISBN: 0-14-003796-9   **$4.95**

☐ **THE THIN WOMAN**
Dorothy Cannell

An interior designer who is also a passionate eater, her rented companion who writes trashy novels, and a rich dead uncle with a conditional will are the principals in this delicious thriller.   242 pages   ISBN: 0-14-007947-5   **$3.95**